# GATED

# GATED

## AMY CHRISTINE PARKER

RANDOM HOUSE 🏠 NEW YORK

Text copyright © 2013 by Amy Christine Parker
Front jacket photograph copyright © Mohamad Itani/Trevillion Images
Back jacket photograph copyright © Tiburon Studios/E+/Getty Images

Visit us on the Web! randomhouse.com/teens

Educators and librarians, for a variety of teaching tools, visit us at
RHTeachersLibrarians.com

*Library of Congress Cataloging-in-Publication Data*
Parker, Amy Christine.
Gated / Amy Christine Parker. — First edition.
p. cm
Summary: Seventeen-year-old Lyla doesn't trust the charismatic leader of her isolated suburban community when he is told that the end of the world is near and when it arrives they must all be ready to defend themselves against the unchosen.
ISBN 978-0-449-81597-7 (trade) — ISBN 978-0-449-81598-4 (lib. bdg.) —
ISBN 978-0-449-81599-1 (ebook)
[1. Utopias—Fiction. 2. Survival—Fiction. 3. Cults—Fiction.
4. Religious leaders—Fiction.] I. Title.
PZ7.P22165Gat 2013 [Fic]—dc23 2012048123

Printed in the United States of America

10 9 8 7 6 5 4 3 2

First Edition

For my loving husband, Jay,
and my two beautiful daughters,
Samantha and Riley,
because they gave me the time
and opportunity to realize my dreams

# GATED

The good in this world, what little of it that remains,
is worth protecting by whatever means necessary.
We can't be afraid to stand up and defend it.

—Pioneer, leader of the Community

# ONE

"Shoot to kill this time, okay?" Will winks and pushes me into the tall corn as we walk through the field to the gun range. I push him back and he laughs. The sky is a perfect cloudless blue and the air is hot from the summer sun. It's a day meant for picnics, not pre-end-of-the-world target practice.

"But that's why I have you," I say. I fiddle with the leather strap attached to my rifle, sliding it back and forth across my shoulder until it rests comfortably in the crook of my neck. Turning my face up to his, I'm sure that I'll see his lips curl into a smile at my routine grumbling, but instead he's frowning.

"What if I'm not with you when we're attacked? You can't assume someone else will pull the trigger for you all the time." His hand tugs absently at his ear, a sure sign that he's not joking anymore.

I swallow back my answer and look out past the corn

to the prairie beyond. The unspoken words drop into my stomach, making it hurt. The gun range is up ahead. Marie and Brian are already there. The popping sounds of their guns carry over the cornfield, punctuating the sudden awkwardness between Will and me.

"I'm just saying that maybe it's time you took all of this seriously." Will reaches out for my non-gun-toting hand. I hesitate, my fingers twitching in the air. He dips his head and gives me a sidelong smile.

I know he means well. He always means well. He cares about me. *I* am the problem. Exactly three months until the end of the world and I still can't muster up the proper response. I pull in a long breath, glad for the abundance of air around me. Thinking about the end of things always makes me feel like I'm suffocating.

Will chases after my hand with his own until he snares it. He laces his long fingers through mine. "I worry about you, Lyla. I can't be with you every second, even once we're in the shelter. I just want to know you'll do what you have to to survive."

I can't keep a sigh from escaping. We've had this conversation so many times. It's intensifying now because of the target shooting. This is only our fifth time out on the range, and his pestering is reaching epic proportions.

"Come on," I finally say, like he's the one who's holding us up. He squeezes my hand lightly. We walk the last few yards to the open grass and the gun range. I fish my earplugs out of my pocket and stuff them in my ears before Will can say anything more. He leans down, his lanky frame casting a shadow over my face. He's like a barometer—constantly measuring my moods and reporting them back to me in his expressions. His stonewashed-blue eyes are troubled and his freckled nose is crinkled with concern. This means that he thinks that I'm overly anxious. I want to reassure him, if only to get him to look away, but it's as if clouds have suddenly formed and gathered over my head.

Brian's standing behind Marie, his face buried in her dark curls. He's gently guiding her rifle to her cheek for what I'm sure is the hundredth time. Together they aim her gun at the large collection of hay bales across from them. Each hay bale has a life-sized cutout of a person bound to its front. They're aiming at a woman. It's a silhouette, but still it makes my skin tingle when the gun goes off and I see a piece of the plywood lady's chest fly out into the grass. Marie grins at us and her cheeks flush pink.

"Did you see that?" she asks. I can't exactly hear past my earplugs, but I don't need to. She says the same thing every time she manages to land a shot. I paste a smile on my face and walk toward them and out of Will's shadow.

"Nice!" I holler back. I take my usual spot in the grass, across from the hay bale with the man cutout. I'm pretty sure this makes me sexist, but the man target is the only one I can stomach shooting. I lower the rifle from my shoulder and try to psych myself up.

*Not enough room for everyone. We can't take them all. They had their chance. We have to protect ours.*

I play this litany over and over in my head, hoping that somehow it will make my heart understand. It didn't work the last time and I don't hold out much hope for this time either. How can I take someone's life when he's just scared and looking for help, even if it saves my own?

I glance over at Will. He's shooting at two plywood cutouts: a man and a woman. His rifle is tucked into the space between his chest and his shoulder, and his cheek is welded to the gun's stock. He keeps both eyes open, lines up his sights. There's no hesitation once he gets the sights level. The rifle jumps as he takes the shot and the plywood man's head flies backward. His featureless face searches the sky. Will readjusts and shoots the plywood woman in almost the exact same spot. Her head stays upright, but it's missing its rounded top. He smiles as he lowers his gun and looks at me.

I turn back to my own hay bale and the silent man-board waiting there for me. I pull my rifle up into position and ready my stance. I can feel the others watching me, hoping that for once I'll shoot one of the mandatory targets: head or heart. My bangs are plastered to my forehead and sweat tickles my back as it runs down my spine. I still my body, put my finger on the trigger, and pull. The recoil makes me wince and I shut my eyes. When I open them and look out at the silhouette man, I let out my breath in one relieved rush. The bullet hit exactly where I wanted it to.

"Really, Lyla? The kneecap again?" Marie has her hands on her slim hips and one foot jutted out as if she's suddenly become a seasoned assassin. She can't seem to wrap her mind around my continued reluctance to shoot right.

"It's her tribute to *Terminator Two*," Will says. "Where the kid orders the Terminator to take nonlethal shots all the time." He doesn't look at me as he walks back to his spot and aims at his target again, but I know that our discussion isn't over. It won't be until I manage to find a way to do what they want, to give in and fight.

We keep shooting until we each go through our ammo cartridges. My plywood man is the only one with a chance at life by the end. The rest of his silhouette friends have been dead since the first round of bullets. I set my rifle on the ground and start helping the others pick up the shell casings littered around our feet. I'm moving faster than everyone else. If we get done early enough, I might be able to get in some painting time before dinner.

Marie crouches down next to me and plucks a shell casing out of the tall grass between us. "So what gives, Lyla? Why don't you shoot right?"

I shrug and drop shells into my pouch. "I don't know. It's just that every time I look at those stupid people targets, I see *actual* people—like you or Brian or Will. What if somehow we got stuck outside the Silo and needed help? I mean, how do any of them out there even know it's the end? Pioneer chose to save us, but does anyone else have any idea that the end is coming? Wouldn't they already be here, fighting to get in?"

Marie stares at me. Her face is as clear of concern as the sky is of clouds. "I don't know, Lyla. You worry too much. You're safe and so are your family and friends. Isn't that enough? Besides, the Outsiders are supposed to die. It's their destiny, not ours."

I don't know what to say. Yes? No? What's the right way to feel when you know that everything's about to go so wrong for billions of other people? "Forget it," I say instead. "I'm just in a weird mood today, okay?"

Marie shakes her head and goes back to collecting shells. I start to do the same when the Community's beat-up red truck emerges from the far end of the cornfield. It's too far away to see the driver clearly, but his rigid posture gives him away anyway. It's Pioneer, our leader.

*Terrific.*

He's come to check up on our shooting. He'll see that I'm not improving. He was patient with my reluctance to kill the last time we practiced, but he made it clear that I would have to do better, and soon. My hands start to shake. I'm dropping more shell casings than I manage to pick up.

Pioneer stops the truck and slides out of the driver's seat. Immediately the field around us seems closer, smaller. Pioneer seems to fill most of the space now. It's not like he's a particularly big man or really muscular or anything. In fact, he's pretty much the opposite—pale and rail-thin.

It's what is under the skin that's large. His intensity isn't contained in his slight frame. It pulses all around him like sound waves or beams of light. He almost seems to glow most of the time. He's the only person in Mandrodage Meadows—or anywhere else, for that matter—who does. I can't seem to look away when he's around; he just doesn't leave room for that option. He rubs at the scruff along his chin and ambles over to us.

Marie, Brian, and Will glance at me. I ignore them and pretend to search for more shells, wishing for a hole to bury myself in.

"So how'd it go today?" Pioneer's voice is mellow and warm, practically filled with sunshine.

"Um, good," Will says.

I hold my breath. Wait. With any luck, Pioneer will simply let this be it, take Will at his word, and go . . . but I'm holding out very little hope for that. I sneak peeks at Pioneer and the others as I continue to pick up casings. Despite his pleasant, conversational tone, his blue eyes are sharp, cutting into each of my friends in turn. He knows something's not right.

Marie bounces toward Pioneer—all curls and energy. "I hit the head and the heart twice in a row!"

"Without Brian's help?" Pioneer sounds skeptical. Out of the corner of my eye, I can see his hand go up to pat her shoulder.

"Yep. The last couple shots, I did."

"She really did," I hear Brian say.

7

I look up again just as Pioneer beams at Marie and then bear-hugs her. "Well done. I knew you'd get it . . . eventually."

Will and Brian both let out a snicker, and Marie sticks her tongue out at them.

Pioneer's gaze swivels to me again, catching me watching them. I try to smile, fake excitement that he's here. The others begin to move so that they are between Pioneer and me. They're trying to distract him, have been for the past few minutes, I realize, and I feel a rush of affection for them. Even though they've been pressuring me to shoot right every time we're out here, it's only because they don't want me to get in trouble with Pioneer.

"Shall we examine the targets?" Pioneer says from behind the wall of my friends, extra loud so that I know he means mine specifically.

I drop the shells I've been gathering into a pile on the ground, stand up without a word, and join the others. The air feels charged, like there's an approaching storm, even though the day is still clear and beautiful. I ball my hands into fists and follow everyone to the targets.

Brian shows Pioneer his target first. Will rushes in with his next. Pioneer nods, clearly pleased with them both. Then Marie shows him hers—chattering the whole time about how she's improved her stance and doesn't jump anymore when the rifle goes off. I know she's trying to stall, distract him just a little longer for me, but it's irritating Pioneer. He's practically vibrating, like a tuning fork that's been struck particularly hard. I grit my teeth and come forward. Marie's voice winds down immediately and she backs away until she's between the boys. She looks scared. I swallow a laugh. *I'm* the one in trouble and *she's* scared. Typical.

"Lyla," Pioneer says slowly, "show me your target, please."

I can only manage a tight nod. I'm about to disappoint him, but what can I do about it now? I point at my plywood man like it's a particularly lame prize from that game show Pioneer lets us watch sometimes. Then I try to square my shoulders and wait for his reaction.

Pioneer stands in front of the target for an uncomfortably long time. I fidget from foot to foot, bite my lip, and pull on my braid. The others huddle together silently.

"This target looks relatively unharmed," Pioneer finally says. "Why?"

Will opens his mouth to speak, but Pioneer shushes him with one glance. "My question was directed at Lyla."

His eyes bore into me, searing my skin. Why can't I shoot right like everyone else? There's no answer that I can give that'll make him understand, when I don't even understand myself. So I panic, like always, and say the first thing that pops into my head.

The wrong thing.

"Um, I guess I have a soft spot for the tall, dark, and

faceless?" I let out a short, nervous burst of laughter. As soon as the words are out of my mouth, I know how flippant they sound, but it's too late to take them back now.

Pioneer's voice is ice. "This is not a joke. You are a liability to the Community if you can't help defend it."

He takes a deep, measured breath and his eyes soften. His lips curl into a smile. "I just want to keep you safe." He gestures to the field and the targets. "All of this is meant to keep you safe."

He walks over to Brian's target, stoops, and picks it up off of the ground. He knocks on it. "They're just pulp. Wood. Not people. This practice should be easy. It's meant to be easy. You have to desensitize yourself. If you can't hit the targets, you won't hit the actual people. And we need you to, Lyla. We most certainly do."

Pioneer moves to where Brian is standing and gestures at his gun. Brian hands it to him. He turns to me and raises the gun so that it's pointing at my stomach. His eyes flash as he stares me down. I know he won't shoot me, but it still makes my muscles tense, my nerves thrum.

"Those people out there don't know you. They don't care about you. They will shoot you to take what you have if it means saving their own." He swings the gun around and points it at Will. Will flinches. I can see him fight the urge to take a step back. "They'll murder the ones you love if you give 'em the chance." He looks back at me. "And they will not hesitate. Ever. So you can't either." He drops the gun and we stop holding our breath.

Pioneer takes my arm and guides me to the space across from the unused target. It's the silhouette of a woman holding hands with a child. I tense. It's silly, I guess, but I can't help it.

"You can't see them as people like you or me. They're already ghosts. The Brethren will save only us, their chosen ones. When the earth's rotation reverses in three months, most folks'll be wiped from the planet in a matter of minutes, swallowed up by tsunamis, earthquakes, and volcanic eruptions. So the Brethren have told me and so I've told you. Time and again. It's their destiny, just as it is ours to survive. Do you not believe my word? Do you not believe that the Brethren, our all-knowing creators, in their infinite wisdom, have seen who is and who is not worthy to start again? Has doubt taken hold in you?"

I shake my head and swallow. His words cut me to the quick. He's right. If I resist this, I am as good as spitting in the faces of those who have helped show me the light. *What's wrong with me?*

"Would you let them take some of us with them while you hesitate? Do you not care for us as we care for you? Shooting those who would hurt your family and endanger the Brethren's plan shows your love for us, your faith in the Brethren." He pats my shoulder. "You are a gentle spirit, Little Owl. It's why you are one of their chosen. But even lambs have to be lions sometimes."

He's using my nickname—the one he gave me because

11

I'm always watching everything, taking things in. Usually I like it and the way his voice warms when he says it, but not now. Today it just makes me feel weak.

He guides my rifle back up onto my shoulder and gently moves my braid from between it and my cheek. I focus in on the woman cutout first and level the gun. I have to do what he's asking. I owe it to him, to all of us.

"When you pull the trigger this time, you will aim for the head or the heart," Pioneer whispers in my ear. "Show me, show them"—he points at Will, Brian, and Marie—"how much you love us."

He backs away to stand with the others. I can feel their eyes on me. I chew on my lip. *Get ahold of yourself. They aren't even real.* I aim at the woman's chest. Breathe in and out. Then I close my eyes at the last second and pull the trigger. When I open my eyes, there's a hole in the cutout's chest.

"Good. Now again," Pioneer commands.

I aim at the smaller target. I try not to see its small hands and feet. I concentrate on the black middle of the plywood. Still, when the bullet explodes out of my gun, my chest tightens. Pioneer makes me shoot both targets again and again and again. They are mangled and unrecognizable when I'm through, but I'm not as sick as I was to start with. I still don't like the shooting, but I can at least do it now without flinching each time.

Pioneer's grinning widely at me. "That's my girl!" He pulls me to him and kisses my forehead. His shirt smells like hay and grass and gunpowder. "Your sweet nature is what I love most about you. But unfortunately, until this world is no more, that nature is dangerous. To you and to all of us. You have to prepare for the months ahead of us yet. Get strong." He tilts my chin up and looks me in the eye. "Let me prepare you, Little Owl. The more you fight what I tell you, the harder things will be for you." There's an edge in his voice now that undercuts the warmth of his embrace. It makes me shiver.

"You all will help her come around, won't you? You'll let me know if she needs my undivided attention again as we go forward toward these last days?"

My friends nod obediently. I swallow and focus on the grass beneath my feet. I'm everyone's project now. I can't look any of them in the eye. I'm just too embarrassed.

"Well, now, afternoon lessons begin in twenty minutes," Pioneer says. "Hurry and clean up. I'll be expecting you all to be on time." He turns and heads for his truck without looking back.

Silence settles over us. We pull our targets off their mounts and replace them with new ones from the shed at the far end of the field. Dust still swirls in the air from where Pioneer's truck kicked it up. I cough as some of it goes down my throat.

When the range is back in order, Will and I follow Brian and Marie to the cornfield and the road beyond. The air between all of us is still awkward and tense. I hate that I'm proving to be such a failure at defense—even Marie is more reliable at it. I'm not sure how to readjust my instincts, be as quick to shoot as everyone else. Pioneer's help hasn't changed this.

Halfway to the road, Marie turns and points her gun toward the range again. She lowers her voice, makes it sound vaguely mechanical. "I'll be back," she says. Her face is perfectly deadpan. It breaks the awkwardness between all of us, and I want to hug her for it.

Brian rolls his eyes and laughs. "What is it with you two and the Terminator movies? I thought they were supposed to be for guys."

Marie and I look at each other and she grins. "Um, it's impossible not to quote them when Pioneer's shown them to us about a zillion times. And besides, when there are guys in them as totally hot as that Kyle character, they most definitely become girl movies."

Brian plugs his ears. "Not listening," he says a little too loudly, and we all start laughing.

Any remaining tension in the air floats away. I give Marie a grateful look and she winks. I know that I owe it to her—and to Will, Pioneer, and everyone else, for that matter—to come around. These are my people. My Community. My family. I can't trouble myself anymore with the rest of the world. Their fate was decided a long time ago—as was mine.

> If I can manage to help just one other person find peace
> and contentment, well then, I can die a happy man.
> —Pioneer

# TWO

The first time I laid eyes on Pioneer, I was just five years old. He went by another name back then, one closer to the kind the rest of us have, but I don't know what it was anymore, since for as long as I can remember, we've called him Pioneer.

We lived in New York City back then, in the brownstone my parents bought just before my older sister was born. I remember the pink-and-white-striped wallpaper in Karen's and my room and my sister Karen's brown suede school shoes, the ones that she always left right in the middle of the front hall. My mom was holding those shoes when we found out that my sister had disappeared. Karen and I had been out in front of the house playing—well, fighting over what to play, anyway. Karen wanted to draw and I wanted to do hopscotch. I'd run in to tattle on her for pulling my hair, and when I came back with Mom, she was gone. No one saw anything. There were no clues to show where she'd gone or who might've taken her. There was only one bright yellow piece of chalk and a half-drawn picture of our family on the sidewalk out front. In the drawing, only our feet weren't completed. I used to think that whoever took her made her stop there on purpose so we wouldn't have a way to follow.

My mom cradled Karen's shoes to her chest nonstop after that—when the cops showed up to ask questions, and especially a few days later, when the two big buildings downtown got hit by airplanes and the cops stopped looking for my sister and started looking for survivors.

Pioneer came to us not long after. I remember my father letting him in the house. The way he smiled seemed to brighten up the entire room. I hadn't realized how dark it had become, even with the lights on, until he was in it. Something about the way his eyes filled with some unseen candlelight when he smiled made me think of Santa Claus or maybe even Jesus—even though he looked nothing like either of them. He was pale, with close-cropped black hair—nowhere near handsome, but he was kind. I could just feel it.

The few times my mom's spoken about those days, she's mentioned that Pioneer heard about us on the news. He'd told her that he couldn't get Karen's face out of his mind and that my mom's pleas for help haunted him. When the towers fell and the world went crazy, somehow it was my family he felt drawn to. He thought that maybe helping to look for Karen might be a way to focus on one small piece of the giant tragedy surrounding all of us, that this might make it less overwhelming somehow. He offered to help continue our search, and for the next few weeks he made good on his promise. He even brought others along with him. Later, some of those people came with us to Mandrodage Meadows.

I'm not sure why we all took to him like we did. I think maybe we just knew he was special. My family was pretty shy. Quiet. We never needed anyone else around until one of us was gone. But we couldn't find Karen on our own. We were too scared and sad to know what to do. Pioneer never seemed scared or sad. He seemed so sure of everything.

Almost every night, Pioneer sat with my parents in our kitchen for hours while my mom cried. I could hear their voices from my bed when I couldn't sleep, when the emptiness on Karen's side of the room seemed to grow until I was sure it would swallow me whole. I would concentrate on all of their voices, especially the deep tone of Pioneer's voice, like it was the only thing keeping me out of that darkness.

The first time he talked to me, I was spread out on the living room floor underneath the window, where the sun kept the carpet toasty. By then it was the only place in the house where I didn't feel frozen—inside and out. I was drawing the same picture over and over, finishing what Karen had started. I had to. If I hadn't wanted to play hopscotch, if I'd only just decided to draw too, she wouldn't be gone. I kept making my parents, my sister, and me, standing in a row on a thin green line of grass with our hands connected in an unbroken chain. I think maybe I thought that if I drew us this way enough, it would make Karen come back. She was there on the page. Our family picture was complete. She couldn't be gone, not really, not for good.

I'd never been very interested in drawing, not like Karen, but for days I did nothing else. I was hoping that maybe she was just mad and hiding, making me pay for leaving her all alone. If I could only draw enough, she might forgive me and come home. Besides, I couldn't help look for her. My mom wouldn't let me outside, not alone—and after the towers fell, not at all. My mom and dad spent most days on their phones or staring out the window at the sidewalk. It was like they didn't see me anymore, or worse, saw Karen instead. Nothing was the same. I didn't know what would happen if we didn't find my sister. I just knew that what everyone needed most was for me to stay quiet and be good. By the time Pioneer showed up, I had filled four whole sketchpads with drawings.

"What do you have there?" Pioneer asked on that first afternoon as he entered the living room and discovered me. He pointed at my pile of drawings.

I studied the ground and shrugged. I liked him, but he was a stranger, which made him scary.

"May I take a look?" he tried again, and this time held a hand out.

My mom tapped me lightly on the shoulder. Her face was puffy from crying. It made her look scary too. "Go on, sweetie, let him see your pictures."

I took a breath and handed one of my notebooks to him without looking directly at his face. I concentrated on his hands instead. They were soft and his nails were shiny. It made me want to turn his palm over and see if the skin there was just as smooth.

Pioneer held the notebook up in front of him for a while, flipping through the pages. His eyes got shiny and wet, making the light in them extra intense. He whistled softly and let the corners of his mouth turn up in a gentle smile. "Looks like we have a budding artist here. I bet your sister would love these. She looks exactly like she does in her pictures." He pointed at the mantel, where my favorite picture of Karen and me was.

I looked down at the black stick figure that was my sister with spirally yellow hair and no real nose to speak of and felt my lips turn up all on their own. Even I knew that my sister looked nothing like the twig girl I'd created, but somehow what he said made me picture her that way—less real missing girl, more smiley cartoon character. It made me want to laugh. It was like I forgot for just a moment that she wasn't coming back. I bit my lip and my face twisted with the effort to smother a giggle, which made his lips turn up a little more.

"Go ahead, let loose with that smile," he said softly. "You are just too sweet to look so sad."

I scuffed a sneaker against the carpet and tried not to smile. It didn't seem right, not when Karen being gone was all my fault. But then I just couldn't hold it in anymore. I looked up at him and grinned.

These last days leave little room for fear.
Fear eats away at faith, and so it must be
immediately rooted out and stomped underfoot.
—Pioneer

# THREE

My dad is on guard duty when we get back. He's standing by the little one-room station just outside the front gate when we walk up. I concentrate on the wooden sign beside it. It says WELCOME TO MANDRODAGE MEADOWS. It's painted so that the name is floating above a sun-filled field. A lot like the one we've just come from, minus the guns and targets.

I don't want to meet my dad's eyes. I don't want to tell him that I'm still struggling with target practice, but out of the corner of my eye I can see his shoulders fall slightly and I know he's already figured it out.

"It'll be fine," Will says quietly, and takes my hand in his. My dad notices our joined hands and his eyes light back up again. Ever since Pioneer announced that Will was my Intended—the boy he's decided I'll marry next year when I'm eighteen—my mom and dad have celebrated every tiny gesture of affection between us. I wonder if they've noticed that Will's always the one making the gestures, not me. *Will* has definitely noticed, but he hasn't brought it up so far. I doubt I have long, though, before it becomes the next problem Will—and everyone else, for that matter—feels I need to work on.

"Hey, kids, beautiful day, isn't it?" My dad claps Will on the back and tries to tousle my hair even though it's in a braid. I grimace and let go of Will's hand so I can smooth the wayward hairs back into place.

Marie giggles behind us. "As if *that's* going to help."

I pretend to glare at her, but really she's right. My hair has never cooperated with me, not even once. It always lands where it wants to despite my best efforts to tame it—a stick-straight mess. Pointy pieces of hair poke out of my braid like they're trying desperately to keep from bending.

"Headed to class, right?" Dad says with a smile. He leans into the guard station and presses the button that opens the large iron gate to our development. The gate groans loudly as it shudder-slides behind the high brick wall that borders all of Mandrodage Meadows.

"Unfortunately." Marie frowns. "It's too gorgeous out to be cooped up in the clubhouse."

Dad looks at Marie the same way most of the adults in the Community do—like he's not sure whether to hug her or punish her. "Your lessons are important. How do you expect to accurately remember all of this"—Dad gestures to the wide-open spaces beyond the gate—"and learn from its mistakes if you don't understand its history?"

I roll my eyes skyward. We don't have time for one of my father's impassioned lectures on how we are the only future this world has, the keepers of its doomed history and culture. *Blah, blah, blah.* He used to be a structural engineer back in New York, but I'd swear that he really should've been a history teacher, he's so over the top about it.

"We're gonna be late, Dad." I point to my watch. Pioneer has the entire day scheduled, even our free time. Not showing up where you're supposed to be when you're supposed to be there only brings punishment. And I've messed up enough for one day, thank you very much.

"Yeah, okay, sorry," Dad says with an embarrassed smile. "Go on. See you at dinner, Lyla."

I lean up and give him a quick peck on the cheek, and then we rush through the gate. I can hear it rumble closed. I wave at Dad one more time before he disappears behind it, and then we pick up our pace even more.

Mandrodage Meadows looks like any other suburban gated development in America—at least that's what my mom says. Beyond the entry gate is a large circle of houses, twenty in all, one for each of the families that live here. They're made to look like mountain cabins, with lots of stacked stone and log siding. I've always kind of liked the woodsy feel of them.

In the center of the circle is a large green space with a pond, gardens, and picnic area, and beyond that—where the houses end—are our clubhouse, pool, wood shop, barn, and stables. The orchards are at the very back and border the brick wall just beyond the fields where the animals are let out to graze. And just below them is the Silo, our underground shelter, silently waiting for the next three months to go by and for the apocalypse to arrive. It makes my chest tighten to think about it, so I try to ignore it most of the time, but it's hard, since some part of it is underneath just about every inch of ground we walk on here. I look up at the wide-open sky, take a deep gulp of fresh air, and try to focus on the upcoming lessons or Marie's endless chattering. It doesn't work very well.

Sometimes it seems like our families have put out a lot of wasted money and effort to make it so nice in the aboveground buildings, since everything will be destroyed in the end. Pioneer says that apart from giving our families a comfortable place to live for the past ten years, the cushy normality of it serves as a distraction to anyone who happens to find us. Visitors here would see us as very reclusive, eccentric suburbanites. They certainly wouldn't expect us to have an underground shelter hidden beneath the orchards or an armory of guns to protect it. Even our development's name enhances the illusion. "Mandrodage Meadows" sounds kind of uppity, vaguely French. We're the only ones that know that it's an anagram for "Armageddon Meadows"—a private joke that Pioneer made up.

We jog all the way to the clubhouse, making it to the meeting room just in time to take our seats before Pioneer arrives. He takes his place at the front of the room, sitting cross-legged on top of the Formica table there. He leans back on his hands and smiles at us. There are thirty of us in all—every child in the Community—all of us around the same age. There are equal numbers of guys and girls—something the Brethren had Pioneer be sure of when he picked families to move here. This way we each have an Intended. Will with me, Brian with Marie, and so on. No detail of our lives has been left to chance.

Pioneer picks up one of the thick books beside him and opens it on his lap. He clears his throat. "Today we will focus on history, specifically the characters throughout whose bad decisions—their . . . hesitations—jeopardized their countries as well as their fellow man." He pauses and looks at me, his lips curling into a smile. "Historical cowards is our topic for today. Any thoughts on this . . . Little Owl?"

His words blindside me. My face burns all over. All eyes are on me, waiting. Even though Will, Brian, and Marie are the only ones who could possibly know what happened at target practice, I feel exposed. *Is he really going to out me to everyone?*

"Um, not really, no," I say. The others laugh nervously. The air feels charged. I know I'm not the only one who senses it. But then Pioneer chuckles and launches into a detailed lecture about George B. McClellan, a Union general during the Civil War who kept refusing to engage in battle even when he had the clear advantage—my historical counterpart, I guess. Pioneer is obviously not done reforming me yet.

I want to find some excuse to leave, ask to go to the bathroom, fake sickness, anything so I won't have to keep sitting here. Will puts his hand on my leg. He's holding it a little too tightly—agreeing with Pioneer, forcing me to stay. He nods emphatically as Pioneer talks. His devotion to protecting the Community is borderline manic sometimes.

I fight the urge to wrestle my leg out from under Will's hand. If I run, I will only prove what they're starting to suspect—that I'm a coward and that it's their duty to try harder to rehabilitate me. That kind of attention frightens me more than anything else.

After class, I rush out without a word. I want to paint by the lake or head out to the corral and saddle Indy, but I know Will will just follow me there and I don't want to see him right now. His need for perfection in all things, even rule following, is frustrating to be around sometimes, and the way he acted in class has me more than a little angry. I don't need him to remind me of what I need to work on, so I head home instead.

My mom's in the kitchen preparing dinner. It's Sunday, the one day a week when we eat in our own homes. Every other meal is eaten in the dining room at the clubhouse with the rest of the Community. For once I'm glad it's

Sunday. Not having to face Will and Pioneer tonight is the one bright spot in this whole wreck of a day.

I linger in the doorway and watch my mom chop vegetables. She lifts her foot and scratches the back of her leg with one toe. Her hair is pulled back into a haphazard ponytail. The light from outside enhances the red-gold in it, effectively camouflaging the gray that's started to come in. She's tinier than I am, and although we're both pale, she's much thinner, more fragile looking. Standing behind her, I feel taller, curvier—sturdier—like a coffee mug placed next to a china teacup.

She turns to drop her pile of cucumbers and tomatoes into a bowl of cold pasta noodles and sees me. "Hey there. Dinner's almost done. Would you mind tracking down your father?"

"Sure." I come up beside her and reach into the bowl to grab a cucumber and she swats at my hand. Part of me wants to talk to her about what happened out on the field . . . but can she understand? When she practices shooting, I know she's like me and also imagines the targets as actual people, but for her it's different. She sees the person who took Karen and she's never missed a shot. Not once.

I decide to just walk away and leave her to finish making our meal. She's humming to herself as I leave the kitchen. I'll have to try to imagine whoever took Karen when I shoot next, but I know I won't be able to draw from the same emotions that she does. Karen is all faded for me, not a flesh-and-blood girl anymore, just one more thing to feel guilty about. Is it because I'm missing some crucial part of my heart that I can't keep feeling the pain the way Mom does? Am I really just like McClellan, cowardly and selfish? The worst of it is that I *want* to be good, to do what's expected. So why do I still hesitate?

"So how'd target practice go today?" Dad asks between mouthfuls of pasta salad once we've sat down to dinner. I sigh heavily and set my fork down on the place mat. When I look up, the first thing I see is the picture of Pioneer that we keep on the kitchen wall. I always feel like the real Pioneer's watching me through it somehow. *There goes my appetite.*

"Something tells me you already know how it went," I mumble.

"I have an idea." Dad leans back in his chair and looks at me. Mom looks from me to him and back again. Now I get the rare privilege of telling her what happened after not telling her as soon as I came home and then getting a double dose of lecturing from both of them. *Wonderful.* I push down on the tines of my fork with my fingers, making the handle bang against the table.

"Kneecaps," Dad says in explanation, and my mom makes an "Ooohhh" face. My shooting habits aren't exactly a surprise to either of them, I guess.

"Look, I shot the heart today, okay? Pioneer already

talked to me about this. I get what I have to do." I lean back in my chair and look up at the ceiling.

Dad wipes his mouth on his napkin. "We've never doubted that. But can you do it when there's a face staring at you instead of black plywood?"

"If I have to, yes," I say, but I'm not the greatest liar. I don't even convince myself.

"That'd be easier to believe if you actually shot accurately without being prodded by Pioneer first," Dad says.

I glance up at my mom. I was sort of hoping that she'd take pity on me and change the subject, but she's holding Dad's hand now, making them a united front.

Dad goes into lecture mode. "Look, none of us want to hurt people. You get that, right? But we may have to make some hard choices pretty soon in order to survive. The Community's stayed safe for a lot of years, but we're still a point of curiosity for the towns around here. Don't you think they wonder why we're out here all alone? Do you think that once the earth's rotation reverses, they won't figure it out? We only have enough supplies stockpiled for our own people, and even then we might not have enough. If people start showing up here looking for shelter, they aren't just gonna take 'Sorry, we're full up' as an answer and walk away. They'll fight," Dad says, the volume of his voice gradually increasing with his enthusiasm for this subject. "Would you really risk one of us dying to ease your own misguided conscience?"

"You're being too soft speaking of them that way,

Thomas." My mom's eyes are rippling with tears. "Those people out there are monsters. Evil. Each and every last one of them. They need to be wiped from this earth. Not one deserves our mercy. The Brethren watched all of us for years. They know the Outsiders' motives. We are the chosen, the ones who showed true goodness and compassion. We are meant to survive, not them. And if they come here before the end—or just after the disasters begin—we cannot feel sorry for them. Not ever. We would only be helping to keep evil alive, and all of this, all that we've done here, would be for nothing." She's started trembling now. I watch as she looks over at Pioneer's picture. She puts a hand out and touches the frame with the same kind of anxious strokes that she uses when she rubs Karen's shoes. If somehow Pioneer really can watch us through that picture, she probably sees it as comforting.

I stare at my plate. Tears blur my own vision, making everything look like an abstract painting. "I don't know what's wrong with me, okay? I want to do what I'm supposed to, believe me . . . but I just, I don't know. I just freeze up or something."

Mom puts a hand on one of my shoulders and Dad puts his hand on the other, their other hands still tightly clasped together. We are all connected now in one unbroken circle.

"It isn't wrong to defend yourself, honey. What would be wrong is not fighting to keep the people you love alive," Mom says.

They're right, of course. I couldn't live with myself if something happened to them, to Will or Marie. I've been selfish, and worse—stupid. I have to do better.

"I'll shoot right from now on." I speak my words like a vow—to them and to myself. I'm not a little kid anymore. I can't choose to ignore what's happening. It's time I grow up.

> It's a foolish person who keeps putting himself in danger.
> We must do what we can to survive, to protect those we love.
> —Pioneer

# FOUR

We never found Karen. We buried an empty coffin along with many, many other New Yorkers that fall and tried to tell ourselves a funeral without a body was somehow just as final. When it was over, my mom couldn't go home, not to a place with nothing but reminders of what we'd lost. The city was starting to feel like a foreign country, not ours anymore.

We spent a few months in a rented apartment while my parents tried to figure out what we should do and where we should go next. My mom took me out of school and promised to teach me my letters herself, but she spent most days under the covers staring out the window, leaving me to wander around the apartment alone all day. I drew pictures nonstop. I guess I was still trying to make things right.

My mom was scared all the time too—scared someone would take me, scared that there'd be more terrorist attacks. My dad didn't say much, but he didn't have to. His eyes were as empty as that coffin had been. We were alone a lot of the time. My parents didn't have many friends even before Karen went away. And since Mom grew up in foster care and Dad was an only child with parents who died before I was born, there weren't any grandparents or aunts and uncles to come help comfort us.

Pioneer was the only one who came around. He didn't stop visiting us, helping where he could. He seemed to think that he could solve our problems. He said that we weren't alone. Many of the people he knew were scared all the time too, fed up with living in a world that felt like it was teetering on the edge of destruction. He said that they were pooling their resources to build what he called the Community out west, charting their own course just like people did so long ago. My parents liked the idea of uninterrupted land and sky, of a place where you could see trouble coming a mile away and deal with it before it ever made it all the way to your doorstep. Pioneer said that they could use my dad to help build the place there, since he was a structural engineer. Pioneer wanted to make it safe, so safe we would never need to leave.

My dad left the city first. He moved with Pioneer and some of the others almost right away. My mom and I stayed behind to sell the house, the furniture, and anything we couldn't carry with us on the plane. We began our new life with as little of our old one as possible, but I didn't mind. My parents were acting a little more like themselves again. I felt for the first time in more months than I could count that life was really starting for us. And I wanted it more than I could say out loud without feeling guilty for wanting anything after Karen.

Mandrodage Meadows looked nothing like it does now. The basic skeletons of what would become our homes and the clubhouse were there, but mostly it was a large open field peppered with trailers and tents. I loved it. It was like one big adventure, like something out of a book.

While my mom got us settled into our tiny trailer, unpacking our few things and making up the beds, I got out my sketchpad and started walking in a wide circle around the trailer. I didn't want to watch her tuck Karen's shoes by the front door. She called to me from the window and told me to stay close to our trailer, and I did, but I was itching to explore. So I sketched instead and tried to put all my restlessness and excitement onto the paper.

"Hey, you're the new girl," a boy who looked about my age yelled from between two nearby tents. He was heavily freckled and his hair stuck up in a dozen different directions, but I liked it. Everything about him made me want to smile. He jogged over to where I was.

"I'm Will." He held out his hand to shake mine, a weirdly formal thing for a kid to do. He seemed to be trying really hard not to scare me. It made me wonder how much he knew about my family already.

"I'm Lyla," I said quietly.

Will bobbed his head, and we stared at each other for a moment before he laughed. "Wanna play?"

I was a little shy. I hadn't had many friends up to that point. I had mainly played with Karen before. I nodded and studied the ground.

"Well, come on, then. The others are out at the lake playing ball. You ever play baseball?"

I shrugged. "No."

"I'll teach you. It's not too hard." Will reached for my hand to pull me along with him just as my mom opened the trailer door and peered outside. I thought she would panic and pull me inside with her, but instead she smiled faintly.

"Looks like you're making friends already, sweetie."

"Will wanted me to come play ball," I mumbled— almost too low for her to hear. I was so sure she would say no. After all, I hadn't been out of her sight for the better part of a year, but she surprised me by smiling a little wider.

"I think that would be fun," she said slowly. I looked up at her, studied the pattern of shadow and light in her eyes, and tried to decide if she really meant it.

"I'll just come with and read a book while you play. Give me one second." Mom ducked back inside and I stared after her. She was going to let me play. Sure, she was coming too, but I didn't care. I was going to be with other kids again. I put my sketchbook in the grass by the front door and skipped between Mom and Will the whole way to the lake. There were loads of kids there my age tumbling through the grass, hitting baseballs, and shoving each other as they ran the bases. For the first time in a long time, I didn't want to draw what I was seeing—I wanted to be a part of it.

We played until it was too dark to see. My mom stayed and watched me for hours, but eventually she started to drift back toward the trailers and some of the other adults who were gathered there. She hadn't given me such a long leash of freedom since Karen. It felt good, like stretching my legs did after the long plane trip we took to get there.

That night we ate our first meal with the Community. I loved it because the table was never quiet, not like back in New York. We ate outside, with Pioneer grilling up burgers and my dad leaning over site plans with some of the other men.

Later, I ended up sprawled in the grass with a belly full of potato salad and watermelon. I was too tired to sit up any longer. I couldn't remember ever being this utterly spent. Will was lying beside me and we were throwing grapes into each other's mouths. All around us, people laughed and talked and ate. I couldn't stop smiling. I had a new best friend and plenty of room to run around. I never wanted to leave. I was home.

I watch over these people. They've put their safety,
their very futures, in my hands. It's an awesome responsibility,
to be sure. But I wouldn't have it any other way.
—Pioneer

# FIVE

As soon as the sun starts filling up my room in the morning, I throw on some clothes and head for the stables. I want to forget about yesterday, to put a mile of prairie between me and any thoughts of self-defense. Of course, I'll have to settle for riding Indy around the corral instead.

Riding always clears my head and calms me down. I'm sure that if I ride long enough now I'll be able to get my head straight and dedicate myself to what I need to do. Plus, I love the smell of the barn. It's a medley of sweet hay and warm saddle leather with a not-so-subtle undercurrent of manure, which sounds disgusting because of the poop but is actually really nice. I wish there was a way to convey this smell in my paintings. Somehow it's as much of what makes this place beautiful as the scenery is.

Indy's in the last stall on the right. He's already snorting and kicking at his door. He knows I'm coming and that I always bring carrots.

"Hey, boy. Ready to ride?" I say. He nuzzles my fingers while I feed him.

We ride out into the center of the corral. It's still pretty quiet, which makes me feel like I'm completely alone. Most of the rest of the Community is still getting ready for the day. There's just Indy and about a dozen lazy flies to keep me company. I ride early on purpose. I love it when I have the place all to myself.

I nudge Indy in the flanks and he lunges forward. We go from a bouncy trot to a rocking canter, and I sit back into the saddle and let my mind go blank. The only way this morning could get better is if there was enough space for Indy to gallop, but the corral's too small and we're not allowed to ride out on the prairie alone. We have to go in a group, which for me defeats the purpose of riding, really. Still, I settle for the corral and pretend that it's bigger than it is and not just a horse-sized hamster wheel. And I feel better, more relaxed, by the time some of the other Community members are beginning their morning chores. I can do what I'm supposed to. I *will do* what I'm supposed to. From now on I will stop resisting what Pioneer wants.

An hour later I'm on guard duty at the front gate with Brian. I've never understood why we have round-the-clock coverage here. It's not like we ever get visitors, at least not with any regularity. Except this time there is a visitor. A car trailing a cloud of dust is heading down the dirt road that leads to the development.

Brian notices it first. I'm just about to lay down my

winning hand in Uno when he leans forward in his chair and squints out the front window. He grabs the binoculars, then curses under his breath and gets the walkie-talkie from the built-in table beneath the window.

"Pioneer, we got a live one headed this way." He lets go of the speaker button and the walkie-talkie crackles for a moment.

"One car?"

"Yes, sir."

"I'm on my way."

I grab the binoculars from the table where Brian left them and try to get a better view of the approaching car. It's a police cruiser, maybe a few miles away at most. I can see it after I focus the binoculars a little more, but the bar of lights on top isn't flashing. Still, it sends a chill up my spine and my stomach flutters.

"Brian, take another look." I hand over the binoculars.

"Well, crap," he mutters, and grabs for one of the guns hidden beneath the table and tucks it into his belt, pulling his shirt out and over it. He calls Pioneer again.

"Treat it as a welcome rubbernecker right now. No need to panic yet," Pioneer says. Anybody who wanders into our development out of curiosity we call a rubbernecker. A welcome rubbernecker is someone we don't turn away at the gate.

I jump as our development's siren lets out three short bursts at half volume—just loud enough to hear within our walls—our code for unexpected company. Basically, it means be alert, but carry on as usual. A few people will need to head to the orchard and drive a truck across the path that leads to the Silo's entry door, just to be safe, and our guns will have to be quickly tucked away. In other words, we have to take out the apocalyptic and leave in the suburban.

I straighten my shirt and shorts, then my hair. Not that any of these things gives away much more than my inability to look anything other than ordinary—which is a good thing right now, I guess.

"Be calm, Lyla," Brian grumbles. "Quit fussing with your clothes."

I paste a smile on my face and then realize it looks all wrong, so I bite my lip instead. Brian rolls his eyes and groans. "Oh, man, you suck at this. Just stand behind me, 'kay?"

A few short minutes later, the police car comes to a stop beside the guardhouse.

"Stay here," Brian says as he opens the door.

There are three people in the car. I can see the two men in the front clearly, but the person in the back is hunched behind the passenger seat. All I can see is the top of his head. The driver's-side window rolls down as Brian gets closer to it. I lean around the door to see and hear better. The man in the driver's seat is about my dad's age. His eyes stand out more than anything else. They seem to be on alert, watchful—sharp inside his softly rounded face.

"Hello there." He smiles up at Brian even as he sizes

him up. "I'm looking for a Mr. Gerald Brown. He lives here, correct?"

Brian puts a hand on the top of the car and leans down. "Yes, sir. May I ask what you need him for?"

"His sister's looking for him. Family business." The man looks Brian up and down, takes in his broad chest and untucked shirt. "Nothing to be concerned about. I'm assuming we're welcome?" There's a challenge in his voice even though he's smiling brightly, and Brian recoils a little. I retreat back into the guard booth and put my hand on the gun hidden underneath the table. I'm not sure what I'll do if I need it, but it's what Pioneer's taught us to do.

"You are absolutely welcome, sir." Brian sounds convincingly casual, and I allow myself to relax a little, but still I keep my fingers on the gun. "We just like to keep a record of our visitors."

The man nods and settles back against the seat, content for now. Brian turns to me and points at the gate. I take my hand off the gun and press the button that opens it. The car slowly begins to roll forward, and the driver waves to me as they pass. The person in the back has moved to sit behind the driver and now he's looking out the window at me. He's about my age.

I stare in at him. He's handsome—it's not something I know because I've cataloged his physical features already. In fact, I can't say what his eyes look like or what color his hair is. It's more of an immediate knowing in my gut—breath-stealing and unsettling. And I can't look away. He smiles at me and I stumble backward a little.

Brian gives me a look. "Cut out the nervous nonsense and get over here. You're being really weird."

I make myself follow him. We trail behind the car as it moves toward the gate, now halfway open. Beyond it is Pioneer. He's got his biggest, warmest smile on and is motioning the car forward, pointing to where they should park. I try to ignore the boy in the backseat. I don't want to look at him, but I can tell he's looking out the back window at Brian and me. I focus on Pioneer instead and let Brian walk slightly ahead of me, effectively hiding me from the boy.

The two men in the front seat get out quickly. They look a lot alike in their uniforms, but you can tell that the driver's in charge by the way the other man stands slightly behind him. They take turns shaking Pioneer's hand and exchanging pleasantries. Brian and I are lingering just outside of the gate, still unsure whether we are supposed to come in or remain on duty.

The boy in the backseat of the car gets out slowly. He's not in a uniform like the other two. His hair is even more unruly than I originally thought now that I have a clear view of it. It's about a dozen shades of brown, lightest along the top where the sun hits it. He moves a piece of it out of his eyes and nods at us before he goes to join the others.

"What do you think this is about?" I whisper to Brian.

He shrugs. "Can't imagine it's anything good."

"What could they want with Mr. Brown?" I wonder.

"Got me. Maybe he did something he shouldn't last time he went for the supplies."

"He hasn't been in town for a long time, though," I say.

Pioneer looks over at us like he's deciding something before he calls to me. "Lyla, could you come here, please?"

I nod and walk over to Pioneer, careful to keep my pace steady, relaxed, and confident. After yesterday I want to prove to him that I can do whatever's necessary without hesitation. He pulls me off to one side.

"Mr. Brown's relatives sent these men to check up on him. His brother passed on recently and they wanted to let him know."

"Oh, I'm sorry," I say to no one in particular. I guess I should say this to Mr. Brown, but since he's not right in front of me, I feel the need to say it to Pioneer. He nods and continues. "I will be taking them to see Mr. Brown and his family now. It may take a while."

Our guests are staring at me. I squirm a little, I can't help it. Pioneer's eyes harden slightly—his subtle warning to quit acting strange. I swallow and smile. "What can I do to help?"

The man who was driving the car steps forward and offers me his hand to shake. "Lyla, is it? Nice to meet you. I'm Sheriff Crowley. I asked your . . . Pioneer if you'd do us a favor and take my son, Cody, on a tour of your development here. He's helping out at the station right now and is on a ride-along with us today, but he's liable to be bored by this bit of business. Would you mind showing him around and letting him ask you some questions about Mandrodage Meadows?" He says our development's name carefully and smiles at me. I can feel everyone watching me. I have to fight the twitching in my lips. "A tour might prove to be a good deal more interesting for him," the sheriff says like he's not sure that I'm on board with playing tour guide to his son.

Cody's staring at me, his face tilted like he's curious about my reaction. My face turns red and I glance at Pioneer. He nods his consent, but he doesn't look entirely comfortable with the idea. "Sure, I guess," I say.

"Brian, please return to the gatehouse. Lyla will rejoin you when she's through here," Pioneer says. Brian looks disappointed, but he heads back to his post anyway.

Pioneer gives me a look that's heavy with meaning. "Make sure he gets a thorough tour."

I can tell by the way that he emphasizes "thorough" that he means the opposite. I turn back to Cody. Pioneer is already ushering the older men toward Mr. Brown's house. Cody's standing beside me with his hands in the pockets of his low-slung jeans. I let my eyes linger on his chest just long enough to see that it's muscular. He's smiling widely now, obviously aware that I'm studying his chest, so I focus on the faded words spread out across his T-shirt.

" 'Save Ferris'?" I ask.

He looks down. "Yeah. It's from this old eighties movie. *Ferris Bueller's Day Off.*"

When I don't respond, he looks a little embarrassed. "It's kind of a joke. My mom used to play it whenever I was sick. My sister and I've always sort of liked that movie. She bought me the shirt."

"I don't get it, what's the joke?"

"My sister calls me Ferris sometimes. And since I want out of Culver Creek as soon as possible . . . she just thought it was funny, like I need saving from our town."

"Oh," I say, but then I still don't totally understand. "Why do you need saving from Culver Creek?"

I think about the neatly painted shops downtown with their hanging baskets filled with flowers and the old homes lining the main road, all elaborate Victorians complete with gingerbread trim. It's beautiful there. I've always thought it was bizarre that inherently evil people would want to live in such pretty places.

Cody seems to consider my question as he looks up and down our street. It's oddly empty for this time of day, but I can feel a dozen or more pairs of eyes peeking at us from inside the houses. *Are my parents watching, or even worse, Will?* The thought makes me nervous and strangely guilty, like talking to Cody is somehow wrong, even though Pioneer told me to.

"I want to work in movies and they don't exactly make them in places like Culver Creek," he says. "At least not so far."

"As an actor?" I guess. That's what Marie's brother wanted to do when he left us. It makes sense. Like Drew,

Cody's every bit as cute as any of the actors I've ever seen on movie night.

He looks at me strangely. "No. I want to work in visual effects."

"Huh?"

"Think *The Wolfman* or *Lord of the Rings*—the makeup and creation of characters—monsters and stuff."

"Those are movies . . . right?"

"Um, yeah. You haven't seen them, huh?"

"We see movies," I say quickly. "But not lots."

"What's the last movie you watched?"

"*The Day After Tomorrow* and *The Terminator*. Last weekend. Double feature. You know—'Are you Sarah Connor?'" I try to say the last part with the proper accent, but it comes out sounding utterly corny. Cody laughs, though, and once my initial embarrassment wears off, I join him.

"Wow, okay, those are good examples, albeit *old*, of movies with visual effects. *Day After Tomorrow*'s a little more current, though. I'm hoping to be one of the guys who makes characters like the Terminator look realistic. So, you don't go to the movies while they're in the theater?"

"We don't leave Mandrodage Meadows very often," I say, and hope he'll let it go at that.

"I kind of knew that," he says quietly. "You like to keep to yourselves out here, don't you?"

"Something like that." I look away. "Ready for your

tour? I'm afraid it won't be overly interesting." I'm anxious to get started and focus on a less dangerous topic.

"Really? 'Cause I'm convinced that it'll be *very* interesting," Cody says, and winks at me. "You guys are kind of a hot topic in town. It'll be nice to finally see for myself where you're hiding the dead bodies and child brides."

"Excuse me?" I stop walking and stare at him.

His grin widens. "You have to know that people think you're some kind of crazy cult out here. It's a small town. You've been coming into town and leaving again like ghosts on and off for years. We're the closest town to you and none of us even know exactly how many of you there are out here. It's only natural that folks'll start thinking you're up to no good."

I don't know what to say. I walk ahead a little and wrap my arms around myself. "It's not like that. We like to live simply, that's all. There's nothing interesting here unless you count farm animals and gardens as gossip-worthy. And for the record, no one who lives here is under fifteen and the only married people are way past their teens— trust me, there aren't any child brides."

Cody's smile fades. "Hey, I didn't mean to make you mad, really. I was trying to be funny."

"Well, you weren't," I grumble.

He looks so disappointed that I immediately soften. "Forget about it. It's fine. Let's just get started."

I take Cody to the clubhouse first and show him the

pool, our lessons room, and the room where we eat most of our meals together. Then we head over to the corrals. Only the animals are there, watching us with mildly curious faces as they munch on their feed. I wonder if Cody notices that there aren't any other people around.

"Sheep, pigs, and goats, fascinating," Cody says dryly. He turns and looks in the opposite direction, his eyes resting on the dirt road that leads to the apple orchards. "So, what's down there?" He starts moving toward it.

He can't go down there. Even with the truck blocking the road further in, if he gets too close he might see the Silo's entrance. Before he gets far, out of desperation I grab his arm and loop my own through the crook of his elbow. It feels really, really bizarre to be this close to him, an Outsider. I can feel the curve of his forearm under my fingers—a bit smaller and leaner than Will's. My stomach flutters and my face gets hot. He looks down at my arm and then at me. He raises one eyebrow at me. Marie is better at this type of thing than I am. I have no idea how to flirt effectively. I paste on what I hope is a friendly (but not too friendly) smile. "There's just a bunch of apple trees and old farm equipment back there. Come inside the stable. Please, I want to introduce you to someone."

Cody looks at the orchard one last time, but allows me to lead him past the corrals and into the stable. One by one, the horses look up as we pass. Their ears flick back and forth. One or two poke their noses out into the walkway between the stalls. Cody leans in closer to me each time, and our shoulders keep touching as we walk. Every time it happens I get the same thrill inside my chest. This boy is making me nervous, and I don't think it's because he might see something on our tour that he shouldn't.

I look up at him, trying to see if it's happening to him too, but his face is pinched and uncertain.

"What?" I ask. I'm surprised at how disappointed I am that he doesn't seem to notice the strange tension between us.

He won't look at me now. His eyes are glued to the stalls on his side of the stable and the horses inside them. "Um, I'm not exactly a big fan of these guys," he says, and his face goes pink.

"Really? Why?" I stop just before Indy's stall and drop Cody's arm. Cody stays in the middle of the walkway. He still won't turn fully to face me.

It hits me then. "You're afraid of them," I say slowly. I have to work at keeping my face straight because I have a feeling I'll really embarrass him if I start smiling—or worse—laughing.

"Not afraid exactly . . . just not a fan," he says. *He is scared of them.* I shake my head and try to process this. This boy is quite possibly stranger than I thought he'd be. But his fear makes me feel better, less nervous.

I turn toward Indy's stall and grin. *Wait till I tell Marie about this.* Indy's already by the door, his neck straining out into the walkway toward me.

"Hey, big guy, how's your morning going?" I coo at

him, and he puts his head into my shoulder and leaves it there—the closest thing to a hug hello that he can manage.

I can feel Cody watching me, watching us. My fingers start to tremble in Indy's mane. Cody's eyes on me have every part of my body on high alert, but I'm not scared. In fact, I think I like it. I look back at him and try to be calm. "They're really gentle, you know. And smart. So, so smart." I run my hand across the top of Indy's head, let my fingers toy gently with one ear. He moves his head up and down against my shoulder.

"This is Indy. He's mine. We kind of grew up together. He's about the gentlest horse there is. If you come say hello to him, I promise he'll behave. It's impossible to be scared by this guy." I hug his head.

Cody's still in the same spot, but his face isn't as tense. The corners of his mouth are turned up into the beginnings of a smile. "He really loves you, doesn't he?" he says.

"Not nearly as much as I love him." I plant a kiss on the blaze running down the center of Indy's face. "He's a better listener than anyone else I know. And he's easy to please. Give him a carrot and take him for a ride and he's ecstatic." I can't help thinking about target practice yesterday. "He never expects anything more than that." I realize that I'm not smiling anymore and that Cody's looking at me strangely all of a sudden. I chew on my lip and try to quickly pull myself together.

"Come here." I motion for him to get closer to Indy and me.

"I don't know . . . ," he begins.

"He'll be sweet, I promise."

Cody still looks skeptical, but he inches toward me anyway. I'm not sure if it's because I was that convincing or if it's just that he doesn't want to seem like a giant wimp. Either way, he ends up next to me. I take his hand and put it to Indy's nose. I can sense more than see him smiling at me.

"Feel that. Isn't it the softest thing ever?"

Indy doesn't hesitate. He buries his nose in Cody's hand, happy to have so much attention. Cody stiffens and I let out a little laugh as Indy moves a little closer to Cody and nuzzles his Ferris shirt, leaving a wide smudge of slobber and dirt across his chest. Cody makes a face and we both burst out laughing at the same time.

By the time we say goodbye to Indy and leave the stable, I'm feeling less wary. Indy doesn't warm up to just anybody. He never nuzzles Will. I try not to read anything into that. All I know for sure is that Cody's funny and nice and I'm having more fun than I've had in a while.

We walk in silence at first, but Cody doesn't let it last long. He launches into a story about his first time around horses, when his mom put him on the back of one to take a picture and it took off running. He was stuck holding on for dear life until it ran itself out. It was probably terrifying for him, but he makes it sound hilarious instead. I watch him talk, the way his hands move as he does. There's something almost painful about being around him. He makes me so nervous that I can barely stand still. I'm pretty sure that I'm smiling way too much and laughing way too loud. Still, I can't stop myself, and even stranger, I don't want to. I look for the evil that has to be lurking just underneath the surface, but all I see is a boy . . . and an extremely cute boy at that.

"How long have you lived here?" he asks.

"Ten years."

"And you've been to Culver Creek before? Because I'm sure I've never seen you there."

"Yes. We all take turns getting some of the supplies we need, like clothes and batteries and stuff," I say. "But since there's so many of us and not enough trucks for us to take to town all at once, we only go twice a month. My family's only been to town about once or twice a year since we moved here." *What am I doing? SHUT UP, blabbermouth!*

"And I thought I had it bad. How do you cope with being stuck here all the time? I think I'd go out of my mind."

"I don't really think about it." I don't add that Mandrodage Meadows has always felt the opposite of confining when compared with our future living quarters in the Silo . . . or that Culver Creek always feels too large and dangerous. So many Outsiders and there's no way of knowing which ones pose the biggest threat, which ones might do one of us harm, like the person who took Karen.

He's walking close enough to me that we keep touching shoulders again. I can smell his cologne or shampoo—it's citrusy and spicy at the same time. I like it. I wonder what he thinks of me. I'm liable to smell like hay and horse manure after this morning's ride—not nearly as pleasant a combination as his is. I put a little space between us.

I show him everything but the orchards. He doesn't seem to care when we pass the road that leads into them without stopping. We finish up by the pond and settle into the grass to wait for his father. I'm surprised we've been left alone this long. A few other members of the Community are out in the garden, and there were a few others by the stables, but mostly the entire place feels quiet, almost deserted. I wonder if he's noticed and thinks it's strange. I'd half expected Marie to ambush us somewhere along the way. It's not like her to stay away—not that I'm complaining. She would've taken over the tour and I'd have been left to tag along behind her. It's been nice not to be part of her background for a change.

"So, unless you're on a supply run, you never leave . . ." His voice trails off.

"Right," I say, and chuck a rock into the water. It was really stupid of me to tell him all of that. We both watch the rock skip across the surface three times before it sinks.

"Nice." He grins. "But I can beat that."

I watch as he gathers up a handful of rocks and then chooses one to throw. It skips twice and disappears. I smile.

"Okay, best out of three," he says, and then, after his second throw is equally unsuccessful, "I guess you can't get some kind of special permission to leave any other time?"

"Special permission for what?" I ask, and he looks shy for the first time since he's gotten here.

"I don't know, maybe to hang out . . . with me?" He smiles and my mouth drops open. I've messed up. I've been too nice and gotten myself into trouble once again.

"I can't," I say quickly, and take a step away from him.

"I sort of figured, but it didn't hurt to ask." His lips curl slightly into a half smile. He chucks the last rock. This one doesn't even skip once. It just sinks.

He doesn't look at me right away and I feel awkward and squirmy. For some reason I feel the need to explain myself. It bothers me that he looks a little hurt by my answer, but there's no way to do this without giving away too much or completely insulting him in the process. *Gee, I think you're really, really cute and all, but I can't go because you're an Outsider and probably have the potential for serious evil and I'm chosen and pure and about to enter a shelter that'll keep me safe while the world implodes and you die. No hard feelings?*

"Kind of seems like you're trapped here, Lyla. Are you?" Cody tilts his head and studies me.

"No, I like it here," I say automatically.

I'm not supposed to feel trapped here, but now, in this moment—and if I'm honest, more and more all the time—I do, I can't help myself. I *am* trapped. For good reason, sure, but trapped all the same. But it isn't like any of us can really change our minds and move away from here. We have no money of our own, nowhere to go. And it doesn't make much sense to even consider it, since the world is about to end. Still, I can't help wishing that I could go out with Cody and maybe see what a kiss feels like when Will's not on the other end of it . . . but this kind of wishing is foolish and I can't indulge it.

"Lyla." Pioneer's standing by the picnic tables with the sheriff and the other man. He looks irritated and ready to be rid of our guests. Cody's father hands a piece of paper to Pioneer, and Pioneer nods and puts it in his front shirt pocket. I stand up and brush the grass from my shorts. Cody gets up more slowly and stretches.

"It was nice to meet you," I say loudly in a more formal tone than I used when we were alone. And then I surprise myself, lean closer to him and whisper something I know I shouldn't.

"You know, my family's assigned to the next supply run into town this Saturday." I can't quite look at him afterward. *What am I doing?*

He shoots me a sidelong glance and a slow smile spreads across his face, lighting up his gray-green eyes. "Maybe we'll run into each other. Could happen . . . especially if I have a general idea of where you're going to be."

My breath quickens. I can feel his smile becoming contagious and I return it with one of my own. "We'll probably be at Walmart for most of the morning."

"I happen to love that store. Where else can you get a haircut, goldfish, and camping gear all at the same time?"

He winks at me and I have to clamp my mouth shut to

keep from laughing. I've never felt so reckless. It's terrifying, but exhilarating too. I look over to where the adults are standing. Pioneer is watching us now, so I force myself to sober up.

"I hope you enjoyed your tour."

Cody catches on quickly and shakes my hand stiffly. Still, his thumb strokes the top of my hand for half a second and my stomach takes a free fall to my shoes. "I did, thank you very much."

I turn toward Pioneer and together we walk Cody and the other two men the rest of the way to their car. We wave. The car turns toward the gate and then rolls slowly through it. I know that as soon as the gate is completely closed, Pioneer will want a detailed accounting of my time with Cody. I should tell him everything, right down to the "chance encounter" Cody and I might have on Saturday. I can redeem myself, and shake off this awful temptation before it takes root. I promised myself after target practice that I would follow the rules from now on, that I wouldn't knowingly put the Community in danger. *So why am I already preparing to lie?*

We can't let the propagation of humanity be decided
by a fickle rush of hormones.

—Pioneer

# SIX

I was thirteen when I found out that Will and I would get married someday. Will had just celebrated his fourteenth birthday the month before, and Jessica, the youngest kid in the Community, had just turned twelve. Now no one was under what Pioneer called "the age of accountability." We were all finally old enough to know who the Brethren meant for us to pair with, and the Community was abuzz about it.

I was all knocking knees and shivery insides as I walked the other girls to the clubhouse. Pioneer was planning to announce our Intendeds before that night's movie and just after dinner. We were dressed up for the occasion, something we rarely ever did. Pioneer had our moms order us new dresses and our very first high heels. They were all exactly the same, right down to their colors, because we bought them in bulk just like everything else, but it didn't really matter—at least not to me. I loved the staccato click my heels made as I walked toward the clubhouse. Our parents, along with the boys, were waiting for us there.

When we entered the dining room, the boys stood up. They were equally dressy in shirts, ties, and black pants. They seemed to stand straighter in them, grow older before our eyes. These weren't the dusty-faced boys we'd just played baseball with the other day. They were suddenly strange and far more serious. Grown-up, or at least trying to appear that way.

I fiddled with my hair, which was curly like Marie's for once. I tried to fluff it up. My mom had rag-rolled it the night before, and while the curls had been tight and springy when she first undid them, now they were already starting to droop and go straight. Silently I cursed my stubborn, straight hair.

Marie swatted at my hand. "Leave it or it'll just get straighter."

Together we looked up and down the row of boys. We'd spent the last few weeks obsessing over who we'd be paired with. Marie was hoping for James, the oldest boy in the Community and also the most handsome. Most of the other girls were hoping for him as well, and he knew it. I watched as he preened at the front of the line. His arrogance annoyed me. He was the one boy I most definitely did not want.

Actually, there was only one boy I hoped for. Will. He was my best friend and felt like family already. I looked for him. He was standing midway down the line with Brian.

I smiled at them both and Will smiled back. I knew he wished for me too and it gave me hope that maybe that made us destined to be Intendeds. I crossed my fingers and willed it to happen.

Marie nudged me and tilted her head toward Brian. He saw her and his face reddened, making it look like a giant tomato. Back then Brian was short and sort of pudgy, the exact opposite of what he is now. His good looks were still hibernating.

"Let's hope neither of us gets stuck with Extra Beefy," she whispered. I stifled a giggle just as Pioneer—formal in a pair of black pants and a blue tie—walked to the front of the room, his hands clasped behind his back, and we were ushered to our seats.

Pioneer had a speech prepared. He droned on and on. I'm not even sure what he talked about. I can't remember. I just know that every person in the room was distracted and fidgety, even our parents. We were all trying to see past that moment and into the next one, when we would know. When Pioneer finally finished lecturing and started calling our names in pairs, everyone seemed to let out a breath at the same time.

"A tiny bit nerve-racking, right?" Pioneer asked, wiping at his brow dramatically. Several people chuckled.

Each couple rose together and went to stand at the front of the room when they were called. Parents congratulated each other when their child's Intended was named. Moms dabbed their eyes with tissues. Most everyone looked pleased with their pairing, if a little embarrassed. Pioneer went down each row of girls. It wasn't long before his eyes met mine.

"Little Owl," he said, smiling widely, "your Intended will be . . . Will."

I felt my whole face smile, a big, goofy relieved one. I would've hugged Pioneer if he hadn't been too far away. Marie squeezed my hand as I stood up. I went to stand by Will. We were both grinning like idiots. For the first time, he took my hand in his. It was work calloused but warm, already comfortable.

Marie was next. I widened my eyes at her and she put her hands together palm to palm as if in prayer.

"Marie, your Intended will be . . . Brian," Pioneer said loudly.

Marie's face fell. She hesitated and I could see that she was having trouble standing up, but finally she managed and walked toward Brian on stiff legs. He was even redder now. Marie stood next to him without managing to seem near him at all. Her eyes traveled across the room to where James still sat waiting for his Intended. He never even looked her way.

Afterward, we ate cake and then gathered in the meeting room for the movie. Will and I sat together. It didn't feel awkward or strange. It felt like it always had since the day we'd first met. Right.

Boundaries are good for people; they make them feel safe.
If their world's too wide open, they're liable
to wander and get up to no good.

—Pioneer

# SEVEN

I'm in bed for no more than five minutes that night when I hear something hit my window. Actually, a lot of somethings—pebbles from our garden. I look out into the backyard. It's dark, but I can see movement, shadows rearranging themselves in the bushes just below my window. My heart squeezes in my chest and I press my face to the glass to try to see better. For one wild moment, I hope it's Cody. Maybe he's found a way to come back and see me . . . *but no, that would be impossible.*

A flashlight blinks on long enough for me to see Marie's grinning face; it seems to be more skull than skin in the yellow light. She waves for me to come outside. I have no idea why she's here, but I slip on some shorts and shoes anyway and hurry down the stairs, being careful to avoid the creaky spots.

*What is she up to?* Being out after curfew is a huge no-no.

I head out into the yard. Marie's in the far corner by the rosebushes. She has a blanket thrown over one arm and a CD player hanging on the other.

"Full moon's tonight, remember?" she whispers, her face bright with excitement.

I'd completely forgotten. We've been planning this after-hours trip outside the development for the past month.

"Brian and Will are waiting by the wall in my yard," Marie says. "We have to hurry."

"After what happened today—those guys showing up—you still think that tonight's a good night to sneak out? Are you crazy?" I whisper. "Pioneer and all the other adults are probably on extra alert right now. There's gotta be twice the amount of people guarding the Community tonight."

"It's the *perfect* time for this. They're preoccupied," Marie says as she pulls me further into the shadows and out of my backyard. "Brian already scoped out who's on guard duty tonight. It's Mrs. Brown, so you know she'll be more concerned with her knitting than with keeping watch. Everyone else is asleep. Who's gonna know? We'll only be an hour or two. Come on! Just go for a little while. If you're still freaked out once we get there, we'll come right back. I promise."

In theory, this is the safest possible time to break the rules, because most of the Community is asleep. And no one's ever attempted it before now. The development's wall is high enough to make scaling it risky, and the only other way out is through the front gate, which is guarded 24/7. Plus, there're always at least two other adults roaming around inside the development, making sure that curfew is enforced. Once our parents check to see if we're in bed and our lights are out, they can usually feel pretty confident that we'll stay put. Their overconfidence is to our advantage.

I drag my feet as we leave my yard and head into Mr. Whitcomb's. Marie's yard is two more over. "Marie . . . ," I begin.

"Aw, come on, Lyla! This is probably our only chance for something resembling a date with the guys. You know, that ritual the rest of the world enjoys but we don't?"

I shoot her a look and try to ignore the flash I have of Cody's face. Marie grilled me for details once he was gone, but I brushed her off. I can't talk about him. I'm afraid that she'll figure out that I thought he was cute and tease me about it. And besides, what does it matter? I'm not supposed to see him again. I need to put him out of my mind.

"Don't you want to hang out with Will when someone isn't watching your every move?" Marie throws up her hands in exasperation.

"I have hung out with him alone, lots of times. We had dishwashing duty together just the other day," I say. I know what she means, but I can't help giving her a rough time about it.

Marie's mouth sets itself into a thin line. "Whatever.

Forget it. I don't know why I even try. How can you be all nonchalant about disobeying when you're shooting—when actual *lives* are at stake—but be so high-strung over this?"

"Ouch."

Marie walks a little ahead, then stops and turns around. "I'm sorry, just . . . please, Lyla. Just this once. Please." She gives me her best puppy-dog eyes.

I glance back at my house, at the windows. There are no lights on inside. My parents have been asleep for hours, and they haven't checked on me in the middle of the night since I was ten. If I'm ever going to sneak out, this is as good a night as any—maybe even better. Smart, almost. No one would ever expect it.

"One hour," I say. "That's it."

Marie hugs me so hard I cough. "Yesss! Thank you."

"Can't breathe," I groan, and she lets go and laughs.

Brian and Will are waiting for us when we get to Marie's yard—the absolute best place to attempt a sneak-out. Her parents hate to garden, so her backyard is completely overgrown, probably more jungle-like than an actual jungle. There are lots of places to hide.

Will is over by the wall, holding the makeshift ladder he built special for tonight. When he sees us, he smiles and props it up against the bricks. It's a thick piece of plywood we smuggled out of the wood shop, with various bits of scrap wood nailed to it to make the rungs.

"Ready for this?"

"As I'll ever be," I say, and try to look excited. I'm

supposed to be excited. *This* is the date I should be looking forward to. This is the boy who should be stealing my breath and making my heart race. Cody was just . . . someone new, and that's the only reason I can't stop thinking about him. Maybe this is the perfect thing for me to be doing right now, a way of refocusing.

"Heard you had to give a tour today," Will says as if he's reading my mind. "Smart of Pioneer to send you to do it— not that I'm glad he did, but I'm sure it made it hard for that guy to see anything around here besides you."

"You're crazy." My cheeks flush.

"No, just honest," he says, and kisses my blush-heated cheek. "By the way, nice bed-head."

"Shut up." I punch him in the stomach and he grunts.

"No, really, I like it. It kind of goes with the little bit of toothpaste you've got right there." He wipes a finger against the corner of my mouth.

"Thanks for the heads-up, Marie," I whisper, and pretend to glare at her.

She giggles. "What're friends for?"

I smooth my hair and run my own finger across my lips.

"So, we're really going to do this?" I ask Will.

"Absolutely," he says.

"I can't believe you're actually on board, Mr. Consummate Rule Follower."

Will pretends to look wounded. "Are you saying I'm uptight?"

"No, just boring," Marie answers for me.

"That's unfair," Will says with a look of mock hurt on his face. "I follow the rules that make sense. The ones that keep us safe. But an hour or two by the river . . . to talk"—he raises both eyebrows here—"isn't exactly life-threatening."

"Something tells me being alone with you in the dark isn't exactly *safe* either," I say.

Will chuckles and leans in to kiss me softly on the lips. "I promise I'll be good . . . or at least not *very* bad."

I roll my eyes and put a little distance between us. I like it better when he's just my friend like he used to be before we were Intendeds. Flirting like this always feels a little like target shooting. I'm more likely to want to shake his hand than I am to bat my eyes and aim for his heart.

"Can we get going already?" Brian grumbles. He's the first one to scramble up the ladder, pulling himself up and over the wall in one fluid movement. I can hear the dull thud as he lands on the other side.

Marie goes next. She has a little more difficulty hoisting herself up onto the wall, but she's still over it quickly enough to keep my fear of being found out to a minimum.

"Your turn," Will whispers into my hair.

I climb carefully up the plywood. I have to grip the sides to keep from falling as it bows under my weight. The ladder ends a little more than two-thirds of the way up the wall. I have to practically do a pull-up to get myself up on top of it. It takes me a few tries, but finally my feet find purchase between the bricks and I manage to pull myself up onto my stomach so that I'm lying across the top of the wall. I feel dangerously exposed on the thin cement ledge, so I swing myself around and let my legs dangle on the other side before slowly lowering myself as far as I can before I have to let go.

"Oww!" Brian yelps as I fall into him, throwing both of us backward into the grass. Thankfully, I land on top of his solid chest and not the other way around.

Will's already at the top of the wall. He's got a rope in one hand, the end of which snakes back into Marie's yard. He must have tied it to the ladder so he could drag the whole thing over the wall with us. We won't be able to sneak back in without it.

The plywood makes a scraping noise loud enough to make all of us cringe. Will leans back and pulls faster, the noise slightly louder now. Once it's over, we can't help hovering by the wall, looking for lights from inside Marie's house or from people in the yard investigating. I can hear my heart thudding in my chest.

After what feels like hours of listening so hard that my ears ring, we turn away from the wall and rush headlong into the woods. I'm grateful for the tree cover, feeling a bit calmer with every step forward. We work our way to the river. It's not far from the development, just far enough so that we can have a little fun and not worry about being heard.

Pioneer sometimes lets the Community go there. It's

a treat he reserves for exceptionally beautiful days. We bring picnic lunches and swim. Brian's dad put up a rope swing. Even though there's a pool inside Mandrodage Meadows, I like swimming at the river best. The water is crisp and smells like sunshine mixed with earth. And the noise it makes as it rushes over the rocks and slaps against the riverbank relaxes me. I can feel it soothing me now. The tension of the past two days flows out of me. I hadn't realized how badly I needed this until now.

Marie and I spread out the blanket and Will sets up the CD player. There's only one CD in it.

"Sinatra?" Will rolls his eyes at Marie and groans.

"What? It's romantic. And besides, be happy I smuggled any music out at all."

All of our music is housed in the clubhouse library. Pioneer carefully selected each CD, making sure that most every style was represented. We will move all of it into the Silo when the time comes so that we can preserve it for our children. For now, we can check it out along with the players during the day, but they have to go back each evening. I'm not sure how Marie managed to keep it for tonight—it's nothing short of a miracle, really, but I'm glad she did. Music is a definite bonus.

Marie and I sprawl out across the blanket and stare up at the stars. Will and Brian set the player under the nearest tree and start arguing over which song to play first. "It Had to Be You" finally drifts out of the speakers and into the air.

"Dance with me," Will says from above me. He offers me his hand and I groan.

Marie giggles. "This should be good."

I'm a horrible dancer. It isn't that I don't like the music or feel the rhythm. It's that to do it well, you have to be able to let go, get lost in the song and feel it inside you. I'm not sure I'm built to let go of anything, no matter what it is. Ever. Letting myself go is as foreign to me as thinking things through is to Marie.

Will puts one hand on the small of my back, his thumb lightly stroking my pajama top. He takes me out into the grass. The moon silvers his blond hair, making him look almost distinguished, mature. He twirls me around in a slow circle. I grip one of his hands and the opposite shoulder so tight it has to be uncomfortable for him, but I can't make myself relax.

"Just let me lead you, okay?" he whispers, his eyes strangely soft in the moonlight. The way he's looking at me makes me shiver. There's a hunger to his gaze. He pulls me closer, his chin resting lightly on my hair. I concentrate on not stepping on his feet so I don't have to think about how close he is to me.

"Not a complete disaster. Good, Lyla!" Marie calls over Brian's shoulder. She looks perfectly content. Once Brian finally slimmed down and muscled up, she fell for him hard. It shows in the way she looks at him now.

Marie and Brian are dancing too. I watch as she moves in his arms. It's hard not to watch her when she dances.

She's beautiful. I mean, she's not exactly unattractive when she's *not* dancing; it's just that right now she's mesmerizing. If it wasn't almost the end of the world and if we didn't live in Mandrodage Meadows, I know she would be studying dance full-time somewhere with a proper teacher, not memorizing the old ballets and Broadway dance numbers that Pioneer has archived in our library. I wonder if she's ever sad that she'll never get the chance to dance the way she's obviously meant to—on a stage in front of hundreds of people. I've never asked her about it. Regret is a given here, the price of survival. No one wants to dwell on it.

"Glad you came?" Will asks, pulling me in closer.

I nod into his shoulder. "I think so, yeah." There's a strange kind of magic out here by the river. It's muddling my thoughts, making my mind drift into a current of what-ifs. What if my family never moved to Mandrodage Meadows? What if I didn't know that the world is ending? Would I be here with Will or Cody?

I'm so caught up in my own thoughts that at first the high-pitched scream of our Community's emergency siren doesn't register. But then the meaning of it hits me like a cold blast of river water.

This is it.

The end.

And it's early.

"We have to get back. Now!" Will yells.

My heart is so icy all of a sudden that it hurts. *How could we have been so stupid?* The world spins around me.

The stars seem way too bright. *Can we make it back in time?*

None of us speaks. I rush to gather up our blanket. My hands are shaking so hard that at first I have trouble picking up the thin fabric, separating it from the grass.

"Just leave it and move!" someone says, but I can't make myself stop trying to pick up the blanket and I don't know why.

Will's next to me in a flash. He's yelling at me to go. I can see his lips moving, but the alarm seems to be sounding off from inside my chest now. It's all I can hear. Will jerks me to my feet and we sprint toward the trees. We leave everything behind us, including the ladder we used to get out. My breath is so shallow now that I'm light-headed. I try to take a deep breath. Fainting is not an option, there's no time.

"Head for the front gate," Will barks as we run.

The alarm is one long, uninterrupted howl. It hasn't ever gone off like this before—not in the middle of the night without a practice drill scheduled. It's only supposed to go off if the last days begin early—if Pioneer is somehow wrong about the exact date. But we should still have three months. *Can his visions be that far off?* I try to hold in the sob struggling to escape my chest. *I'm not ready, not yet.*

We are still almost half a mile from the gate to Mandrodage Meadows. I feel like my legs are breaking down, like any minute I'll lose all my strength and go boneless right there in the middle of the trees. But even if that doesn't happen and I manage to keep running, if we all manage to keep running, we might not make it. If they close the shelter door before we get there and this is real, they won't reopen it—not even for us. We will be locked out, left to die with the rest of the world.

My breath is coming hard. I can't keep pace much longer. Will takes my hand and starts to pull me along. I can't match his long-legged stride, but he pulls me anyway, forcing me into a jumping run.

Marie is screaming, her face white with panic. Brian is pulling her along just like Will pulls me. The tall grass is making shushing noises as we run through it. For some reason the noise and the running strike me as funny— like Will and I are suddenly part of a life-and-death three-legged race against Marie and Brian. I feel hysterical laughter bubbling up in my throat. *This can't be real, can it?*

Will veers off to the left, leading us to the front gate. We make it there just as the siren hiccups and almost dies. Will sucks in a breath and slows. We all freeze. I feel as if the sound of the alarm has been controlling our motion. For a moment I hope it really is a false alarm, but then the siren winds back up again. We stop at the guard station just long enough to figure out that no one's in it. Everyone is already inside the high walls of our development— either on their way to the thick steel door of the Silo or already deep inside the underground cement structure itself. Still Will rattles the station door's knob, tests it to see if it's unlocked.

"Leave it, there's no time!" Brian yells.

"The gate's closed. We need to get it open if we want in," Will yells back. My heart stutters the way the alarm just did. The station is supposed to get locked up tight before it's abandoned. We can't open the gate if we can't get in and hit the button. I close my eyes and silently will it to be unlocked, but it isn't.

Will roars and kicks at the door until it slams open. He runs inside. Pioneer will not be pleased that he's destroyed the guard station door. But then again, does it really matter if we never need it after this? I shake my head. I can't think straight anymore.

The large iron gate screeches on its track. We don't wait for it to open all the way or bother hitting the button that shuts it again before we slip through. The entrance to the Silo is on the other side of the development. We have at least another mile to run before we'll even be close. My heart pounds in my chest and I put my hand over where it sits under my skin, hoping to somehow calm it. Marie slows and comes to stand beside me. I'm pretty sure that she's thinking about the distance too, because she starts to cry.

"We can't make it." She sobs between ragged breaths. "It's too far. Oh, God, we're gonna die." No one tries to comfort her, because she's right. We are out of time. As if in confirmation, the siren wheezes. Stops. This time it doesn't start again and suddenly everything is still.

"No, do you hear me? No!" Will shouts at the sky. He turns and runs toward his house, then disappears inside.

We watch him leave and then Brian sort of shivers and puts his arms around Marie. She collapses against him, utterly hysterical now. I wrap my own arms around myself and spin in a circle to try to keep from screaming. My eyes rest on trees, houses, yards, as if somehow focusing on them will calm me down. *What do we do now? Seventeen feels too young to die. I need more time. We all do.*

Will's garage door rumbles open just as I'm on my fourth spin. He erupts from the dark space behind it in his father's golf cart and swerves to a stop in front of us.

"Get in!" he barks. I slide in next to him and Brian throws Marie onto the backseat before climbing on himself.

"Hold on!" Will yells as he stomps on the gas pedal and we start to pick up speed. The golf cart can only go twenty-five miles per hour, but it's fast enough to almost throw us off as we whip past the center lawn where the greenhouse, lake, and picnic tables are. Still, it's not fast enough to make my heart quiet or to make Marie stop screaming. I grip the tiny rail pressing into my thigh and hope that I'll be able to stay put, that we'll get to the Silo in time.

"Go faster, you stupid piece of crap!" Will hollers.

We're halfway through the development now, almost to the stables. Some of the animals are in the fields beyond it. Several of the horses lift their heads as we pass. Their ears are flicking back and forth like they can't figure out what all the fuss is about. I give them one last long look. I wish I could find Indy, put my hand on his nose, and feel his steamy breath on my fingers one more time, but it's too late for that now. My eyes are wet with tears, but I don't bother to wipe them away. Will slams on the brake and we throw ourselves out of the cart and toward the clump of apple trees that disguise the entrance to the Silo.

Will makes it to the door first. It's set into a low hill in the center of the trees. I don't have to catch up to know that it's already locked up tight. Will's head is in his hands and he's on his knees in the grass. Brian and Marie come up behind us. When they see Will, Marie loses what's left of her composure. She runs up to the reinforced steel door and pounds it with her fists.

"Let us in! Please, let us in! Don't do this!"

She screams and pounds and none of us say a word. They can't hear her. To the people beyond the door, we are already dead.

If a man is too confident in his salvation,
he'll lose his passion for it.

—Pioneer

# EIGHT

Once Marie gives up and stops pounding, the world settles into an eerie quiet, holding its breath. I'm not breathing either. I don't think any of us are. I look up at the sky, search for some sign of smoke or fire or both. What'll happen first? Solar flares? Pioneer's never been very specific about what exactly will kick things off. Maybe it'll be the earth. It could shake and crumble and erupt all at once like a bomb that folds in on itself rather than out. A minute goes by. I clench my fists and try to be still so I can listen.

No one talks.

No one moves.

Two minutes.

Still nothing happens.

I'm sweaty and chilled and panicked to the point of immobility. What do we do? There's no place to hide out here that'll be safe. Our only option is sealed off and just beneath us. It's maddening that we're this close, but we might as well be one hundred miles away for all the good it

76

does us. I need to move, run out into the field, to do something, but I can't. There's nothing we can do now. Nothing.

"Please God, please God, please God." I've been muttering these words under my breath without really realizing that I'm doing it. They startle me. I'm praying and it isn't to the Brethren. It's like a reflex reaction that I didn't know that I had. In my panic, am I hoping Noah's god will take pity on me, since I'm pretty sure that Pioneer won't? But don't I already know how Noah's god answered the prayers of those left outside the ark, those wicked unbelievers? He let them drown. And it makes sense. They disobeyed his command. If Noah's god exists, why would he take pity on us?

My pleas should be to the Brethren. We're their chosen people. At least we were before today. But maybe we aren't anymore.

"What d-d-d-do we d-d-d-do now?" Marie stutters in between wails, her face contorted with fear.

"I don't know. I . . . I tried, but . . . I don't know," Will says, more to himself than to her. He sinks down onto his knees and puts his face in his hands. *"Why?"* he hollers at the ground. *"Why?"*

"I can't die. Not like this. We're supposed to be inside. They left us. They just left us," I mumble, but no one's listening.

Marie's crying gets louder and she starts shaking. Her tears collect along her chin before they drip onto her shirt. She looks up at the sky and opens her mouth to say something more, but she can't get the words out, she's hic-cupping and crying too hard.

"They have to know that we'd be close by. Why couldn't they've waited a few more minutes? Nothing's even happening yet. They could've let us in." Brian glances at the entrance to the Silo, but there's no hope in his face. He knows that his questions don't matter anymore. We all want a different answer than the one we've got. We want a way to make things okay.

Will lets out a hard laugh. "You think so? What's Pioneer's first rule? Huh? When that door shuts, it doesn't open again for five years until the Brethren come for us. For any reason. We all knew that."

I can't look at any of them. I want to blame each of them for this. Marie convinced me to break the rules. Will and Brian made that stupid ladder. I didn't even want to go in the first place. If we'd been where we should've been—in bed—we'd be safe right now. These thoughts settle into my chest and expand until I'm afraid that I can't keep them to myself. But what good will it do to start yelling at them now?

Marie is sniffling loudly. She's cried herself out for now. She's leaning into Brian and he's holding her arms with his hands as if he can keep her from falling to pieces this way. Will isn't holding me and I don't want him to. What I want is to run, or grab Indy and race out onto the prairie, try to get ahead of the destruction, but I don't know which way it'll come from. So I stand still and wait.

*Bang!*

Every other minute or two, Will kicks or pounds at the door. There's no rhyme or reason to what sets him off, but each time he starts back up, the rest of us jump.

"Could you quit doing that?" I finally snap, because if he doesn't stop soon, I might go crazy.

Will shoots me a look and I stiffen because now I've managed to direct all of his anger at me instead of at the door. He shouts, "What should I do? Give up? Just stand here and look stupid like the rest of you?"

"Ease up, Will," Brian warns.

"No, I'm not gonna ease up. Unless you have a better idea—in which case, I'm all ears. Tell me what you think we should do." He glares at Brian and then at me. When his eyes meet mine, his face softens just a little.

"All right, look, I just can't . . . stop . . . I mean . . . They locked us out. They left us to die." He takes a few steps away from the door and yells, "*Nothing's* happening! Open the door!"

"They don't know that," Brian says quietly. "They have no way of knowing from down there—or of hearing us. And you said it yourself, even if they did, they wouldn't open it."

"Well, then we have to make them hear, make them change their minds," Will shouts before turning to rush past us and away from the orchard.

"Where's he going?" Marie wails, and Brian closes his eyes like he's about a half second shy of losing his patience.

"Pull it together, babe, please? Look at Lyla. She's not freaking out."

*I'm not?*

I haven't given any thought to how I seem to everyone else, because I feel like my insides have gone all loose and jiggly inside my skin. This wasn't supposed to happen. I still can't quite believe that it has. We're supposed to be in the Silo. We're supposed to be part of the future, not still-breathing relics of the past. I wrap my arms around my body to try to physically hold myself together.

Marie is just beginning to quiet down as Will charges back down the path toward us with an ax, his eyes targeting the shelter door. He raises the ax over his head and we all duck as if somehow he'll hit us by mistake even though we're nowhere near him. He swings the ax at the door. It connects with the iron and makes an impressive sound before it bounces off. The ax handle vibrates in Will's hands and he curses as he almost drops it. But then he's swinging it at the sides of the door, striking at the cement walls on either side. He's grunting and yelling and swinging over and over again, but making very little progress. He sort of reminds me of one of those Looney Tunes characters—Yosemite Sam, maybe, when something isn't going his way and he throws a massive fit. Then Marie winds up again, wailing and crying louder than ever as the ax hits the wall and the door . . . and I just can't stop the crazy laughter building up inside of me. I start giggling because the whole thing is just too surreal.

And then I'm smack in the middle of a full-body laugh, the kind I get when I'm really nervous. I clutch at my stomach. My eyes are leaking and my nose is running. My sides ache, but I can't stop the waves of hysterics that keep crashing over me. It's enough to stop Will from hacking at the door and Marie from weeping. Brian is actually holding her closer now, like he's afraid of me or something. They're all looking at me like I've gone ahead and totally lost it, which only makes my laughter worse. Pretty soon Will has to come up behind me and pat me hard on the back to make sure that I'm managing to breathe between laughing seizures.

"Um, Lyla, are you okay?" Brian says. He looks more frightened now than he has the last half hour.

I gasp and try to calm down. "Yeah, I'm sorry, but watching Will hit that door and then Marie with the wailing . . . and the orchard is so quiet, everything else is just so normal . . . This whole thing feels impossible. I mean, are we wrong? Maybe they're just in the clubhouse. It's not like we checked. Maybe the alarm stopped ringing because it was just a *false* alarm. This whole thing could be a really big mistake. Couldn't it? Please, this can't be happening right now. Not when it's all our faults that we didn't make it." Now I'm crying in the midst of laughing, which is really terrifying because it makes me realize just how close I am to losing it completely.

Will lets out a long, slow breath. "Okay, so it's our fault we're out here. So what? What's crying about it gonna do? We need to figure out what comes next."

"What do you mean 'what comes next'? Like we have options? We're gonna die," Marie shrieks, and Brian pushes her off of his lap and shakes her shoulders.

"Shut up!" he shouts, and we all startle because he hasn't really flipped out at all up until now. He's been eerily calm, actually, but I guess since the rest of us have freaked out, maybe it's his turn.

"We're stuck out here." He stands up and kicks at the ground, uprooting a small patch of grass with the edge of his shoe. "We can't do anything about that part. But we can stop feeling sorry for ourselves and figure out how to survive for as long as possible. I'm not gonna just sit here and wait to die. We either find a way to get them to let us in or we start figuring out what the next step is. So what do you guys want to do?"

Will paces back and forth a few times before he looks at me and then back to Brian. "We need to find out how much time we have. Then we can decide."

Marie wipes her hand across her nose and exhales shakily. "We need, like, a phone or a radio or something."

Brian nods and looks at the ground. "Pioneer keeps a radio and computer in his room, right? We need to get them and start seeing if there's any news about the end yet, if things are already starting."

"But we're not allowed in his room. *Ever*," Marie says with something like awe. Pioneer lives alone in two small rooms at the back of the clubhouse, but no one's ever even seen them, because they're strictly off-limits. I can't remember hearing of anyone actually being invited inside of them.

"Like he'll even know. He's in the shelter. Whatever's left in his rooms can't be forbidden anymore," Brian says.

"Then let's go," I say. Staying in the orchard is becoming unbearable. I can't keep still knowing that my family is just beneath my feet, safe within the Silo. I'm never going to see them again. I didn't get to say goodbye. None of us did. Will finally shrugs and takes my hand. Brian takes Marie's and together we start down the path toward the clubhouse and Pioneer's rooms.

At first when we hear the lock clicking, we can't track where it's coming from. I jump because the sound doesn't belong with the other, more natural ones around us. Without really thinking about it, we all huddle closer together. In the space of half an hour, we've become completely dependent on one another. Turns out impending death will do that. I'm shaking and Will's grip tightens on my hand. *Did we just imagine the sounds?*

The Silo's door groans and slowly swings out into the orchard. For a moment everything seems to freeze; even the crickets around us have quieted. And then we see Pioneer filling up the space behind the door.

"Oh, thank you, thank you, thank you." Marie throws herself at Pioneer. He doesn't return her hug. His face is solemn. "You weren't where you were supposed to be tonight," he says quietly, his eyes resting on each of us in turn. His expression is unreadable. I can't help shivering. I'd feel better if he'd yell. His calm is spooky.

"Hurry up," he says as he motions us inside.

Brian and Marie rush into the space before he's even stopped talking. Will lets go of my hand and moves toward them. I follow, but I'm moving more slowly. *Why did he open the door?* It goes against everything he's taught us up until now. Why now after letting us pound for so long? I'm glad for the sudden safety, but I can't help wondering what's really going on. We don't deserve to be let in. We broke the rules.

I look at Pioneer. He stares into my eyes and smiles softly. "It'll be okay, Little Owl. I'm here. You're safe. Come inside now." He puts his arm around my shoulders and gently moves me into the Silo. Then he shuts the shelter door and locks it behind us. When the lock snaps into place, I can feel my panic start to fade a little. Pioneer gives my arm one more pat before he moves to the front of our group. "Okay, my wayward flock, follow me."

Suddenly I know why he did what he did. He let us in because he cares for us, because he wants us to have a second chance, even if it means breaking his own rules. Of course that's why. He's always done everything he could to keep us safe. This is just one more example of his devotion to us. And my questioning is just one more example of how undeserving of it I am.

He doesn't speak another word as he leads us forward,

and his quiet rubs off on all of us—either that or everyone else is drowning in guilt over our ill-timed trip outside Mandrodage Meadows right along with me.

We follow him down the first flight of steps, through the radiation-showering area, and past the armory. I'm dizzy with the sudden change of fate we've been dealt. I still can't quite wrap my head around the fact that we've been spared when Pioneer's always vowed to keep the Silo's door sealed once we reached the last day. His timing was so odd. Just as we were about to give up trying to get in, he opened the door. Why then and not right away? Wasn't waiting far more risky? I keep stealing glances at everyone else to see if they are wondering about the same things, but Marie is grinning like an idiot and Brian and Will are staring blankly ahead, their faces giving nothing away.

We walk to the stairwell that runs the length of the cylindrical shelter. We have all started calling it the Silo because that's exactly what it looks like—a farm silo buried underground. Below us are six floors of communal living spaces in the main cylinder along with twenty personal compartments poking out from the two middle floors like the spokes of a wheel. The main cylinder includes a common meeting area complete with a large library and music space, a medical center, a hydroponic garden and fitness track, a theater, and a storage area; in the wheel spokes are bunks, tiny kitchens, and sitting areas—everything we need while we wait for the world to become safe to be in again.

I know that there are definitely worse ways to wait out the destruction that's coming. Some people have prepared small one-room bunkers in other parts of the world—tiny shelters behind their houses. Our Silo is like an underground city compared to those, but still it has walls, and every time that I'm in it, they seem closer together. I should be happy to be inside now, grateful that we're safe, but the tension I felt outside hasn't gone away. In a strange way, I feel like I've merely traded one death sentence for another. How long can any of us really survive down here away from the sun and the wide-open spaces of the prairie? I guess the only answer is for as long as we have to. We have no other choice.

We go down one level before Pioneer stops us at the door to where the meeting area, library, and music rooms are. He opens it. Beyond the door are the rest of our family and friends, their faces streaked with tears and full of concern. At first there's silence as we stare at each other, but then someone cries out and our families rush at us and everything blends into a tangle of hugs and kisses and more tears.

My mom and dad sandwich me between them. They're shaking and their voices are thick from crying. I nestle deeper into their arms. My mom's shirt scrubs back and forth across my face, giving off the scent of her favorite lavender soap. I inhale it in tiny sniffs, my breath hitching as my own sobs start. Being here now is almost enough to make me hysterical all over again. I was so sure that I would be left outside.

The room is loud with the sounds of reunion. It's strange to think that we've only been separated for an hour or so. The Community surrounds the four of us, patting our backs and crying along with our parents. I look over at Marie and she grins at me, her face beaming with all the attention she's receiving. Will and Brian look embarrassed by the sheer volume of love coming at them, as if they would wipe off their cheeks—moist with everyone's kisses—if they could manage it without hurting someone's feelings. I can't decide how I feel. Awestruck, maybe? I can't quite believe that I'm safe, that we all are.

Pioneer speaks only after we've settled down some. "Brothers and sisters, sit."

The room quiets quickly and we all move to the rows of armchairs and sofas spread out across the space in groups. My mom won't sit in a chair of her own. She perches on mine instead. She puts her hand on the top of my head. Will's family hovers around him as well, and Marie is practically wrapped in her mother's arms like a butterfly in a cocoon, both of them squished into the same armchair. I bite at my fingernail and try not to cry. Now that we're safe, our punishment for sneaking out has to be imminent. What we've done is so bad that I can't even imagine what it will be. I just know that it will be horrible.

I look over at Pioneer. He's calmly watching us settle

in, his face smooth and still. He's the only one who seems to know what's going on, what will happen next. I grip the arm of the chair and try to brace myself for the bad news that has to be coming. Does this mean we will be living underground longer than we originally thought? The space around me is wide enough to hold the Community comfortably. There are five more floors of living spaces besides this one, but I'm still breathing shallowly like somehow it is no bigger than a clothes closet.

Pioneer paces the length of the room, eyes on the floor and hands clasped behind his back, before he clears his throat and speaks.

"For months now I have been plagued every night by concerns over the last days, about our preparedness to face them. I have begun to fear that we are not ready. *Complacency* has settled in among us, friends. Our commitment to survival has faltered." He pauses here and looks into all of our faces, his eyes suddenly glistening. "My heart breaks when I think of how far we've come, how much we've done to survive, only to have it jeopardized when we are so close to the end. Tonight, I tested our readiness, hoping that somehow I was wrong, that we haven't grown indifferent to the doom this world will face, that we are still on the right path, but deep down I feared that you would fail this test. And these fears were realized this evening."

His eyes bore into mine and I'm convinced that he

knew the exact moment that we snuck out. From the corner of my eye, I catch Marie squirming slightly in her chair. She knows it too. The alarm went off because of us.

No one talks, which only accentuates how quiet it is down here, how insulated. Pioneer's eyes close and tears start to streak his face. "If today were truly the last, we would have lost four of our own. Four." His face contorts with pain and he hides it in his hands. My mom lets out a small sob and I pat her hand. We wait as he struggles to regain his composure. "A few months are all we have now. There is no room for complacency. For *rebellion*. Not here, not anymore." His lips pucker around these last words like they carry a bitter taste.

"We didn't spend the last ten years planning, building, and sacrificing to lose Community members on that last day. And as much as I would love to tell you that I have the time down to the exact hour, I don't. None of us are sure when we will move in here for good—when the Silo will become the only safe place we have left."

"So you're saying that this was all a *drill*? You let us think we lost our children for a *drill*?" says Mr. Wallace, Brian's dad, and his face reddens. He leans forward in his chair like he's having a hard time staying put.

The rest of us back away from him almost on reflex. Questioning anything that Pioneer does is practically unheard of, and the few times that anyone has tried, they faced one of his more intense punishments—sometimes in front of the rest of us. I've never actually done something bad enough to warrant one of these punishments myself. That is, until tonight.

I wince and try not to think about what punishment Will, Brian, Marie, and I face now. Sneaking out is even worse than questioning Pioneer. The hardest part is knowing that whatever it is, we deserve it.

Pioneer stops pacing. His face pales and his eyes go from glistening to hard and flat so fast I wonder where the rest of his unshed tears have gone. Out of nowhere, he pounds the podium in front of him with the flat part of his hand, and we all recoil. He moves until he's right in front of Mr. Wallace, staring him down until the poor man squirms and looks away. Brian and his mother shrink into their seats. I silently will Brian's dad to be quiet. The last thing any of us needs is for one of our parents to be punished too.

"Yes, I made you think your children were gone! God knows I didn't want to, but I had no choice. You needed to feel what it would be like to lose them in order to truly understand how dangerous this time is. We are hanging onto the very edge of a cliff here! Your children dangle from the safety ropes that *we* provide them—this Community, this shelter. If you don't keep the ropes in your hands at all times, they will plummet into the abyss with the rest of this forsaken world and there is absolutely no getting them back then! Did you know where Brian was when the alarm went off? Did you have any idea where to look first? No! None of you knew. You trusted that they were where they were supposed to be. *You* somehow made it into the shelter. *You* made sure that *you* were safe. Then you sat here blubbering, wringing your hands and begging me to open the door." Pioneer stabs his finger at the ceiling to the place where the Silo's front door would be if we could see it. "You put the whole of their survival in my hands, where it cannot be, because on that last day I will not be responsible for anything more than shutting the door and locking it tight. And I won't open it back up for *any* reason next time. Do you understand?"

He says this last part directly into Mr. Wallace's face and then hauls back and slaps him. Hard. I gasp; I can't help it. It always shocks me when he does something like this in front of us. My mom shushes me. I watch as Mr. Wallace's family moves a little farther away from him as if their proximity will bring Pioneer's wrath down on them too. Mr. Wallace gulps like a fish and nods.

Pioneer's shaking now, as mad as I've ever seen him. His salt-and-pepper hair, normally smooth and neatly combed, is sticking up in a dozen different directions where he's raked his hand through it. Even his eyes have taken on a frustrated glow. Maybe he has a right to be mad. He can't take the burden of all of us on his shoulders, not when they're already heavily weighted down with running the Community and preparing the Silo. He had the courage to step up and buck the disbelievers, to gather us here to save some remnant of humanity. If not for him, we would be as doomed as the rest of the world. He's our only hope for a future.

Around me heads dip and eyes study the floor—including my parents'. My mom rubs her thumb across the tops of Karen's shoes—which made it into the shelter even though I didn't. My parents avoid looking at me. What made them come here without me? Did they stop to look for me at all or did they just run for the shelter and trust that I would somehow be there, knowing that there was at least a chance that I might not? And worse, would I have done the same in their shoes? I wish that the answers to these questions were automatic. I want to say that I would never do what they've just done. I've always believed that they mean more to me than my own life ever could . . . but after this past hour, I can't say that for sure. When the siren went off, I didn't think about anything but surviving. They were only on my mind when I realized I wasn't going to make it. And it's this realization—that we are all one panicked moment away from cutting the bonds that tie us—that chills me to the bone.

"Go home," Pioneer says. He doesn't soften the edge of disappointment in his voice as he talks. My parents wince at this. "Get your minds and hearts right, because in a few hours we start preparing in earnest."

The Lord saw how great man's wickedness on the earth had become, and that every inclination of the thoughts of his heart was only evil all the time. So the Lord said, "I will wipe mankind whom I have created from the face of the earth."
—Genesis 6:5, 7

# NINE

When we first moved into Mandrodage Meàdows, the grown-ups hardly mentioned the end of the world to us at all. I can't remember ever sitting down with my parents, Pioneer, or anyone else and discussing just why we were way out in the middle of nowhere digging the largest hole in the earth that I had ever seen. What I *do* remember is roaming the prairie and the hills beyond them with Will and the others. I remember picking wildflowers in the summer and sledding in the winter. I remember feeling like New York was a million miles away and that all the darkness that came before we moved here was no more than a fading nightmare. If it weren't for Karen's shoes still sitting by our front door, I might've chosen to forget that before time altogether.

When I turned ten, that all changed. That was the year that Pioneer sat all of us down at school and showed us the taped newscasts our parents had seen but we hadn't. He brought out charts and maps of space and taught us how to decipher them. I started to realize that the sky hid dangers far greater than I had ever imagined. Asteroids. Solar flares.

He read us the story of Noah. He said that we were just like Noah and his family. Their god had told them that something was coming, something most of humanity wouldn't survive, and so Noah prepared his people. He braved the chiding and disbelief of the rest of his community, gathered those few who did believe to him, and built them an ark to ride out the coming storm, just as Pioneer had us build the Silo. When Noah's flood finally came, the scoffers finally saw the hand of Noah's god on him and fought to enter the ark, but by then it was too late and they were lost, just as the people beyond Mandrodage Meadows would be one day.

"You are all chosen, specially selected by the Brethren, the higher beings that have watched our planet's progress since before humans occupied it. They chose me, gave me the visions of what's coming, so that in return, according to their instructions, I could choose you, the people most worthy of surviving. My Community."

I had lots of questions, we all did—about the mysterious Brethren, about what Pioneer saw in his visions, about how our families were picked. Pioneer laughed, his deep booming one that always made us want to laugh too— even when we weren't sure why he was laughing. He laid one of his hands on my shoulder and the other one on Will's. Then he told us stories about the aliens that waited for us across the universe. He showed us drawings he'd made of their slim bodies and large black eyes, pointed to the galaxy where they lived on a map, and described how wonderful their world is. He said that he'd seen it all in visions the Brethren gave him. He spent the better parts of weeks and months showing us how to search the Bible for the messages that they had embedded inside for those clever enough to recognize them.

We started walking around the development with a new lift to our shoulders and a secret smile playing on our lips. We were special. We were chosen. We would be the survivors.

If you really love someone, you have to be prepared to do
what's necessary to help them learn and grow,
even if it's painful for the both of you.
—Pioneer

# TEN

The air outside the Silo is sweet and not just because it's
laced with the aroma of apples and honeysuckle. It's fresh,
not recycled—unlike the air inside the Silo. I can't stop
taking deep breaths and holding the air in my lungs as we
walk back home. All of us are silent, serious—as if we're
part of a funeral procession, as if we haven't just been
given the best gift we could possibly get: more time—time
to do things differently, time to say goodbye again. Still,
Pioneer's speech has woken me up. It's strange, but I think
that up until now I haven't thought enough about what it
will really mean to let go of the sun, the sky, our development, the world. I've been so busy *preparing* for the end
that I haven't exactly stopped to consider what's beyond it.

I hurry toward home even though I probably won't be
there for long. Pioneer will have to send for me soon. He
didn't need to announce that he would punish Will, Marie,
Brian, and me for us to know that it's coming. We broke

the rules. We left the development without permission. We told no one where we were headed. We disobeyed our parents and, even worse, Pioneer. The false alarm was only part of our penance. Pioneer never lets something like what we've just done go. It will be extra painful, whatever it is. He'll make sure that we're not tempted to screw up like this ever again.

By the time we reach our house, I'm restless with dread. I don't want to wonder about what's coming. I need to get past this night. I need to stare at the sky, paint the sunrise—memorize everything good about the world so that I won't forget it.

We don't bother going inside the house. Instead we sit on the porch swing. I'm in the middle. My parents press in on either side of me. Mom sets Karen's shoes on her lap, her hands still roaming them nervously. The suede's been worn smooth across the top from all the years she's spent handling them when she's stressed. Holding them seems to be her default in a crisis. It used to make me sad to watch her, but now it worries me. Dad and I stare at the shoes as she rubs, but neither of us says anything. What is there to say, really?

Even though Will's house is across the street and up by the gate—too far to make out the faces of the people milling around out front—I know he is the person leaning against the porch rail. I watch as he turns his head in our direction. He doesn't wave, though, and neither do I. This is not the time for casual greetings. Marie is two houses over in the other direction, pacing her porch like it's a cage. Brian's house is too far down the line for me to see clearly, but I'm sure he's doing the same thing we are, waiting to be punished. People pass us on their way to their own homes, but they don't stop to talk or even look up at us, save for the occasional furtive glance. We're as good as marked right now, outcasts until the punishments have been doled out. Later, no one will speak of it. Things will go back to normal. But it doesn't make their avoidance any less hurtful. In a way, it's like the uncomfortable punishment appetizer before the more brutal main course.

"Best to take it willingly and silently," Dad finally says, his eyes focused on some point in the front yard. His foot pushes off of the porch and slowly sets the swing in motion. "Crying won't help."

I feel my insides tremble, my breath catch.

Mom says, "He loves you. Like we do. Sometimes when you love someone, you have to do things you don't want to do—to teach them something they need to know. It's that way with kids. You have to be firm." Her fingers travel the shoes a little quicker. "If we'd done a better job of it with Karen . . ." Her voice trails off. She looks down the road in the direction of the front gate.

Dad opens his mouth to say something, but then drops his head and shuts it again. He pats my leg. "I'm sure you won't do anything like this again. Whatever happens now is just the consequence. The lesson's already hit home, right?"

I nod and he puts an arm around my back. His fingers

rest lightly on my shoulder. I lean into him and we grow quiet, each of us lost in our own thoughts. I've always tried to be good since Karen, to make up for leaving her alone. I've worked pretty hard not to worry Mom or Dad. They've worried enough already for a lifetime. It bothers me that I'm failing now.

The night begins to fade around us by degrees, but we stay where we are. We swing silently, our legs pressing together and apart with the motion of the swing, and wait.

Mr. Whitcomb and Mr. Brown are on our front porch just before dawn, before any of us have had a chance to really settle down. The Community's doctor, Mr. Kincaid, is behind them, standing on our sidewalk with a first-aid kit in his hand. My stomach clenches. I have an overwhelming urge to run. Whatever Pioneer's got planned, it's going to hurt.

My mom walks me down the porch steps and hands me over to them without a word. I look over my shoulder at my dad. He stays where he is. He's tensed but still. His hands grip the swing's seat, but his face is set, determined.

I bite my lip to keep from crying. I don't want to be a baby about what's coming. Still, my legs won't move at first and Mr. Whitcomb has to nudge me toward the road. My mom makes these tiny sounds in her throat as we leave her behind and head up the street. I know she wants to get me out of whatever's coming somehow, but she can't and I won't encourage her guilt by looking back.

Brian, Will, and Marie join us on the road. They're

being prodded along by several more adults. I try to say hello, but my voice is caught in the tightened muscles of my throat. Will moves to walk on one side of me and Marie positions herself on the other. Brian squeezes in on her other side. The adults bring up the rear.

For a brief moment I imagine us linking arms like the characters did in *The Wizard of* Oz when they were preparing to meet the wizard. I'm the Cowardly Lion for sure. I can practically hear my knees knocking together. Will's definitely the Scarecrow with his extra-long arms and legs; Marie, the ruby-lipped Dorothy; and Brian makes a perfect stiffly postured Tin Man. I wish we really were headed down that long hallway in the Emerald City, but instead we're making our way around the stables to the corral. Pioneer is standing in the exact center and beside him are multiple buckets and wood beams.

"Come here."

We walk as one. The adults linger by the corral gate where they can watch. None of our parents came with us. They're being kept away on purpose so that they can't intervene, a common practice for punishments.

*Lions and tigers and bears, oh my.* These absurd words fill my head as we walk. I press my nails into my palms to keep from chanting it out loud. Somehow I don't think Pioneer will find it funny.

Pioneer waits until we're directly in front of him before he picks up four of the beams one at a time and hands them to us. They're notched on either end. We look at each other and then back at Pioneer.

"Put them behind your necks."

Pioneer's voice is harsh enough to get us moving immediately. The beams are heavy and awkward. I balance the wood on my shoulders and try to find a comfortable spot for it to rest on, but there is none. Pioneer picks up two buckets and puts one on either end of Will's pole. They're almost completely full of water and Will has to scramble to get them balanced before they can spill.

"You will carry these buckets around the corral until I say you can stop. Keep the water in the buckets and today will be your only day of punishment. Spill too much and you'll do this again tomorrow."

I can already feel the wood cutting into my neck, the roughness of it rubbing my skin raw. When Pioneer hangs my buckets, it only gets worse. I'm not sure I can do what he wants, but I don't have a choice. I struggle to get my balance right, then start following Will. Together we begin walking along the fence that borders the corral.

"Slow and steady, Lyla," Will calls back to me.

"No talking!" Pioneer shouts from behind us.

I grit my teeth and take careful steps forward. We're not even halfway around and already I'm sweaty and shaking. How long before the beam becomes too heavy for me?

Pioneer and the others watch as we do lap after lap

around the corral. I've lost count of how many we've done after a while, but the sun has slowly climbed a third of the way up the sky. The only thing I can concentrate on is balancing the pole. At first I was able to keep it steady enough that the buckets barely swayed, but now they're slowly rocking back and forth. My entire back is cramped. I'm crying and so is Marie. I'm not sure if we're going to make it. But I can't do this again tomorrow, so I readjust the beam for the hundredth time and take another step. My neck seizes. I try desperately to stretch and still keep the beam steady.

"Please. I can't keep going. I need to stop." Marie doesn't wait for Pioneer to answer her before she stops walking. Her beam is listing back and forth. The buckets are sloshing violently. I suck in a breath. Marie lets out a little wail and drops to one knee.

"Stand up!" Pioneer yells.

"I can't," Marie cries.

"You will stand up now!" Pioneer hops the fence and charges over to where she is. Marie closes her eyes. Tears stream down her cheeks. The back of her neck is bleeding. I can see the trail of blood along her collarbone, a gruesome necklace. I shudder and try not to think about what my own neck looks like. All I know is that it's getting harder and harder to think about anything other than the pain I'm in.

"Get up!" Pioneer pulls Marie to her feet. "You have no one to blame for this but yourself. You left without permission. You put yourselves and your families in danger. Our rules are not a joke, something you can blithely disregard. Did you think for one second that I wouldn't find out? I *always* know where you are. I carry the Community in the same way that you are carrying these beams. If I can't falter, then neither can you. Now walk!" He gives her a shove and water spills out of both buckets.

Marie cries out again and stumbles forward. Pioneer wheels around, comes to each of us in turn. "You will follow each and every rule that I set down from now on. Without question. Step out of line again and this punishment will seem like a light scolding compared with what comes next. I will not have troublemakers in the Community."

"We honestly didn't mean to cause a problem," Brian says.

Pioneer stops beside him. "Neither did Adam and Eve, but their god still kicked them out of Eden, didn't he? The Brethren demand more from you—and so do I."

I've never seen Pioneer so worked up and angry. It scares me. Is he threatening to kick us out of the Community if we mess up again? *Where would we go?*

Pioneer continues to walk beside us for the remainder of our laps. He talks on and on about the Brethren's plan for us, our duty to them, but I can't concentrate. I hurt too much. We do three laps more before he finally lets us stop. When the beam comes off my shoulders, I struggle not to throw up. I try to put my fingers on the sticky, wet skin just beneath my hair, but the slightest touch makes me want to pass out. I look at Will's neck instead. It's bloody and raw—so are Brian's and Marie's.

Mr. Kincaid enters the corral with an armful of towels and medical supplies. He places them on the top of the fence post next to Pioneer, but before he can come over and examine us, Pioneer waves him away. Without a word, Pioneer motions me forward and then begins gently tending to my neck. He makes little clucking noises as he works.

"I hate this. More than you do. I love you all so much. It kills me when I have to help you learn such a lesson." He smooths my hair and kisses the top of my head. "But you'll never learn, will you, Little Owl, if the lesson isn't memorable?"

I swallow hard. I can't say anything. Right now I'm pretty sure that I hate him and what he's done to us. If I open my mouth, I'm not sure that I won't tell him so.

"Be a good girl now, Little Owl. Please don't make me do this to you again." He's obviously sensed my rage, because he's looking at me intently now.

After a moment, he puts a hand on the center of my back and rubs it in a slow circle the way my mom sometimes does when I'm sick; then he moves on to Marie. Marie hasn't stopped crying yet. I watch Pioneer whisper in her ear and kiss the top of her head like he did with me. Her eyes meet mine, but there's no anger in them, just pain mixed with relief. Does she think our punishment was just?

We spend the rest of the day on work duty, first at the stables and then in the kitchen. Bandages cover our neck wounds, but everyone stares at them. Many of the adults shoot disapproving looks our way. I can almost hear them chastising us.

Will keeps his head down as we pass everyone, his hand wound tightly around mine. Marie covers her face with her hands. I don't hide. I stare right back. We've already been punished. We've *bled*. What more do they want?

We're excused from dinner with the rest of the Community that night. We have to eat our dinners alone in our rooms. I can't stomach the food, even though it's my favorite stew. My body hurts everywhere. I ease my way onto my bed and stare out the window at the sky. The stars are clear and bright above the trees, twinkling portals. Are the Brethren up there watching me now? When they finally travel here after we've survived the end, will they say I'm worthy to be with them or leave me here alone, a survivor of humanity but an outcast of its successor?

The nations and kingdoms will proclaim war against each other,
and there will be famines and earthquakes in many parts of the world.
But all this will be only the beginning of the horrors to come.
—Matthew 24:7–8

# ELEVEN

Pioneer sets the Community siren off—four short bursts just after we've woken up the next day. It's a call to gather in the clubhouse. There's some kind of important news to share.

I grab some aspirin on my way out of the house and walk toward the clubhouse with my parents. I have to alternate squishing my eyes shut to keep out as much of the harsh sunlight as I can and opening them so I can still manage to not fall on my face. I can't help yawning over and over. It makes my neck and back tense up—which is painful to the point of unbearable. Yesterday's punishment didn't stop out in the corral; it followed me home. It still feels like the wood beam is on my shoulders, weighing me down.

I'm tired because I didn't sleep well last night. Every time I closed my eyes, I was back outside and running for the Silo—only this time I was being chased by the rest of the Community. They were trying to drive me in the opposite direction, away from the shelter. I kept startling awake, breathless and panicked.

The air is already hot and heavy with humidity. I regret wearing my hair down to cover my bandage now. It feels like a heavy wool rug on my back. I wave limply at Marie as she leaves her family so she can walk with me.

Her hair and face both look smooth and neat, like the weather and our recent punishment have had little to no effect on her appearance whatsoever. The speed of her steps is the only thing that suggests that she's still hurting as much as I am. They're slow and measured.

I watch her get closer. She's wearing the exact same purple-T-shirt-and-white-shorts combo that I am, but she manages to make it look sexy—even coupled with her white bandages—whereas I just manage to look rumpled. I don't care, though. She tries harder to look nice than I will ever want to. She earns her sexy.

Wearing the same thing as someone else happens a lot in the Community, since we buy all of our clothes in bulk and each of us has the same limited choices to pick from each day. There will be at least five to six other girls dressed to match us this morning. It doesn't really bother me, but I can tell by the way that Marie has tied off her shirt around her waist and carefully shredded the hemline of her shorts that it bothers her. She almost always alters her clothes to make them original creations. Once she even used beets from the garden to dye one of her shirts just so it wouldn't look like anyone else's.

Marie grabs my arm and pulls my ear to her lips. "Come to my house today after chores, okay? I have something I want to show you."

"What is it?"

I have to work to sound interested. My neck is still shrieking at me. It feels swollen and my muscles have tightened up, making it difficult to turn my head. All I want to do is stay still, lie down, and wait for the pain to stop. And this heat isn't helping. The sweat on my shoulders stings and makes me fidget—making my desperately wished-for stillness impossible. I'm tired and hot and in pain—not to mention worried about what Pioneer has planned for us now. He'd hinted that things were going to change today, and I can't imagine that those changes will be good ones. I can only hope that it won't mean more chores, because my head is starting to feel like it's wrapped in a hot, wet towel filled with spiky nails. I swallow the pair of aspirin that I've been carrying and hope that they start to work on my headache soon. My throat is so dry that they stick halfway down and I have to work to swallow them.

"Can't tell you now, not with all the parentals around," she murmurs, and turns to wave to my parents, who are watching us. "Hey, Mr. and Mrs. Hamilton."

"It's not something that's gonna get us into trouble, is it? I mean, after yesterday . . . ," I begin.

Marie laughs—a light, breezy giggle. "You worry too much. It'll be fine, just meet me, all right?"

I look back at my parents and then move in a little closer to her. "No, I won't. One punishment is plenty, Marie. I'm not risking another one and you shouldn't either." Her refusal to acknowledge what happened in the corral is freaking me out a little.

I give her my best stern look, the one I learned from Pioneer. If she's going to try to pretend that everything's cool, then I'm going to try even harder to remind her that it isn't.

Marie likes to put unpleasantness behind her as quickly as possible, always has, but especially after her brother, Drew, and his Intended, Kelly, decided to leave the Community last year. Pioneer said that as far as we were all concerned, Drew and Kelly didn't exist anymore, just like all the other family members everyone in the Community left behind when they came here—only worse because they knew the truth and turned their backs on it on purpose. To Pioneer, they were no better than traitors. But Marie pretended that they were on a special supply run that we weren't supposed to know about or something. Of course she knew that that really wasn't true, but she pretended it was anyway. Maybe so we wouldn't ask her about it or maybe so she could keep seeing her brother as one of the chosen or something. And it looks like she's trying to do it again now.

I get why she does it, which makes me the best person to try and call her on it. I know how tempting it is to try to pretend things aren't what they are. I used to do it all the time after my sister disappeared. But it never brought her back. After a while, the pretending gets too hard, changes you in a way you can't change back. I only have to look at my mom to know that that's true.

Marie stares at me and her lips quiver a little. "I'm not trying to get punished again. If we had any time left at all, I'd wait. Swear. But, Lyla, the end is getting really close now. If last night's false alarm did anything, it was to remind me of that." She looks past me at my parents, who are now starting to look suspicious. "I need to check some things out before . . . and what I'm planning isn't a big deal, really. Not like sneaking out. I just want us to hang out and have a little fun. Right here, safe and sound, behind the gates. Talk and stuff with the other girls. Try to just forget about this." She points at her back. "It'll be fun. Come on. Don't tell me you don't want to at least a little."

"Well, I don't," I say, and not too kindly. But when I see how disappointed she is, I cave. It's impossible to deny her. Maybe because she's the same as me, an only child by default now, a sister in misery, our bond forged out of an all-too-similar pain. I want to get past all of the bad memories too. The only difference is that I don't want to deny them altogether.

I nod at her and she goes to hug me, but I wince and then so does she and we end up just smiling at each other instead. Then she spots Heather and Julie and quickly turns away from me before I have a chance to say anything more. Her black ponytail swings back and forth as she trots over to the other girls and begins whispering in their ears. Looks like it'll be a party, whatever it is.

I push out my bottom lip and blow air at my bangs to try to cool off my forehead, but they're already hopelessly plastered to my head and won't budge. I can only hope that whatever Marie has planned includes a trip to the pool, because after the past twenty-four hours, I am more than ready to cool off.

On the outside, the clubhouse mirrors our homes, with its wood-and-stone front and deep porch. Inside, there's a banquet space for when we come together for holidays and special occasions, and beyond it is the meeting room. Mom says it reminds her of a conference room, the kind found in most hotels, but somehow I doubt that any of those rooms have pictures of natural disasters and their aftermath papering the walls. To me it's more like a shrine to pain, a reminder of how fragile our world really is.

One of these pictures is of a tiny girl dressed in pajamas holding a filthy stuffed animal in the middle of the rubble that once was her house. It calls to me every time I'm in here. I'm unable to look away from it now as we wait for Pioneer to arrive. I think it's something about the girl's face that attracts me the most. She has this look of bewilderment mixed with defiance, like she's daring the tornado that crushed her world to come back again. I've always wondered why she isn't crying. She has nothing except a bedraggled bear—and yet there's an eerie calmness in her expression. I want to be like this girl when the end finally comes—mad or brave, not cowering in fear.

Pioneer enters the room flanked by Mr. Whitcomb and Mr. Brown, his two constant companions at meetings and most of the rest of the time too. They were the first ones to sign their families up for the Community and have always been the most supportive of Pioneer's plans. They're both quieter than usual. They motion us over to the rows of metal chairs set up to face the front of the room church-style. The room is buzzing with the drone of a dozen conversations. No one seems to know what's going on.

Pioneer watches us take our seats. He looks awful. His face is drawn. Lack of sleep has deflated it. Still, he stands ramrod straight in front of us, eyes glittering. "I trust you have all had time to reflect," he begins.

I watch as all the adults bob their heads up and down in agreement, each one looking a little bit more embarrassed than the last. More than a few people look over at Will, Brian, Marie, and me. I nod along with the others, anxious to put my best foot forward. I've decided that I will try to do whatever is expected of me from now on. I don't want to be the cause of worry for my parents or Pioneer or Will anymore. Even though yesterday wasn't the end of our time above ground, it has to be the end of my pining for it. I can't keep wishing for things that I'll never have.

"I have been up all night trying to determine how best

to serve you, how best to help you protect your families," Pioneer says.

I've heard that Pioneer spends *most* nights pacing the halls of the clubhouse, where his private rooms are. I've always felt a little sorry for him. Being our leader and having no family to share the hardships of the job with has to be lonely, especially when he's puzzling things out. He says that his burden is too great and a family is not his destiny. But right now I'm kind of glad he doesn't have anyone. I'm not done being mad at him for yesterday just yet.

"I struggled last night, brothers and sisters. I found myself looking for a sign or a message from the Brethren— anything at all that could tell me the right way to lead you. They graced me with a vision and that vision helped show me the way." Pioneer hesitates and more than half of the room leans forward.

We're always curious about Pioneer's visions. He's our prophet, so they reveal the last days and many of them seem to confirm what Pioneer's scientific research suggests about what they'll be like. None of us want to miss whatever's next, because it's bound to be important. I wipe my palms on my shorts to dry them.

"In my vision the Brethren appeared in the sky. They told me that the time has come. The world is already starting to experience the pains of change. I saw a great flood, the water high enough to cover whole towns, and a great shaking of the earth. When I woke, I began searching for news from the outside. I searched for anything that might tell me what I could already feel in my bones. And I found what I was looking for. There are very clear signs that the earth is shifting its rotation. The end has already begun."

Pioneer nods to Mr. Whitcomb, who's been standing in the back of the room and now starts fiddling with the electronic equipment there as his wife dims the lights. Pioneer switches on the two televisions in the front two corners of the room. We only use them when Pioneer has some news like this from the outside world to show us, or on Friday nights, when we're allowed to watch a movie he approves of. At first there's just a blue screen, but then it's interrupted by a flurry of sound and movement.

"What you are about to see happened just three days ago," Pioneer says.

My stomach flips over and I grip both sides of the chair as Pioneer steps away from the front of the room and sits down. We've only watched newscasts a handful of times. Pioneer says that we don't need to keep up with the outside world. He says that most of what's on television is lies and junk—time-wasting distractions to keep us from our daily tasks at best and a way to keep us too attached to an evil and dying world at worst. He's the only member of the Community with access to a television on a regular basis, and he only watches it when he's looking for some sign that the end is coming or that the outside world has *realized* that it's coming. It's just another of the many burdens he's willingly taken on for us. Whatever this is is bigger than big.

There are two newscasters on the screen now, a man and a woman. The woman captures my attention first. Her brown hair is streaked with blond. It's beautiful, but impossible, the streaks almost perfectly placed around her face to make the most of her blue eyes. She's wearing lots of makeup, just like the actresses in all the movies we've seen. I can't quite wrap my head around the idea of getting bad news from someone so pretty. It makes everything seem less real.

"We have just learned that there has been a devastating earthquake in the Indian Ocean, resulting in a series of tsunamis which have attacked a number of coastal communities in Indonesia, Sri Lanka, India, and Thailand. Scientists believe that the magnitude of the quake might be as high as nine-point-three on the Richter scale, making this the third-largest quake in recorded human history. There is no word yet as to how many lives have been lost as a result of what many are already calling the Super-Quake, but many experts estimate that the death toll could reach into the tens of thousands. We will have more information about this tragedy for you within the next hour."

I grab my mother's hand. The screen blanks out for a moment before starting back up. There's a new set of newscasters on the screen now and behind them is video of water rushing through the center of a town. I find it strange that some of the people in the street are just walking, not running, as the great wall of water comes up behind them, knocking cars over and pulling whole sides off of buildings. It's almost like they've already given up on surviving or maybe they can't quite believe what's happening.

Before yesterday I might have thought something was wrong with them—that maybe they weren't very smart or something, but now I think I know how they feel. The suddenness of the whole thing must've produced some kind of shock—right up until the time that it reached them and they understood that it was really the end. By then it was too late, though. I can't stop watching as the water reaches them. It isn't long before they've disappeared beneath the wreckage of cars and buildings as the water surges down the street. And all the while I can see other people on the screen, watching from somewhat safer perches on roofs and light poles as this giant wave washes away everything and everyone below them. It makes me think of my parents down in the Silo yesterday, waiting to hear the sounds of the end, waiting to know that I was dead, but doing nothing to stop it.

The screen blanks out again before flickering back to life.

"And this happened two days ago," Pioneer says.

Another newscaster comes on.

"Hurricane Katrina has just hit New Orleans. Water levels are rising fast and many experts now believe that the levy will not hold. Most residents evacuated before the storm hit, but others decided to stay and ride out the weather. It is now feared that those who chose to sit tight are in grave danger, and with winds gusting up to one hundred miles per hour, any efforts to rescue them have had to be put on hold. Please stay with us for up-to-the-minute information in the coming hours."

Behind the newscaster are pictures of trees being lashed by wind and rain. Boats slam up against docks and water washes over stone walls, crashes into buildings. Their walls buckle and then the buildings fold. They move out into the newly created river around them, no sturdier than if they were made of matchsticks.

The screen goes blank again and the room erupts into noise. Everyone seems to be talking over everyone else. Some people look terrified, but others look excited, almost eager. I can't stand to see it, so I look away. I concentrate on the girl in the picture on the wall instead. Nothing about the last five minutes seems real.

Pioneer claps his hands, shushes us. "And this last is from just this morning." His voice is somber, but his eyes are all lit up, just like the others'.

"Japan has been hit with an earthquake today. It looks to be one of the largest in recorded history. Within half an hour of the quake, a tsunami battered the country as well, sending a wall of water that reached almost a hundred thirty-four feet slamming into its shoreline. The entire area is now underwater. Many fear that the death toll will rival any other natural disaster to date. No word yet as to exactly how many are thought to have perished, but as we get new information in, we will update you."

The screen goes blue and then black. Mr. Whitcomb doesn't turn on the lights right away. He looks too stunned to move—and so does everyone else around me. So much destruction has taken place in just the past few days. It's hard to comprehend it all. These reports are concrete proof that Pioneer has been right all along—not that any of us have ever really doubted, but still, there's a big difference between believing and knowing. We're no longer acting on faith.

My parents huddle around me, hold me tight like the very waves and quakes we've just seen on the screen will be arriving at our door any minute to try to separate us.

"This is exactly what I saw in my vision last night. This is what we've been waiting for, the first signs, brothers and sisters," Pioneer says as the lights come back on and he stands in front of us once again.

I can't help noticing that his face is etched with lines and his eyes are rimmed with dark circles. The effects of the end are rearranging the features of his face, changing the once-attractive angles into sharp edges. And his eyes are missing the warmth that they normally have. Right now his usual glow is more like a laser beam, too concentrated and bright to make me comfortable. It's enough to make my fear, an ever-present flutter in the back of my head since last night, an almost unbearable throb.

"This is a flare sent out into the world too late to warn most of them that the end is coming. But there will be those who will recognize it for what it is. They will be hit with the sudden urge to survive, and that urge may very well drive them to our door. They will demand our care, and if we don't agree to give it, they will try to take it by force. And if we fail in keeping them out, they will surely take all of what is ours—our food, our supplies, our very survival. So we are faced in these last days with some very clear tasks: to defend what is rightfully ours at all costs and to make our final preparations for entering the Silo as quickly as possible so that we are already inside before panic can lead others here."

Will looks back at me, his face full of words he can't say across the space between us. Words like *I told you so.* I know that he's thinking about target practice again.

"I am convinced that we have to enter the shelter early," Pioneer says. "I have adjusted our duties so that if need be, we can enter the Silo as soon as the end of next week. Starting today we will be completing all of the necessary arrangements. I realize that some of you may be scared or uncertain . . . and of course you should be. I am too."

Pioneer takes a moment to give us his warmest smile, the one that seems to attach us to him like a lifeline. Some of the warmth missing only a moment ago is back in his eyes. "We need to remember—now more than ever— what the Brethren have promised us. They know what we are facing. They have sent you—through me—a challenge.

Keep to the path. One day soon they will come here to meet us in the flesh. We must be grateful for their care. We must be ready to be what they require, which is a people purified, stripped of our need to be any part of the outside world or like those who live in it—consumers and parasites who take from the planet and from others to feed their own craven desires. Rapists, murderers, molesters, the lot of them."

Someone behind me yells out, "Tell it to us straight, Pioneer! Go on!"

Others clap and laugh out loud. I try to catch the zeal I see in them, to find it in myself, but right now all I feel is fear. My chest is so tight there's no room to feel anything else.

"Brothers and sisters, I'm glad you are excited. You should be. I myself am barely able to stay still." He does a little sideways jig and the laughter and applause increase. "I am so pleased by your conviction. Hold on to it. Keep it tucked in your heart. Don't let this world or its people mislead you. Not now. Not ever again. Continue to meditate on why we are doing this. We must survive. We are *charged* with survival. And if surviving means making sacrifices, then so be it. Let the final countdown begin."

The whole room goes quiet. Then there's an explosion of applause and cheers. I suck in a breath as what Pioneer has just said sinks in. We could be underground in less than twelve days. Even knowing what I do about the earthquakes, tsunamis, and hurricane, I still want to beg the Brethren for more time, like somehow I can talk them out of ending things. Twelve days isn't long enough. I find myself pleading under my breath, hoping that somehow they'll consider listening. I ask for more time, for courage . . . for a miracle.

It's not good for any person to be idle for too long.
In my experience, too much time to think is a dangerous thing.

—Pioneer

# TWELVE

School and all other regularly scheduled activities are canceled for the first time ever. Pioneer posts our new schedule of duties for the week on the large board just outside the clubhouse's front door while we wait inside the meeting room. The duties board is usually comforting to me, a constant reminder that we're all safe. I like seeing all of our names neatly written in the squares. I'm connected to everyone and they to me by a grid filled with purpose, contained in a world small enough to be mapped out entirely on one wall. But not today. Today the board feels like a countdown calendar, a record of how little time we have left.

Marie and I are the first to huddle in front of it once Pioneer's done. Normally we're each assigned a specific set of chores, like mucking out the horse stalls or working the development's gardens. Pioneer says it's vital that we don't let any Outsiders in if we can help it, so everything that needs to get done to keep the Community running is done by us. But now most of us are assigned to the wood shop, and those who aren't are responsible for all of the other chores as well as preparing the evening meal.

"Pioneer told my dad that we have to finish the final furniture pieces on back order," Marie sighs before she kicks at the wall. "I hate the wood shop." She jumps off the porch and starts running after Julie to see if she'll switch duties with her. I can already tell by the way Julie is trying to avoid her that she won't have much success. I can't help chuckling under my breath. I take the path toward the wood shop alone.

Making furniture is our only source of regular income. Other than that, we have only the assets that each family arrived with—which were pretty considerable, I guess, since almost all of us were pretty well-off money-wise before we met Pioneer. Now almost all of that money has been used up in the building and maintaining of Mandrodage Meadows and the Silo. For the past five years, we've been making furniture to cover purchasing supplies and running the development.

We build high-end pieces to sell to the same kind of people some of us once were—the kind who have designers create their living spaces and spare no expense for anything one-of-a-kind and handcrafted. The furniture pieces are mostly reproductions of rare antiques and museum pieces. They cost a lot, so we don't have to make too many to cover our expenses, but even so it takes a long time to make each piece. Usually only a few of us, those most talented at woodworking, are assigned to the wood shop full-time with Mr. Brennan, who was a woodworker even before he came here, but now everything's changed and it will take all of us working practically around the clock in shifts to complete the work we have left before we enter the Silo.

We have fifteen more orders to fill now, which doesn't seem like a lot except that most of the pieces that were ordered are large, complicated, and ornate. Pioneer has set our deadline for the end of this week, when my family will go to town for the final time. We'll deliver the furniture and then use the money we earn to buy all of the last-minute things that will complete the Silo's stockpile. One week to finish fifteen pieces of furniture is crazy, maybe even impossible, but Pioneer feels that we can't risk having any of our families away from Mandrodage Meadows any closer to the last days than this Saturday and so we have no choice.

In less than an hour my hands are covered in saw-dust and my ears are ringing continuously from all of the electric-saw noise. It was hot before our morning meeting, but now it's as if the air is on fire. It must be a hundred degrees inside the workshop, what with the sun beating down on the building and the heat from all these working bodies. We have at least ten large fans blowing, but the breeze is no cooler and my shirt feels like a second skin. My entire body is grainy, like the sandpaper in my hand. I adjust my face mask and try to take a breath, but between the heat and the dust, I'm slowly suffocating.

Marie and I are supposed to be sanding down the carved areas of a couple of dressers with fine-grit sandpaper before they're taken to be stained. At first we work feverishly, but with the heat as bad as it is, it isn't long before we're only dabbing at the carved leaves and roses in front of us. I can barely see out of our safety glasses because they're so fogged up.

Then Marie starts leaning over and putting her fogged-up face extra close to mine, breathing like Darth Vader. From the periphery of my vision, she looks like an alien or a giant bug with curly black hair. It makes us both laugh, especially when we face each other and press our noses together, creating doubles of our giant bug heads as our vision blurs.

Eventually Mr. Whitcomb comes to stand behind us to make sure that we're doing more working than laughing. I try to ignore Marie's presence beside me because every time I catch a glimpse of her hair and those glasses, I start up all over again. Mr. Whitcomb taps the back of my head right where my bandage is, and I yelp. I lean over the dresser and try to focus.

We get a break a little while later when Mrs. Brennan brings large jugs of lemonade and Dixie cups from the kitchen. Marie and I grab two cups apiece and carry them back over to our station to drink them. I put the cool cup to my head for a minute first before I drink. Marie gulps both of hers and then gets up again to get some more.

Will is on the other side of the room, helping to cut wood into the exact sizes needed for the sides and tops of various dressers and tables. Like most of the men, he has his shirt off. He's shiny with sweat, gilded with grime. He's so focused on the spinning saw in front of him and the wood between his hands that he never notices me staring. His hair looks almost gray with its thick layer of sawdust. I can't help wondering if that's what he'll look like when he's truly old. If it is, he'll definitely still be nice to look at. I'd have to be a fool or blind not to know how cute he is, but it's strange how I can know this and still not feel anything. It's kind of like looking at a painting. Sometimes I see one in a book that's beautiful and the artist's use of light, color, and texture impresses me, but the painting never makes me forget about the technical reasons why it's beautiful or makes me feel something deep inside that I can't put into words. To me, Will is like that, technically perfect but somehow uninspiring. My stomach has never jumped around with him the way it did when I was with Cody. Not in all the time we've been around each other.

Cody.

I keep trying to get that boy out of my mind, but he keeps creeping back in. And every time he does, I can't help smiling. I don't even know him, but still I feel kind of happy just thinking about him and how his smile was slightly lopsided or how his chin was just a little bit scruffy. It was shocking how much I wanted to reach out and touch it that day. But I have to stop this. Will is right there. What would he do if he knew what I was thinking?

Marie nudges me on her way back to her seat and I can see her eyebrows arch upward, can practically picture the smile beneath her face mask as she looks at me and then Will. I'm still staring in his direction. I didn't even realize. I nod my head and try to mirror her expression so that she'll continue to think that I'm lusting after Will the way she does over Brian. I've never told anyone—including Marie—that I'm not in love with Will. She's my closest friend besides him, so maybe I *should* tell her. I mean, I've thought of a dozen different ways to bring up the subject, but I just can't seem to. I'm not sure why. Maybe I'm afraid she won't understand or maybe that she'll feel sorry for me. But I think mostly I'm certain she'll think something's wrong with me. I can't face seeing this in her eyes and knowing that what I've suspected is true, that I'm somehow defective and incapable of recognizing love—of feeling anything like it. Ever.

We work right through lunch. My mom and some of the other members who haven't been assigned to the workshop bring us sandwiches and drinks eventually, but I can't really eat. Every time I try to, I feel like I'm eating wood chips instead of egg salad. There must not be any part of me, including my mouth, that isn't coated in sawdust. I drink about a gallon of water instead. The heat is becoming a physical pressure, multiple pairs of flaming-hot hands compressing my head until I feel like I'm throbbing all over, every bit of my skin fevered and swollen.

After we eat, we rotate jobs so no one gets too cramped up from the same repetitive motions, and soon I'm in the back of the shop where the biggest fans are, painting furniture with chestnut-colored stain. The air is nowhere near as stuffy, but the smell of the stain starts to stuff up my nose and increases the pressure inside my head until I feel like it might explode. I feel faint and sick to my stomach, but no one else has stopped working. The few times I've tried to sit back and relax, Mr. Whitcomb or Mr. Brown has come to stand next to me, eyeballing me until I hunch back over my tabletop and paint. I try to imagine that I'm painting a landscape or the horses out in the pasture, but since my brushstrokes have to be up and down and even, it's impossible.

We don't stop for dinner until it is almost eight o'clock. I'm so tired that I can barely stand up. My hands and wrists ache from all the sanding and painting. My lungs are clogged with dust and raw from stain fumes. I wriggle my arms and stretch. Will and most of the other men are still working. It's like they've made a contest out of the day. They keep checking out what the person next to them is doing. Whoever is still working and not complaining about it must be the manliest. Their circular saws haven't stopped screaming all day, and even after I go outside and head toward the horse corral, I can still hear them. It makes me want to rip up pieces of my shirt and stick them in my ears so I can have at least a little peace and quiet.

"There you are. C'mon," Marie says as she tugs at my arm. Her eyes are rimmed with two identical circles of white where the safety glasses have blocked all of the sawdust. She looks like a bedraggled raccoon in reverse and I have to laugh.

"I know, bad, right? I refuse to even look in the mirror right now," she sighs.

"Where are we going?" All I want to do is go home, stand under a blast of cold water in the shower, and then pass out.

"Pool." She grabs my arm.

"But we're filthy and I don't have my suit," I half complain, half laugh. Marie ignores my protests and pulls me down the path to the pool. It's noticeably cooler the closer we get to the water. Pretty soon we're hopping from foot to foot so we can peel off our socks and shoes, and then we hold hands and run across the still-warm cement and jump into the water.

We let go of each other right before we go under, and then I curl into a ball and sink to the bottom, a burning coal in a bucket of ice water. I imagine my skin sizzling as I sit on the cement. The pool lights are on and I open my eyes and stare up at the surface.

Marie is floating on her back above me, arms and legs wide, her hair fanned out in all directions. I stay curled up for as long as I can, relishing the quiet and the way time seems to be suspended down here. I look past Marie to the sky. It is quickly fading to black except for right at the edge of my sight line where the last stripes of the pink and orange sunset are lingering. It's like a beautiful mirage, shimmering as the water moves, precariously close to disappearing.

I don't come up until I start to see spots and my lungs threaten to burst. Then I shoot up to the surface of the water, gasping and dizzy. Marie bobs upright and gives me a look that says she thinks I'm crazy before she turns her face back up to the first few evening stars.

"Do you think if you wish the same wish every time you see the first star each night that it has a chance of coming true?" I ask as I tread water around her.

"I don't know." Her voice is soft and faraway, almost like she's not really listening to me at all.

I press my lips together tightly. "Because I've been wishing the same wish for forever . . . so you think maybe I have a chance?"

"Which is what?" she asks.

I watch my hands cut through the water. "That we never have to go into the Silo at all."

She sucks in a breath.

"He could be wrong, you know. The world could be just fine. I mean he could be . . . confused or something, couldn't he?" The words spill out of me in a rush.

She looks at me carefully, her eyes glued to mine—not

exactly the response I was hoping for. I know I shouldn't question Pioneer's visions, his science. Long ago he showed us the proof of the end and it makes sense. All of his visions have come true. The newscasts today are just further proof. And he's done nothing but good by withdrawing us from a world where people abuse the earth, hurt each other, and try to take what isn't their own. For me to suggest that he's somehow not who we think he is is unthinkable. But then, almost as if it has a mind of its own, my hand goes absently to my neck, reminding me that not everything he does feels right.

"I said that wrong. I just mean that I *wish* he was wrong, you know? But of course he isn't, I mean the earthquakes and the hurricane. Obviously he's right." I'm babbling and nervous. Does she think I'm crazy or bad—or worse, will she decide to tattle to Pioneer?

I open my mouth to say something, anything, to distract her from all that I've said—to reassure her that I'm not thinking of rebelling or something, but I don't know exactly what to say. I try to smile at her instead, but I can't quite get my mouth to turn up. It's like I've become so chilled that my mouth's frozen.

Marie turns her face away from me and starts wiggling her fingers in the water just enough to put a little distance between us. "You have to be careful, Lyla. I wouldn't say any of this to anyone else, okay? Having some fun, getting into a teensy bit of trouble, that's one thing, but what you just said . . . is something else entirely."

"You're right, of course you're right. I'm just heat-stroked, pay no attention to me," I say quickly. I arch my back and slide onto the surface and Marie does the same. I stretch out my hand until I can reach hers. I hold on to it and give it a squeeze. Together, we look up at the sky. I keep her hand in mine as we float across the water. But still, I can't stop myself from silently wishing on the stars and hoping against all odds that somehow it will make a difference.

*Give a child what they wish for most
and they'll put their heart in your hands.*
—Pioneer

# THIRTEEN

Indy wasn't at Mandrodage Meadows when we moved there. As soon as the barn, corrals, and stables were built, we had cows and pigs, chickens and turkeys. The horses didn't arrive until much later.

It was the day after Christmas the year I turned eight. I can still remember the animal trailers coming up the road and how our usual distrust of Outsider vehicles was absent for once. All of us kids were waiting at the front gate. It seemed barely capable of holding us we were so excited. We were downright bouncy.

You can't exactly ride a pig or a cow, at least you're not supposed to. But a horse . . . a horse can take you just about anywhere you want to go. They're special. Different.

I'd drawn horses for years by then, always secretly hoping that somehow the adults would decide to let us have them. I had dozens of sketches of Arabians, mustangs, and palominos papering my bedroom walls. In my dreams I was always riding, hair whipping in the wind, arms flung open wide.

The others were excited too, but I knew that Pioneer had agreed to purchase the horses because of me. He'd whispered it in my ear Christmas morning just after I opened a book on how to sketch them. I knew about them before he made the announcement to the rest of the Community. It was the best present I'd ever received, probably will ever receive.

Once they were unloaded and led to the barn, the other kids scattered to play in the snow, but I lingered by the horse stalls. Indy caught my attention right away. He was the smallest and his bottom lip constantly hung open just a little. He seemed aware of it and would suck it in toward his teeth, but inevitably it would flop back out again like some middle-aged guy's oversized belly, all loose and lazy. It was comical, as if he was constantly gaping at something. I couldn't look at him and not smile.

I spent all of my free time for weeks beside Indy's stall. I'd feed him carrots or apples. The other kids were over their initial excitement by then, especially once they'd spent a day or two mucking out the stalls, but I would have brought my pillow down and slept alongside Indy if I could have. He felt like family from the start.

"Happy, Little Owl?" Pioneer asked after the first week.

"Yes, thank you." I smiled at him.

"You know I love you, right?"

I nodded.

"No one will ever take care of you better than me, will they?"

Pioneer watched as I painted Indy—literally painted him. I had spread out my paint pots along the side of the stall and made blue flowers on Indy's flanks. I was just beginning a garland of ivy around his neck. Indy was happily munching on the sugar cubes I'd brought him, choosing to tolerate my decorations in return. He held his head high and peered over the stall at the other horses as if to let them know that he was special.

Pioneer came inside the stall and picked up some purple paint. He ran a line of it down Indy's nose. "I love you like you were my own daughter, Little Owl. I love you like you love this horse, you know that? All of you are my family. My children. There isn't anything that I wouldn't do for you, no lengths I wouldn't go to to keep us together. When something speaks to your heart like this here horse does to yours, I take great pleasure in giving it to you. And all I ask in return is that you put your trust in me. Can you do that?"

I nodded and threw my arms around his waist. I wanted to tell him how much Indy meant to me, how much more he himself meant to me because he'd given me Indy, but I couldn't think of the right words. I just knew that he'd managed to give me my whole world, everything that mattered. As far as I was concerned, there was nothing he could ask of me that I wouldn't give him wholeheartedly.

Children will stray. It's in their nature to do so. But in my world,
they can only travel as far as my leash will let them.
—Pioneer

# FOURTEEN

We end up at Marie's house after our swim. Both of our
parents as well as most of the other adults are still out by
the wood shop. It looks as if the work will continue long
into the night. Heather and Julie show up not long after
we've changed into some of Marie's clothes and towel-
dried our hair. They look a lot fresher than we do. *They*
spent the day gardening and making meals, but I don't feel
jealous because tomorrow *they* are assigned to the workshop and *we're* assigned to the gardens and kitchen. I've
decided it's much better to be on the other side of a rough
day than anticipating it, and they must feel the same way,
because they keep inspecting the blisters on our hands
and groaning.

I have to admit that in spite of my protests to the con-
trary, I was curious about what Marie wanted to show us
this afternoon—that is, before we found out about all of
the natural disasters and got assigned hard labor. I'm too
exhausted to really care now, but she still seems excited

and I don't want to disappoint her, especially after my moment of inappropriate honesty out by the pool. We all plop down onto her bedroom floor in a sprawling semi-circle. I start to doze off while I wait for everyone to get comfortable and for Marie to stop fidgeting with the door, but when she closes it and drags her desk chair over, tucking it under the knob, I'm wide awake again.

There are no locks in Mandrodage Meadows, at least not in our houses. Pioneer says that secrets breed mistrust and so we aren't allowed to keep our doors closed, much less barricade them. If her parents come home and find us up here like this, we'll be in trouble all over again, which means whatever she wants to show us must be forbidden. I'm starting to worry about Marie. After our last punishment this feels like a death wish. How can she be so rebellious and never actually question anything? It doesn't make sense.

I give Heather and Julie a look. I'm waiting to see if one of them will speak up and remind Marie of all of the trouble we could get in. I know that I definitely won't be the one to do it. What if she tells the others about my wish then? I don't think she would, but then again, I didn't think she'd shut me down when I told her either. Finally, when no one else speaks up, we all scoot closer together and wait while Marie disappears into her closet. After a moment or two of rummaging around, she comes back out again with a stack of glossy paper and a six-pack of Coke dangling from one hand.

"We aren't supposed to have that," Julie whispers. Her eyes are glued to the Coke cans like they're going to attack her.

When we moved to Mandrodage Meadows, our families committed to simple, healthy living. We've always produced most of our own food, avoiding practically everything that isn't straight out of the ground. Pioneer's convinced that most of the world's diseases are caused by the foreign chemicals in manufactured foods. Soda tops his all-time-worst list. Still, I have always been curious about the things on that list—scared, but curious. I mean, why are people determined to drink something like this if they know that it'll eventually kill them? I'm guessing it must taste really, really good.

Marie hands each of us a soda can. Heather won't take hers. "I don't want to get sick," she squeaks, like she's convinced that the moment the stuff touches her lips she'll develop a giant tumor or something.

"Come on, you enormous wimps," Marie groans, "take some. I don't want to drink alone. Besides, if you don't, I swear the next time I get assigned to cut your hair I'm buzzing it—especially you, Lyla." I put a hand over my hair and pretend to cower.

Julie and I glance at each other one last time as we try to decide if we should take a sip or not. Getting caught with junk food is a minor offense. Nowhere near as serious as sneaking out was. And this may be our only chance. And I've always wondered. Finally I shrug and we each grab a can. Heather folds her arms and looks away as the rest of us open our cans and take tiny sips. Marie mimes scissors and pretends to cut Heather's hair, but she's serious about not trying any. Marie's threats aren't working.

The soda is warm and almost alive in my mouth, fizzing along my tongue and down my throat. It's hard to describe what it tastes like, because it tastes like nothing I've ever had before. I just know that I like the way my mouth tingles, and I take a bigger sip the next time around. Julie tilts her can and drinks deeply before she pats at her chest a few times. Suddenly her face scrunches up like she's smelled something bad and then she lets out an enormous burp, her eyes wide with shock. I have to hold a hand over my mouth to avoid spitting my mouthful of Coke on Marie and the floor, but all I manage to do is reroute it through my nose. My eyes water and I have to grab a tissue as Coke snot runs down my chin.

"Well, that was really attractive, you two," Heather grumbles, and we all lose it, laughing until we can't catch our breath. It's only after we've quieted down that I actually remember the stack of paper Marie placed between us. I slide the pile closer to me.

It's a stack of magazines. I've never actually touched one, but I've seen them in the town stores on supply runs. My mom always made me look away if she caught me staring, because Pioneer forbids us from reading newspapers or magazines. The more disconnected we are from the world, the easier it'll be to say goodbye to it. Looking at these is a much bigger, more serious offense than drinking soda. I look at Marie and try to figure out why she's so willing to risk getting caught with them.

"I got 'em last week when my family did the supply run," Marie says, and there's a hint of pride in her voice. "There was this lady with a whole box of them. She put them out by the dumpster behind the store and I just slipped a few into my backpack. It wasn't like stealing or anything. She was throwing them away."

"What about the Coke?" Heather asks sourly. "Find that behind the dumpster too?"

"No." Marie glares at her. I'm pretty sure she regrets inviting her now. "I got it when my Dad had me pay for the gas for the truck. I might've lied, but I didn't steal it."

I study Marie. She's nervous for sure, I can tell by the way her hands shake a little. I wonder why she never told me about this until now. It seems strange that she would do it on her own. She's daring, but not usually this daring.

Marie takes another giant sip of her Coke and opens one of the magazines in her lap so that we can see the pages. The people in them are dressed in elaborate outfits, each one more beautiful than the next. None of us opens our own magazines. Marie glances up at us, at me specifically. "These are movie stars." She points at one page in particular. "See, it's the guy from that one movie we watched last winter . . . I forget the name, but you know what I mean, right?"

I study the guy. He does look familiar. "Yeah, I think . . . wasn't it called *2012*?"

Marie grins. "Yes!" She looks back down at the pages, flips them slowly as if considering something. She opens her mouth and then closes it again, then opens it.

"What?" I ask.

She keeps her eyes on the magazine. "Drew wanted to be a movie star."

It's the first time I've heard her mention her brother in a long time. We all get very still. I wait to see if she'll say more.

"I like to think that maybe when he left he went there, you know? To Hollywood. I mean, wouldn't it be cool if he did and he made it and we just happened to see him in one of these?"

At some point she just stopped talking about Drew altogether, not long after she stopped telling us he was on that special supply run. I'd just assumed that she had accepted things for what they were, but now I see that she just came up with a new, more elaborate lie.

Marie laughs a little. "I know it's a little silly, but it could happen, right? I mean, why not? He's just as good-looking as these guys. He could be in here. . . ." Her voice trails off and she bites her lip. Telling us all of this has cost her; she's afraid that we'll shatter her hope. Even if what she's said is impossible, I can't bring myself to tell her so.

"I think there's a chance," I say slowly, and she beams

at me. I understand her taking this risk now. If there's even the slightest chance that she might see him again and find out that he's okay, it was worth it. I pick up my magazine and start flipping through it. The other two just keep sitting there, eyes wide, too afraid to follow our lead.

It isn't long before Marie rolls her eyes and lets out another groan. "C'mon, you guys, when are you ever gonna get the chance to look at these again? It's the *end of the world*, for crap's sake! Live a little."

Heather sucks in a breath and Julie and I let our mouths hang open. Marie has a weird sense of humor sometimes and just now I'm pretty sure that she's gone too far. Even Julie looks a little uncomfortable for a minute.

Marie sighs heavily. "I'm sorry, you guys, but seriously, this is like the only time we have to do something a little risky together. And believe me, it's not as risky as some other things." She gives me a meaningful look and half smiles. She's already turned the other day into more of an adventure in her mind than a very costly mistake.

"Yeah, well, I hope not. Look what that got you guys." Heather points at my neck. "Getting punished is not my idea of a good time."

Marie gives Heather an exasperated look. "In two weeks we'll be underground. We won't even be able to *sneeze* without the Community knowing about it. Everyone's busy out there. We are not gonna get caught . . . and anyway, you should check out the guys in here. They are

H-O-T." Marie half sings this last part and I grin at her as she fans herself with one hand.

Heather and Julie lean forward to get a better look. And when Marie raises her eyebrows at Heather and wiggles them, we all laugh. The other girls hold the magazines in their hands like they're rare works of art.

I look down at my own magazine and trace a finger around the face of the woman on the front cover. Her skin is so smooth. I'm positive that if I could really touch it, it would feel like baby skin, all soft and perfect. Even her teeth are pretty, straight and white. I put my fingers to my own mouth and touch the little gap between the middle two teeth. I will never look perfect like she does.

We pore over every single page of each and every magazine, memorizing hairstyles and how to apply color to our cheeks. Marie seems to think we can use river clay or crushed strawberries to make our own cheeks glow the same way, but I can't really believe that it'll work. By the time we hear the workshop saws cut off outside, our heads are filled with gossip about people we don't know and beauty tips we'll never actually need. Still, it's fun to pretend that we might, even if it's just for tonight.

Back in my own room, under the covers and drifting, I think about Marie, my wish, and the magazines—about how she's kept them and her hopes about her brother a secret. I hadn't realized that she might have just as many secrets as I do. It makes my stomach twist uncomfortably.

I hate that she felt she had to hold anything back . . . but it isn't as if I've been able to confide in her either. Tonight's proof of that. It's strange to think that even though we have known each other forever, there are still things we haven't discovered about each other, things we don't want the other one to know. And if that's true of us, what don't I know about Will, Brian, and everyone else I've grown so close to these past ten years? Do they all have something that they're trying to hide? Even Pioneer?

Do I trust my people? Without a doubt. I still watch over them, though. Temptation's always lurking like a wolf, and I refuse to give it an opportunity to pick off the weak among us.

—Pioneer

# FIFTEEN

We manage to finish our furniture order by the end of the week. It took five days of almost round-the-clock work, but today all fifteen pieces of furniture line the walls of the wood shop, freshly stained and waxed, gleaming under the fluorescent lights. My hands and nails are chestnut brown from all of the hours spent staining, and my back and shoulders feel permanently hiked up to my ears and sore, but thankfully, it's over now.

The Community has gathered in the wood shop to celebrate. Several of the moms have brought in orange juice and still-warm muffins. We pass them around and wait for Pioneer to show up, to give the furniture order one final inspection before we load our biggest trailer for tomorrow's supply run. My dad is standing by Will and his dad. They're talking and laughing about something with their heads close together. My dad has one hand on Will's shoulder.

Will lifts his eyes to mine and winks before giving his attention back to our dads. All three of them have basically lived in the wood shop the past week, and now they're pale, dirty, and exhausted. They look proud of themselves and their work, though. I can see it in how they keep glancing over at the furniture. I feel the same rush of pride fill my own chest because I know that they've had the most to do with us reaching our goal. My dad and my Intended.

I can see more than one of my friends—Heather and Julie in particular—looking at Will with a sort of hunger in their eyes. They wish he'd been meant for them. I'm lucky that Pioneer chose him for me, that I didn't end up with someone like Mark, Julie's Intended, who is slow to finish any task he's started. I may not love Will the way I'm supposed to yet, but I know that I won't find anyone better in the Community to commit to.

Maybe if I could start looking at Will differently—hold on to the way I feel about what he's done with the furniture—I could stop thinking about Cody and imagining different scenarios where we might run into each other when I'm in town. The truth is, even if we're able to find each other again, we'll only have a few minutes to talk at best. Minutes I won't be able to spend alone with him, because my parents will be there too. He's just a stranger, anyway. A stranger that causes seismic activity in my stomach every time I think about him, but still.

I refocus on Will and try to shake Cody out of my

head, erase the fullness of his lips and the soft crinkle of his eyes from my memory. My future is here with Will. He's smart and dedicated and kind . . . comfortable—like a warm bath. Seismic stomach activity is probably highly overrated. Who can live with that kind of upset all the time? Maybe comfortable is enough to build on. Will's my best friend. Who better to marry than someone who already knows most of your faults and loves you anyway?

Will looks over at me with this half-amused look. My dad probably cracked one of his embarrassingly corny jokes just now. I flash him my biggest smile and his face lights up. It makes me feel that much happier that I've come to my senses—that our relationship is exactly as it's meant to be. Tomorrow when we go to town, I won't look for Cody. I'll help get the last of our supplies like I'm supposed to and then leave him and the rest of the world behind me.

Pioneer arrives a few moments later. He's dressed in a pair of shorts, which is very unusual for him. He's usually pretty modest and prefers jeans. His legs are thin and pale, further proof that they hardly ever see the light of day. I have to stifle a giggle, because somehow the shorts make him seem strange, new and out of place. I can't stop staring at the thick layer of hair on each leg. It makes him look like a severely starved bear. Marie shoots me a look from across the room, and we both have to cover our mouths to keep from laughing.

Pioneer's even wearing a ball cap, a faded blue one with the words MYRTLE BEACH on it. I've never seen it before. It makes me wonder what his life was like before he had his visions of the future and began preparing all of us for the end. I try to imagine what it would be like to walk that beach, imagine painting the waves, my toes buried in sand. I've only been to the ocean once. My parents took my sister and me, right before she disappeared, but I don't remember it much. I just have this feeling that I was sunburned and itchy, but happy.

Pioneer runs his hand across the intricately carved side of a dresser. "Brothers and sisters, I realize that the last week has been trying . . . for all of us. I've asked a lot of you." He pauses and beams at me and several others before his gaze settles on those who spent the most time in the wood shop. "But now I am happy to say that the hardest of our tasks before we enter the Silo is behind us."

I look at my parents and Will. They're all nodding at Pioneer. As physically draining as this past week has been, I doubt that finishing this furniture order is the hardest task we'll complete in the next few weeks. For me, tucking myself underground for the next five years will be so much harder. I feel like the difficult part has barely just begun, but everyone else seems relieved by his words. Why am I not feeling that same sense of release?

"We are primed now to concentrate on preparing the Silo. The money we will make from these final pieces will more than cover the cost of our final supplies." Pioneer smiles. "And now, in honor of all your hard work, I want you to take today off. No duties. No schedule. Enjoy this unusually warm September weather with one another. We're gonna have ourselves a proper cookout."

Pioneer's speech is met with some whoops and hollers from all of the kids and even from some of the grown-ups. I can't remember when we've spent an entire afternoon doing something other than chores or lessons. Of course, a few of us will still have to miss the fun because the guard booth can't remain unoccupied, even for an hour or two. Mr. Whitcomb offers to take a shift, but then Pioneer volunteers himself for the first part of it so that Mr. Whitcomb can enjoy at least some of the cookout with the rest of us. No one could ever say that Pioneer is not self-sacrificing. He's spent almost as much time at the wood shop as the rest of us, but he still doesn't hesitate to make sure we're all able to play and rest.

In less than half an hour, most of the Community has gathered at the pool. I can hear the yells and splashing as I make my way up the path to the pool gate. It's the perfect day for sunning, the sky one long stretch of blue stamped with random mountains of clouds, so perfectly stiff and white that they almost look like pie meringue. I can already see Brian and Marie in the pool with the others. They're playing chicken with Julie and Mark, and from the looks of it, Marie is the reigning champion. Her dark hair swings as she knocks Julie into the water with a high-pitched triumphant squeal. Will is waiting for me just inside the gate, his towel slung over his shoulders.

"Hey, beautiful, ready to cool off?" Will pulls me onto the pool deck and over to the water. "Think we can take Brian and Marie?"

"Absolutely." I tug at the bottom of my swimsuit as we walk toward the pool. It's exactly the same color and style as Marie's and Julie's, but theirs seem to fit more modestly on their frames. Marie is lean with just a hint of curves, and Julie is muscular and slim. I, on the other hand, am more of an explosion of curves—a big bang of breasts and butt. Will says that the guys prefer my body type over theirs, but I don't. I want to curl around myself caterpillar-style, but I settle for an oversized shirt that I don't take off, even as we wade into the water.

The sun is hot, but I kind of enjoy the way it burns the top of my head and back. I sink into the water slowly, my shirt bubbling up in front of me.

"Take it off, Lyla." Marie rolls her eyes. "Seriously, if I had your bod, I'd be tempted to show up here naked."

When she won't let up, I take off the shirt. My fingers skim the thick scab across the back of my neck, a lingering reminder of our punishment in the corral. Marie, Will, and Brian have one too. It's ugly and part of why I was wearing the shirt, but since they seem determined to ignore theirs—and everyone else got tired of staring at them days ago—it's sort of silly to keep covering it up. I throw my shirt over onto the concrete.

"Climb on." Will lowers his shoulders into the water and I clamber up onto them, careful to keep my legs from touching the worst part of his scab. I worry that he'll buckle under my weight, but he stands up right away and heads into the deeper water where Marie and Brian are. I squint at them. I can barely see them it's so bright.

When we get close enough, Brian lunges forward and Marie leans so far over his head as she reaches for me that I'm not sure she'll be able to stay on. Her hands make contact with my chest and she pushes. I grab a handful of Will's hair—not easily done since it's so short.

"Ow!" he hollers as Marie comes for me again. I get my hands up before she gets a good hold on me and push her back. Her arms flail out by her sides for a moment before she regains her balance. It makes her look a little like a bird for a minute, and I start giggling. Soon we're both laughing hysterically and I can't breathe.

"Show no mercy, Lyla," Will shouts up at me as he grips my legs a little harder to keep me upright.

Marie laughs. "Oooh, my kneecaps are *terrified*."

Will and Brian are snickering.

"You're about as aggressive as a ladybug," she says between giggles.

"Even less than that," Will says, and I can hear the smile in his voice. "A ladybug looks downright intimidating next to her."

"The only time she can actually beat the snot out of someone is at cards," Brian says loudly. "She'll Uno you to death." The others laugh so hard that they're practically crying now.

"Who's the last person you want to be assigned guard duty with if Armageddon hits early?"

"Lyla," they say in unison. Half the pool heard that last one and now several other people are looking at me and smiling in that way that says that underneath it all, they aren't completely joking.

And just like that, I'm sick of everyone thinking that I'm meek and mild. I'm sick of trying to be meek and mild. I'm sick of trying to be whatever everyone else *expects* me to be. *Who am I doing it for anyway?* Before I know it, I'm lunging toward Marie. My hands connect with her chest, and when I push, I really throw my weight into it. Her eyes widen but she holds on, which only makes me want to take her out more. I grab both of her hands and fold them in toward her chest before shoving her backward. She lets out a scream and topples off Brian's shoulders and into the water.

Brian laughs out loud as Marie comes up sputtering, her hair blanketing her face. "*Go, Lyla,*" he says. "Impressive. Honestly didn't think you had it in you. The ladybugs better watch out. *Little Owl's* claws just came in."

I stick my tongue out at him. I hate when any of my friends use Pioneer's nickname for me. It doesn't sound as nice coming from them.

Marie splashes water at me. She's miffed, I can tell. In all the years we've been playing, I've never managed to topple her on purpose. Truthfully, I've never really tried. I let her win and she pretends to think that she actually bested me. I think she prefers it that way, though she'd never say it out loud. I guess I never cared enough to do things differently—until now.

"Kind of rough, weren't you, Amazon woman?" Marie pushes the hair out of her eyes and frowns at me.

"It's the new me," I say. I feel good—strong for once. For the first time, I realize that I don't like to be underestimated. I climb off Will's back and sink into the water up to my shoulders.

"Not bad, short stuff." Will pulls lightly on a piece of my hair. His face is equal parts surprise and admiration.

I grin at all of them. "Wanna go again?"


We eat out by the pool at dinnertime—burgers, corn on the cob, and fresh tomatoes—my favorites. There's even ice cream. I sit with Will, Brian, and Marie. We sprawl out on our beach towels, slightly burned and completely waterlogged.

Marie's recovered from our chicken-fight upset, although she didn't want to play anymore afterward. We spent lots of time sunbathing and watching the guys play water volleyball instead. She's happily helping herself to my last scoop of ice cream now. I tap the top of her hand with my spoon and she smiles before launching a glob of vanilla toward my face. I duck and it hits Will in the cheek and everyone cracks up.

After dinner, Pioneer hushes us and stands up to speak.

Behind him, Mr. Whitcomb and Mr. Brown set up the screen for movie night, since it's Friday. We're watching the movie outside tonight, which we do fairly often when the weather's this nice. It hits me that we'll only be able to do this a few more times. I try not to let it put a damper on things. I'll miss this, all of it.

"Have you enjoyed today?" Pioneer asks. Everyone claps. A few people answer with shouted yeses.

"Good." He nods seemingly to himself more than us. "Before we begin tonight's movie, I just want to say a few words about tomorrow and our last supply run. I am positively overjoyed that it will be the last one, aren't you?"

More yeses and claps echo out across the prairie, making it feel like our group is larger, louder.

"I hate sending any of us out there to rub shoulders with the Outsiders. The doomed. The misled. But we have to meet our needs, don't we?"

Marie, Will, and Brian look at me, but I look over at my parents. It's our turn to go, not that I needed reminding. If anything, I've struggled not to think about it all day—that and the possibility of running into Cody again. My chest constricts. I don't want to see him now. Okay, maybe I *do* want to see him, but I don't *want* to want it.

I shake Cody out of my head and stare at my mom. She's listening raptly to Pioneer, her face pale in the dim pool lights. She looks terrified, but that doesn't really surprise me. It's par for the course for her when it's our turn to travel to town. Ever since we moved here, she's seemed to get more and more content with staying inside our walls and never leaving. She practically goes hysterical just before we leave every single time. For her, not having to go anymore will be one of the best things about living underground.

"Each and every time I've sent you out there, I've worried. Your safety has always been my number one concern. But I've also worried about your peace of mind. Folks out there are bent on twisting what's special, what's right about us. They don't want to open their eyes and see this world for what it is. They won't turn away from the rot and stench of it. Heck, they probably don't even smell it. They ignore the infection. The damage. They embrace the evil of it. All because they're slaves to the temporary pleasures it can provide. They've turned their backs on the truth that the Brethren have tried desperately to show them." Pioneer's face is the picture of sadness and regret.

"And I'm here to tell you that misery like that loves company, brothers and sisters, it surely does. They want nothing more than to turn you all away from the truth you've found here so that you'll be as doomed as they are."

Boos erupt from the crowd. Several of the adults shake their heads and cry out, "No!"

Pioneer grins, wide and toothy. "But we're too smart for them, aren't we?"

"You said it!" Marie's dad, Mr. Diaz, stands up and flexes his biceps. He can be really goofy sometimes.

Several people begin to laugh and clap.

"We have our eyes on the future. We have our hearts set on the Brethrens' will. I am so proud of all of you for that. So deeply moved." His voice cracks and he swallows hard. "You have earned your places here. We all have. For those who never have to go to Culver Creek again, tonight's a time of celebration."

The crowd erupts into cheers and Pioneer holds up his hands to quiet them down again. "But it is also a time to ask the Brethren for the safe return of our beloved Thomas and his family, our sisters Allison and Lyla. They are the last of us to venture forth and rub elbows with those fools. We must shield them with our prayers. We must believe for their safe return." Pioneer's voice lowers and his face grows somber. "Because the Brethren have told me that they will face opposition. Evil has a way of sensing its last opportunity. Somehow it will attack. So let us talk to the Brethren, ask them to keep our loved ones safe."

We all bow our heads, and Marie's, Will's, and Brian's hands settle on my shoulders. Others move to stand with my parents so that they can put their hands on them as well.

"Our Brethren, please help our brother and sisters as they travel in among the Outsiders tomorrow. Help them to go about their business, not looking to the right or the left, not stopping until they are safe within our walls once more. Do not allow this family to doubt or falter in their mission. Keep them so that they may join us once more in waiting for this world to be restored and for your return at that time."

I put one hand over Marie's and one hand over Brian's. I'm thankful for their concern, for their pleas to the Brethren. It makes me feel connected to them, loved. I'll do what I can to not let these pleas be in vain. I will leave Cody alone. I won't look for him or wonder about him any longer. I won't allow the evil that surrounds him and the others out there to infect me. This attraction I feel is nothing more than a deception, a trick meant to draw me away from what's right. But I won't be fooled, not anymore.

Pioneer looks up. "We have survived their 9/11, their global warming, their kidnapping, terrorizing, and thieving. We have turned our backs on all of it. We have stepped out in faith toward our creators from our neighboring universe and accepted their calling. We are committed to rebuilding, renewing this earth. We will not be thrown off course. Not now, not ever. No way! Say it with me."

"No way." Our voices join as one.

"Again!" Pioneer shouts.

*"No way!"* we say, louder.

"Again!"

"NO WAY!" we roar. Our voices ring out across the prairie. All around me people shake their fists into the air. My mom comes up to stand beside me. She's crying and laughing at the same time, her hands clasped to her chest. Dad stands on her other side. He leans over until our eyes meet and we say the words again along with the rest of the crowd. We are one voice, one cry, practically one person.

"NO WAY!"

"NO WAY!"

"NO WAY!"

Pioneer closes his eyes. He sways as if to music only he can hear. Then he does a little jig across the pavement in front of us. It's like he can't contain the joy he feels as he listens to our chant. We laugh and clap and cheer.

It's a while before things settle down. First my parents and I are gathered into dozens of fierce hugs and shoulder pats. My mom is bolstered by it, her head high. My dad looks humbled by the outpouring of love and concern. I'm not sure how I feel. I just know that I want it to already be Saturday night. I want the supply run—and Cody and this awful pull I feel toward him—behind me.

Pioneer pulls us aside while everyone prepares to find a seat for movie time. He puts an arm around my shoulders and hugs me. "Feel ready for tomorrow now, Little Owl?"

I nod and look over at my parents. My father looks serious all of a sudden, sobered.

Pioneer gets in front of me, his hands now on my shoulders and his face up close to mine. My parents stand behind him. "You've been disappointing me lately, Little Owl. To be honest, I wasn't at all sure that you should go with your parents." He hesitates. "But then the Brethren spoke to me and do you know what they said?"

I shake my head. I have no idea, but they've never spoken to Pioneer about me before, so I'm curious.

"They said that you had to go. They said that you needed to be tested. To be tempted. They want you to prove your devotion to the Community, Little Owl. They want you to earn your place. They will be watching you tomorrow. There are no free tickets to the new world, no sirree."

I let his words sink in. The Brethren aren't sure that I'm meant to be here? My stomach hollows out. What is he saying?

"I've had a discussion with your parents about this very thing earlier today. They've assured me that they feel that you are up to the challenge of being amongst the Outsiders. They're going to keep a close watch over you and help you prove yourself."

I swallow and look at my parents. Are they at all unsure of where my loyalties lie? I know that I've had some weak moments recently, but I never meant to make them all worry this way.

"I'll do whatever you need me to do to show you that I belong here," I say desperately. I need for them to believe that I belong here. For the Brethren to believe it too. Where else would I belong?

Pioneer squeezes my shoulders. "Make me proud."

He goes to stand with my dad, and my mom comes to stand by me. She puts her arms around me. "No more misbehaving," she says softly in my ear, and kisses my cheek. "I need you with me, Lyla. Always."

I hug her back. As we walk toward the pool to join the others, I hear a snippet of Pioneer's conversation with my dad.

"Keep a close eye on her, Thomas," he says.

"I will."

"And if she falters. What will you do?" Pioneer is starting intently at my dad.

Dad swallows. "I'll do what I have to to keep her in line."

Pioneer pats his arm. "Good. You're a good man, Thomas."

Deep down they're all convinced that I'm weak, not to be counted on to handle the unpleasant stuff that happens here. No one thinks that I'm capable of protecting the Community, of keeping it safe. The same anger I'd felt earlier in the pool resurfaces. Well, I am, at least I think I can be. I just have to try a little harder.

The screen flickers to life and I settle into an inner tube and float out with Will to the center of the pool, where the other kids are. We smile at each other as the light from the screen settles on us. Will holds out his hand and I take it.

The screen slowly comes into focus. I watch, curious to see what Pioneer's selection is. I'm hoping for something funny and happy. I want to laugh tonight, to forget the conversation between my dad and Pioneer. Still, I'm completely blindsided when the title pops up.

*Ferris Bueller's Day Off.*

I look over at Pioneer to see if he did this on purpose. Does he know that Cody talked to me about it? Is this his way of letting me know? Is he testing my strength before I even leave for town? My whole body breaks out into goose bumps. I swallow hard and try not to feel sick.

I keep looking for Pioneer in the crowd around the pool. It takes me forever to spot him—probably because I can't calm down enough to do a thorough search. He's standing back by the projector with my dad. His back is to the screen and they're in deep conversation, probably about tomorrow and whatever it is that they're keeping from me.

*He can't know. It's impossible. Right?* I try to tell myself that his movie choice is just a bad coincidence. Maybe Pioneer simply noticed Cody's shirt and somehow, subconsciously, it made him remember this movie. But deep down it doesn't feel like a coincidence—not the part where it's our turn to go to town or the movie or meeting Cody. It feels more like an attack on my resolve. An omen. A test. I grit my teeth and stare at the screen. This is one test that I'm not about to fail.

Do not set foot on the path of the wicked or walk
in the way of evil men. For they cannot sleep till they do evil;
they are robbed of slumber till they make someone fall.

—Proverbs 4:14, 16

# SIXTEEN

I wake up to a hailstorm. Is a tornado coming? But it isn't the season. . . . Is this it, the beginning of the end? I try to scramble out of bed but get tangled in the covers and fall out instead. I roll over and try to see out the window. From where I'm lying, the sky looks clear. There aren't any telltale back-to-back flashes of lightning.

*Tap, tap, tap, tap.*

Still, something is hitting my window. I get up slowly and peer outside. Marie's down in the side yard. She's doing a sickly version of a jumping jack that looks more like a kid's peepee dance than an actual exercise, and I laugh. When she catches sight of me, she motions for me to come outside. I can't imagine why she wants to talk so early, but I slip out of my room and head down the stairs in a tiptoeing run. She's obviously attempting stealthiness, since she didn't use the front door, which makes me think that whatever it is that she's up to can't be good. Again.

And yet everyone's worried about me and my so-called misbehaviors. *Figures.*

"Jeez, Lyla, it took you long enough. I was beginning to think you were comatose or something."

"What's up?" I yawn and gather my hair behind my neck, twirling it into a rope before I loop it around itself into a loose knot.

"Listen, I don't have much time. If my mom figures out I'm gone, I'll be on permanent house arrest until Armageddon." She half smiles. "I wanted to ask you a favor."

I can't help smiling back. This is classic Marie. "What, no 'Goodbye, my dear, sweet friend and soul sister; I'll hold the Silo door open for you just in case the world ends while you're still in town'?"

Marie rolls her eyes and has the decency to look at least a little embarrassed. "I came to say goodbye too." She sighs and then blurts, "I thought maybe you could try to get us some more magazines?"

I stare at her and she squirms. "How am I supposed to do that? I doubt the same lady you ran into last time will be out there again with another recycling bin, waiting for me to show up."

Marie shoots me a look. "I know that. . . . I was hoping you would buy them."

This time I laugh out loud and she claps her hand over my mouth and shushes me. "With what, my smile? We aren't allowed to have any money, remember?" I whisper between her fingers.

She digs into her pocket and pulls out a napkin. In the center of it is a rubber-banded tube of cash. She takes my hand, uncurls my fingers, and puts it on my palm.

I stare at it like it might sting me. "Where did you get this?"

"I've sort of been saving it. I've been taking a little every time my family's gone to town for the last year or so. I always volunteer to pay for stuff, fake like I'm trying to learn about money so I can explain how we've had to pay for things to my children or something someday. My dad thinks it's kind of smart, actually. He usually lets me go in and pay at the gas station when we fill up the truck. I only ever take a few dollars at a time. At first it was more to see if I could get away with it than anything else, but then I thought it might be fun to buy some stuff."

Marie is looking around and shifting from foot to foot like she's poised to sprint. None of this is really about the magazines at all. It's about this delusion that she has about finding Drew in one of the magazines, famous and happy and safe. Does she think that if she actually manages to find him, she'll be able to contact him and get him to come back? Even if it were really possible, there's nowhere near enough time for that to happen, she has to know that. But then it dawns on me that this is her last chance to try, to hold on to her hope, before we're underground. After that she has to give up this pretense of seeing him again, because he'll be dead for sure. She needs to keep holding on for as long as she can. I can see it in her face. And it reminds me of my mom. It must have taken every ounce of bravery that she has to bring this to me, to risk my disapproval. And admittedly, I'm not making things very easy on her. *Should I?*

Marie gives me this awful pleading look and I feel my resolve softening. If I'm smart, I can just promise her I'll do what she wants and not actually do it. I can say there wasn't a good time to try. She'll understand that. I can keep her safe and help her keep her hope without her knowing that that's what I'm doing.

"Okay, I'll try—but I'm not promising anything," I say reluctantly, and she hugs me.

"You're the best!" she squeals, and hugs me again.

I take the rubber band off the cash and unroll it. There are twelve ones and one five-dollar bill, seventeen dollars in all. It's the most money I've ever held. It almost seems fake.

"I was hoping maybe—if you figure out a way—you could get us one of those romance novels too—you know, the ones with the shirtless guys on them . . . and lots of, um, kissing inside?"

I can't help shuddering a little. Getting magazines is one thing, but buying books with half-naked guys on them and blush-worthy love scenes is quite another. I'm not sure I could survive the embarrassment of taking one up to the cash register, even if I am a little curious about them too.

I glance up at the house. The lights are still off, but it won't be long now before my parents get up. The sky is more blue than black and I can see pink sunlight peeping over the horizon behind Marie. "I'll do the best I can, I promise, but don't get your hopes up too much, okay? You know how my mom is when it's our turn. You'll be lucky if I manage to bring you back a gumball."

Marie hugs me all over again. "I have faith in you. If anyone can do this, it's you. You're the last person anyone thinks is capable of something like this."

She must mean this as a compliment—at least her big smile sort of hints at it—but I feel a little insulted anyway, especially after yesterday.

Now that I've agreed to the magazine mission and everything is settled, Marie seems less jittery, more serious. "Be careful out there, okay? Come back as soon as you can."

She touches my shoulder softly and this one movement seems more affectionate than all of the hugs she's given me in the last few minutes. We stare at each other. I want to tell her to take care of Will for me, just in case—because with the end so close, who really knows—but I can't quite get the words out. I hope she knows that she is my sister in every way that counts even if I can't tell her now without breaking down.

"I'll be back before you know it," I finally say because it's the only thing I can say around the lump in my throat. She nods just as my parents' bedroom light comes on. I close my fingers around the cash she's given me and we turn away from each other. I slip back into the house and up the stairs to my room mere minutes before my parents head downstairs to prepare for the trip.

Once the truck is loaded with furniture and my parents pack the cab with a cooler full of waters and snacks, I say goodbye to Will. He tucks my hair behind my ear and strokes my cheek.

"I hate that you're going. I know you'll be fine, but I don't like having you so far away from me." He kisses my forehead. I close my eyes and breathe him in. I've always liked the way Will smells—like grass and chlorine and sunshine. He's my own perpetual piece of summertime. His smell calms me, makes me happy the same way painting does. He's pure comfort and I tell myself again how lucky I am that he's mine.

His face gets serious all of a sudden. "There's still lots of time before the end. There's no risk in this trip today." He's talking to himself more than to me, reassuring himself, which makes me feel a little shaky. I'd managed to deny the risk involved in making a trip away from the Community this close to entering the Silo, but now that he's having the same thoughts, I can't ignore it any longer. My face must be going pale, because Will notices and hugs me. "You'll be fine. It'll only be a few hours, tops."

Pioneer is speaking with my mom and dad, handing over the list of supplies and tasks along with the usual envelope full of cash. I pat my pocket and try not to think about the stash of money Marie gave me. I feel sure that I already look guilty, that somehow Pioneer will notice and punish my whole family for this little bit of stupidity that I've volunteered for. Even if I'm not going to go through with it, how would they know? I'm having a hard time remembering why I agreed to do it in the first place. Didn't I just promise Pioneer last night that I would do what I'm supposed to and nothing more? I scan the little crowd of people around us for Marie, hoping maybe I can find a way to back out and give her back the money, but I can't find her.

I start to fidget and Will puts his arm around me again. He must think I'm still scared about the actual trip—which I am—but I'm also completely preoccupied with this money in my pocket. I stare at my parents and Pioneer and try not to scream at them to hurry up. I want this trip over with. I want to be back already. *What is taking them so long?*

Finally, Pioneer moves away from my parents and smiles at me, which makes my chest ache. I feel like the money is glowing in my pocket now.

"There's my brave Little Owl," he says, and Will lets me out of his arms so that I can enter Pioneer's. Pioneer hugs me lightly, his hands equally spaced across my shoulder blades. He used to give me great big hugs when I left for town, but now that I've . . . developed, his arms corral me more than they actually touch me. I miss the old hugs, the ones that let me know he thought I was special, but I understand. I'm almost a woman now. I'm definitely shaped like one. In the Community, physical contact between unmarried adults of the opposite sex who are not Intendeds is usually restrained and careful. Given that most people think that I'm Pioneer's favorite among the younger girls already, it's only right that he keeps me at a distance now.

I throw my backpack onto the seat and then climb into the truck with my family. The interior smells like warm vinyl and cherries because of the deodorizer hanging from the visor. I've always liked the combination. It smacks of open road and new adventures. But today it's overly sweet and suffocating.

"Ready, ladies?" My dad turns, gives me a smile, and pats my mom's leg.

My mom sniffles and grabs for her seat belt, clicking it into place carefully before she grips the shoulder harness like it's a lifeline. She closes her eyes and settles back into the seat. Her skin is pale to the point of translucent this morning. Her mouth is clamped shut; I think maybe she doesn't trust herself not to start hyperventilating. Today will be hardest on her.

My father looks out the window one last time and turns the ignition. The truck shudders as he eases up on the clutch. We begin to roll slowly toward the back gate. My nerves thrum in time with the revving engine. This is it, we're actually leaving.

I lean up between the two front seats and look out the front cab window at the gate, which is sliding back on its tracks. Will jogs next to my side window. He's waving goodbye. I wiggle my fingers at him and then shake my head as he pretends to trip and wipe out in the dirt. I lean out the window and smile at him and he puts his fingers to his lips like he's about to blow me a kiss, but then he just leaves them there, his face suddenly serious, and my stomach twists a little. I shake my head and wave one last time before I plop down onto the seat. The disquiet I felt last night settles onto my shoulders again. Does Will feel the same way too? Like everything's threatening to fall apart?

This world houses a million fleeting delights.
I'd be a fool if I denied that. But I ask you,
how can they ever truly compare to a long and safe life?
—Pioneer

# SEVENTEEN

The trip into town takes forever. There's not much to look at on the way, just a ribbon of dirt and then blacktop winding through grass and trees. There are other cars now and then, but not enough to feel like we aren't the only ones on the road. I put my sketchbook and some charcoal pencils in my backpack, but I won't pull them out until we're almost there. There's nothing to sketch here. For now, I sit back and close my eyes and imagine what Will and Marie are doing back home. I drum my fingers against the window and try not to worry about being so far away from them—and the Silo.

This time last week we were all out on the prairie shooting targets. Strange how different things are now. I doubt that there will be more practices anymore. Pioneer will pretty much lock down the development once we get home. The time for practicing is officially over. I don't like how final everything feels today. And every mile that we put between us and Mandrodage Meadows increases my anxiety. It feels like the end is breathing down my neck now.

Once we get to Culver Creek, we drop the furniture off first. I do some quick sketches of the men helping my dad unload the truck. I try to sketch the people I come across in town. It's much more pleasant to concentrate on the slope of someone's forehead or the cleft in his chin than on the idea that he'll be dead in a few months, even if he is evil.

My mom and I wait inside the truck's cab. The windows are down, but it's still extremely hot. I wish we could put the air on, but Pioneer doesn't like us to keep the truck running. He says someone might carjack us if we do. It's safer to leave it off and have my dad keep the keys with him.

My mom's brought a book to keep her occupied while we wait—a collection of poetry. She says it relaxes her, but today her fingers keep flipping the top corners of the right-hand pages. It makes a small *thck, thck* sound that reminds me of a dripping faucet. It's maddening, but I don't ask her to stop, because in her current mood she's liable to bite my head off.

After the furniture's unloaded, we pull back onto the main road and head toward the Walmart where we can get most of our supply-list items all at once. Pioneer says it's the perfect place for us to shop because it's the only big store for miles and miles. Two towns' worth of people come to it fairly regularly, so we're unlikely to attract any attention with our own trip here—except that we'll have several carts. Dad decides we should split up to save time. He'll fill part of the list and my mom and I will fill the other.

I actually really like this store. There are always tons of really unique people in it. There's even a hair-cutting place in front. I like to spend a few minutes there watching the people inside get haircuts. Sometimes they even have tinfoil and other objects twisted into their hair. My mom says that's how they make it different colors, but the process seems ridiculous somehow. Why go to so much trouble just to go from brunette to blond?

I've never had my hair cut by anyone other than Marie, my mom, or someone else in the Community. Usually we're in the backyard, not in some glass-fronted store where everyone can watch. It's weird. Mom knows that I love to watch the goings-on inside and usually stands with me for a few minutes before we get down to business, but not today. Today she's focused on getting in and getting out as quickly as possible. Her eyes already scan the aisles for the location of the first items on the list. I walk as slowly as I can so that I can look into the salon just a little longer.

The stylist in the salon is a big, big woman—and I don't just mean fat. She's maybe the tallest woman I've ever seen, besides being one of the roundest. Her hair is a shade I've never seen on a person before—apricot. It isn't really curly or straight. It's more like a puff of cotton fill, soft and springy. Her face is covered in more colors: stripes of blue along her eyelids and slashes of bright pink along her cheeks. She's clashing in every way possible, right down to her black fingernails and aggressively snug yellow jeans. Her hands are buried in some boy's longish brown hair.

Cody's hair, I realize with a start.

*No, it can't be him, can it?* I did tell him we'd be here today, so it shouldn't be that big of a shock, but I can't help it, it is.

I look over at my mom to see if she's noticed him. Then I remember that they've never met. Pioneer and Brian are the only other people who've gotten a good look at him. I'm frozen, afraid to move and attract his attention. Seeing him again has simultaneously scrambled my brain and shaken my insides. I stop walking and stare.

Cody brushes some hair out of his eyes. The hair lady has combed most of it straight into his face and is trimming the back, her mouth moving constantly either because she's babbling like crazy or really enjoying her gum. Cody puts both hands on his knees. I can see him squeeze them, his fingers taut against his jeans.

He looks up and his eyes meet mine. His eyes widen and then his face brightens.

"Hi," he mouths.

I just stare back at him. I'm still unsure of what to do. I *should* run, but if I do, maybe he'll come out here after me.

*Think of something!*

Then he lifts his eyes in the direction of the woman's fingers and his hair and mouths, "Help me." He grimaces and I can't help it, I laugh out loud. I clap a hand over my mouth and take a step backward, right into my mom.

"Lyla, what are you doing? We have tons to do, let's go." My mom pulls on my arm and I give Cody one last look before I turn toward the maze of aisles and start putting things into one of our two carts. My hands are trembly and I can't stop looking over my shoulder. I'm praying not to see Cody again, but then hoping to see him at the same time.

Shopping always takes a long time for us. Since we only do it once or twice each year, we aren't very familiar with the layout of the store. We can't always find the items that are on our list and spend lots of time walking up and down the aisles. Canned goods and cereals are easiest, but things like aspirin and duct tape are hard. Usually I don't mind, but today I'm willing Mom to move even faster than she already is.

"We'll be done soon, don't worry." Mom pats my shoulder. She must think that I'm nervous for the same reasons she is. Guilt consumes me. I've let this boy infect my brain. I'm weak and susceptible to temptation, especially when it comes wrapped in the body of a boy like Cody. I'm the reason for Pioneer's prayers last night. He must suspect my weakness. Maybe the Brethren—far away but watching me—told him.

I keep searching for Cody as we fill the cart with toilet paper and paper towels, but after at least a half hour, there's still no sign of him. I start to relax a little. We've filled one cart and are halfway through another now. Maybe he had to leave. I try not to let this thought disappoint me too much. It's a good thing he hasn't shown up.

I pat my pocket, the one with Marie's money in it. After we're done here, I might have a chance to get her magazines. Maybe I'll try when we fill up the truck with gas. Even though there are books and magazines here, I won't get an opportunity to buy any. My mom never lets me out of her sight in this store. She says it's too big and that there are too many opportunities for trouble to find me, but at the gas station maybe I can convince her to let me pay like Marie does and get the magazines there. I'm not excited about the idea. I'm more sick than anything else, but it's as good a distraction as any to keep me from obsessing about Cody. Plus, part of me wants to be able to do what Marie did, to do something no one expects of me.

"Grab me that big jar of olives over there." Mom squints at the list in her hand as she nudges me. I scan the shelves, my mind still on the money and my supposed mission and Cody. I turn to hand her the gallon-sized jar, but I let go too soon. The jar slips from between both of our outstretched hands and smashes by my mom's feet. Olives and light brown liquid spread out across the aisle. My mother lets out a little yelp as some of the liquid splashes onto her pants. They are soaked all along the bottom and middle with juice.

"Sorry!" I squeak.

"It was an accident, no one's fault," Mom says as we stoop together to start picking up the broken glass.

A man with a name tag enters the aisle and hurries over to us. "No, no, no, ladies, please don't go pickin' that stuff up on your own. You'll cut yourselves. I've got this." The man waves us away as he pulls out a small walkie-talkie-type thing and starts speaking into it. "Suz, we got a mess on aisle seven."

My mom's pants are stuck to her calves. The air around us reeks of olives. "I need to go and try to get this stuff out of my pants," she says. "I can't smell this all the way home. I'll be sick."

"The bathroom's up front, right?" I ask as I turn the cart in that direction.

"Yes, but it's past the checkout lines. We'll have to check out and then go in, but even then we can't really leave the cart alone, can we?" My mom chews on her lip. "I'll just deal with it for now until we find your father." She shakes her leg out a bit, but her pants are a second skin where the hem meets her ankles. She has to be uncomfortable.

"Why don't we just find a cheap pair of pants and then you can change really quick while I wait with the carts out here?"

My mom looks like she's ready to say no out of habit,

but then she hesitates. The pants must really be bothering her for her to even consider leaving me alone. I know that the smell is definitely getting to me. I hate olives. We both do.

"Fine, but you have to stay right up front. No wandering around and no talking to strangers."

I nod my head. "I think I can handle myself for two whole minutes, Mom." Although at this point, I'm not completely sure.

We pick out a pair of seven-dollar navy pants from the clearance rack and head to the front of the store. I stop just before the checkout, directly across from the bathrooms. My mom pulls her cart up next to mine and heads to the closest checkout line. She glances at me repeatedly while she waits for the person in front of her to pay. I swear she's convinced that a swarm of psycho killers will come running out of nowhere and snatch me up. I shake my head and look around for my dad. It's then that I notice where I'm standing—right in front of the magazine and book section. I swallow hard and look up at my mom. If I hurry, maybe I can grab a few magazines and make it through the checkout line before she comes back out.

I wait while she gathers up her bag and her receipt and heads toward the bathroom. She hesitates by the door. I try to smile at her, but my mouth's gotten very dry all of a sudden and my lips seem to be stuck to my teeth. So instead I wave and hope that I don't look as nervous and guilty as I feel. She waves back and goes into the bathroom.

I look around one more time for my dad, but he's nowhere in sight. I inch toward the display shelves full of books and magazines, sure that at any moment one or both of my parents will come rushing up behind me yelling "Aha!" I wipe my palms on my shorts and walk the seven remaining steps to the magazines. I give them one quick scan before I pick the two with the prettiest people on them. I turn toward our shopping carts and try to decide which checkout line looks quickest when I notice a cardboard book display of more than a dozen books with the kind of covers Marie mentioned.

I stop and pick up one with a cover I know Marie will love. It makes me want to grimace or gag or both. There's a bare-chested man on it and his muscles are so well defined that they look cartoonish, all hairless and tan. His hair is dark and tousled like someone's just run their fingers through it. Next to him is an extremely busty woman with long dark hair and parted lips. Her hand is draped over one of his shoulders and she's swooning into him. I wonder if this is how Marie sees herself and Brian when they're together. I imagine their heads on top of the bodies on the book cover and I laugh out loud. I turn the book over and start looking for the price.

"You're into romance books?" a male voice says.

I startle and almost drop the book. Cody is across the display from me. His eyebrow is quirked up and he's grinning at me.

"Um, no, I mean, sort of . . . it's for a friend," I mumble, and my face fills with heat. A tornado of emotions—panic, joy, and horror—swirls through me.

He holds up his hands. "Hey, no judgment here. My mom loves those things. She's got about a dozen beside her bed right now. Trust me, the one you've got there is tame by comparison." He shivers and then chuckles.

"I thought you'd left" is all I can manage to say.

"I was just waiting to see if I could get you alone. Something tells me your parents wouldn't approve of us . . . talking. Right?"

I smile a little. "Um, yeah."

"Lucky for me you attacked your mom with those olives. I was beginning to think you would leave before I'd get my chance."

I laugh a little and stare at the books in front of me. Cody flips through a stack of books beside him. "You could always get your friend this one." He holds up a book with a bronzed and glistening pirate in pants so tight and low that it isn't hard to guess what's underneath them.

"Who can resist a dude in extra-tight striped pants?" Cody smirks, and we both laugh.

His eyes crinkle and his lips twist off to one side of his face when he smiles. His hair is still damp from his haircut, tousled and soft looking near the nape of his neck. I have the strangest urge to touch the tiny hairs there to see if they feel the way that I think they do, like duck down.

I'm staring and he's smiling at me while I do it. I look back down at the books. I have to get away from him.

Whatever this is that I'm feeling is all wrong. I know it and yet I can't make myself walk away. Instead I find myself trying to memorize his face. How can a boy I barely know interest me this much? Why him and not Will?

Will is chosen, like me. Cody's not. The Brethren have decided that he's supposed to die. If he was good, he'd be in Mandrodage Meadows with us. The Brethren would've seen to it and led Pioneer to him. Instead he's here in Culver Creek, which means that I'm losing it over a guy who's been sentenced to death, inherently damaged and evil.

But who knew someone so supposedly evil could seem so . . . not? Nothing about him screams danger to me. Shouldn't I have some sort of warning bell going off in my head? Shouldn't I have an overwhelming urge to run? I don't. So what does that say about me?

Cody's watching me. He'd been talking about something a moment ago, but now he's just staring at me, his head cocked to one side like he's trying to eavesdrop on my thoughts.

"Where'd you just go?" he asks softly.

"Sorry, I just . . . should probably find my parents." I finally commit to what I have to do and it sucks.

"But we've only been talking for a few minutes." He moves a little closer and leans against the book display. His hand is close enough to mine that our fingers touch. My stomach flops around like a fish on land.

"Why don't we just walk the aisles? If your parents show up, you can tell them that you went looking for them and got turned around," Cody asks. He hasn't moved his hand. It's still touching mine.

I move over a little to put some space between us. "I can't. I promised my mom that I'd wait right here with our carts. We're just about done shopping anyway. So this is kind of it, sorry."

His face falls a little. "You're sure?"

I nod.

"Lyla!" Mom shouts my name. Her face is the picture of panic. People turn to look at her and then at me. My face flushes and I fight the urge to go hide under one of the clothing racks.

"See? I've really gotta go," I mumble at Cody. I can't meet his eyes as I talk.

Mom's already closed the distance between us. "Are you all right?" she asks loudly enough for Cody and several other people standing nearby to hear.

"Mom, I'm *fine*," I say through gritted teeth.

"I'm Cody." Cody offers my mom his hand to shake, but she looks at it like it might sting her. "Lyla gave me a tour of your neighborhood when I was there with my dad last week. Sheriff Crowley?"

Mom just stares at him.

"Anyway, I saw her over here and just thought that I'd say hello." He smiles, but my mom's face is pinched and suspicious. I want to die.

"Yes, well, I'm afraid we've got a busy day ahead of us.

No time for chitchat. Come along, Lyla." She pulls at my arm. Her fingers grip it uncomfortably.

I look at Cody one last time. Our eyes lock for a second. I shouldn't feel disappointed. I knew something like this would happen. I barely know him. My chest squeezes and I feel dangerously close to tears. Whatever this was, it's over before it could even start—which, according to everything that I believe, is only right. I just wish it didn't *feel* so wrong.

"Hey, wait! Don't you want your magazines . . . and books?" Cody calls out, and I cringe. He holds the magazines up where my mom can see them. Mom cuts her eyes at me. I won't look at her.

"Lyla?" She looks at me like she's never seen me before in her life.

"Um, I was only looking at them. He must've misunderstood."

Cody looks ready to bring the book and magazines to me, but then he looks at my mom and thinks better of it. Instead he shrugs and sets them down. Mom pulls my arm a little harder.

"Mind telling me what's going on?"

"Nothing, nothing's going on," I say woodenly. It's true. Nothing is going on, not anymore.

# EIGHTEEN

I follow my parents back to the truck. We eat a little lunch
in the cab while we're still in the Walmart parking lot.
Usually we try to go to the park and eat outside, but my
parents are anxious to get back on the road, so our last in-
town meal overlooks shopping carts and cars.

I'm not all that hungry, so I sketch instead. I start
off sketching a bird that's wandering around the parking
lot, but before long I flip to a new page and start drawing Cody. I work on getting the shape of his chin right,
the angle of his jaw. Maybe if I can get him on paper, I
can flush him out of my system. I promise myself that I'll
throw this sketch out once I'm done with it. Then I'll forget all about this morning and concentrate on the morn-
ings that'll come after this one, on all of the things big and
small we still have to do before we go into the Silo.

By the time I'm done sketching, my parents have finished eating and are busy tidying up the truck. I feel a

little better, more centered. I push Cody toward the back of my thoughts and nibble on a cheese sandwich as we stuff all our garbage into a plastic bag. Only a few more stops and this day, this town, will be a thing of the past as far as I'm concerned, no more than a dream.

We have to stop at the post office next and then the gas station before we leave town for good. My dad starts the truck and my mom hands me the bag of trash she's gathered so I can throw it away. I hop out of the cab and walk the trash to the front entrance of the store. I watch the continuous stream of people coming out and begin to search for the trashcan.

I've just crossed the main thoroughfare between the parking lot and the front doors when Cody appears. The automatic doors slide open and there he is. I smile almost on reflex. I take a step forward, my hand already coming up to wave. Then I wonder if my parents are watching, if they see me doing the one thing I shouldn't, and I turn around. I start to take a step back into the parking lot. I can throw our stuff out at the post office.

I have about a second to register sunlight glinting off something metal. There's a flash of green. Something strikes my left side. Hard. My body flops against it. I realize with a detached sense of wonder that it's a car. I walked in front of a moving car.

The world tilts. I'm falling. My butt smacks the asphalt. My hands scrape across loose gravel before my head snaps downward. There's a strange cracking sound inside my head. I blink. Then I open my mouth to breathe, but my lungs won't work. The car screeches to a halt a few feet away.

I'm flat on my back on the road. My shirt has ridden up and my lower back is burning, melting into the ground. I can't move, can't make myself get up. There's noise and people all around me, but I can't make sense of any of it. Then it's as if the asphalt expands, wraps around me until there's nothing more than blackness and the sound of my mother's screams in my ears.

When I open my eyes next, there's a ring of heads looming over me. I can't make sense of their faces, can't decide if I know any of them. My head hurts—enough so that I keep closing my eyes again to block out the colors and light. The flashes of movement around me feel as abrupt and disturbing as gunfire. My ears are ringing. I can still hear, but the noises are muffled. People are talking. None of it makes sense. I try to sit up, but hands hold me tight to the ground. It hurts to fight them off, so I stop trying. I lick my lips instead and try to speak.

"Sweetie, you have to stay very still for me." My dad's voice breaks through the haze in my head. He's next to me, right by my shoulder. His face is all fear. It scares me.

"Car," I manage to mumble. My eyes are either watery from the pain or I'm crying. I can't tell which.

"Yes, we know. The ambulance is coming now." My dad looks up and I follow his gaze. He's staring at my mom. She's leaning over my other side. My head clears a little. They're scared because I have to go to the hospital. This is bad. It means unwanted attention for all of us. I struggle against my dad's hands again. I have to get up. We have to leave before the ambulance actually gets here. We have to get back to Mandrodage Meadows.

"I'm all right," I croak.

"No, sweetie, you're not. You have to lie still." Dad leans over, close to my ear, and whispers in it. "Don't worry. We'll handle the people at the hospital. The only thing that matters right now is that we make sure you're okay."

I look out at the crowd of people standing around us. Most are whispering to each other, their faces openly curious. Do they already know who we are? Where we're from? I look for Cody. He was there. In the store. Right before I got hit. I don't see him anywhere now, though.

Good.

At least he had enough sense not to get involved.

My mom smooths my hair and kisses my forehead. Her face goes from reassuring to crumply and half hysterical, then back again. She's barely holding it together. I've made her face her worst fear all over again. I can see her reliving Karen's disappearance as she looks down at me.

"I'll be fine, Mom. I promise." I try to smile, but wince instead. My head and neck are pounding.

My mom finally loses the battle and lets out one long wail just as the ambulance comes tearing through the parking lot, its siren mixing with her cry in a terrible duet.

*Why do we avoid the outside world?*
*Because they can't conceive of a people as beautiful,*
*kind, and loving as ours. And because they don't understand us,*
*they will surely make it their mission to destroy us.*

—Pioneer

# NINETEEN

I've never been in an ambulance before, but I've seen them in the movies. Usually the person being rocketed to the nearest hospital is seconds away from death, and the EMT next to them is holding electric paddles over their chest. They're always injured doing something worthy of a hospital visit—gunning down bad guys or falling from buildings before they blow up. But not me. I manage to get knocked on my butt by an old lady driving an even older car in the Walmart parking lot. It would almost be funny, actually, if my parents hadn't been there to see the whole thing. My mom's probably in worse shape mentally than I am physically.

The EMT crouches next to me and busily wraps things around my arms and hooks me up to some machines that make beeping noises. I'm still not really sure why I'm even in the ambulance. I don't feel like anything's really wrong.

I guess I hit my head on the road when I fell. The EMT said I lost consciousness for a little bit. I do have a pretty wicked headache, but other than feeling like I've been run over by a car—which I have, ha, ha—I'm pretty sure nothing on me is broken. The old lady couldn't have been driving that fast. I mean, maybe it was faster than she was supposed to be going, but it wasn't highway speed. I basically stepped into her bumper and ricocheted off.

I want to sit up. I feel sort of silly lying down. I'm still holding out hope that I can convince the EMT to stop the ambulance and let me out so I can climb back into the truck and head home, pretend like none of this ever happened. I'm sure my parents would be relieved if I did. They have to be panicked that I'm hurt enough to be hospitalized, and also because we've attracted unwanted attention—and not just for us, but for the Community as well.

I try to avoid looking at the EMT. She's asking me questions, lots of them. I'm not sure how to answer them without my parents close by to help me. I close my eyes. I'm tired and shutting them against the bright overhead light feels really, really good.

The EMT taps my arm. "Hey, Lyla, try to stay awake, honey."

I open my mouth to answer her, but talking seems like such an effort. If I can just close my eyes, I know I'll feel clearer. . . .

The ambulance ride becomes disjointed. I keep opening

my eyes when the EMT jostles me, but the minute she stops, I close them again. This happens over and over before the ambulance lurches to a stop and I'm lifted out and into the even brighter afternoon sun. It's strange being moved around this way, lying down, strapped to a very skinny bed.

The hospital is another first for me—all bright lights and funny smells that aren't entirely covered up by the bleach they've apparently cleaned with. I don't like it, not that I had any real illusions that I would. I get poked and prodded several times over and then taken to a few different rooms for various tests, the names of which I either haven't quite caught or can't retain. Eventually I end up in a room with a view of a single tree and a brick wall. I'm in the only bed and my mom is sitting stiffly on the edge of the chair beside it. There's a television in the upper left-hand corner of the room, but it's not on.

"They say that you have to stay here tonight," my mom says as she brushes my hair off my face and onto the pillow.

"But I feel fine." I try to say this with a smile, but moving my face intensifies the thunder in my head. I grimace instead. My left leg is tender all along the thigh where the car hit it. I'm starting to realize that I'm a little achy everywhere now, like my whole body rearranged itself on impact. My tailbone and head hurt the worst; both struck the ground pretty hard, I think.

My mom kisses my forehead in that overly glommy way of hers. I always have to make myself not recoil when she does this, because I know it will only hurt her feelings, but it's too frantic and smothery.

"They want to make sure you're okay. They said you have a concussion and they want to monitor you in case there's swelling." She's smiling, but the hand on my forehead is shaky.

"But we aren't supposed to be here," I whisper, my eyes straying to the open door in case someone's already there, eavesdropping. "Pioneer says . . ."

"If we try to leave, it'll only make things worse. If we're smart about this and give them as little information about the Community as we can, we might be able to get through this without making anyone too curious. But you have to leave the talking to your father and me. Just stay calm, okay?" My mom's voice is harsh. It confirms what I know in my heart to be true. Our situation is precarious. One wrong answer or slip of information and we will single-handedly make the Community too much of a curiosity.

"What do you want me to do?" I say, and throw one arm over my eyes to block out the light and the possibility of more of her kisses.

"Be polite, but quiet. Don't offer any information that they haven't asked for directly. And above all, make sure to let them know that we are just a simple farming community focused on growing our own foods and living a simple life. No matter what, don't mention anything about Pioneer's dreams or anything else."

"I'm not an idiot, Mom," I say, but then maybe she sort

of has a case for my being one, since I've started walking in front of moving cars. "Where's Dad?"

"They needed him to fill out some forms." She sighs heavily. "There's no health insurance . . . which complicates things."

"What about all of the supplies? We're supposed to be on the way back right now."

"Your father's going to drive them back after he's done and then come back in the morning. He has to let Pioneer know what's happened."

"What about you?" I ask, and am surprised at how clingy I feel. I don't want to be here alone.

"Staying here with you, of course." She tilts her head toward the chair. "The nurse is bringing me blankets. Supposedly that thing turns into a bed." She points to the chair and we both eyeball it.

It gets quiet for a moment.

"I'm sorry," I finally say, my voice tighter in my throat than usual. I feel like there's so much I should say, but the words pile up inside my throat. There's too many of them trying to get out all at once. I have to work to swallow. It feels like I'm choking.

My mom breathes in and out slowly. "I know."

"I just don't like worrying you."

"You've never done it on purpose, Lyla, I know that. But you're a child. Worrying me is part of your job description. Just like the actual worrying is part of mine. That's why

I'll be so glad to finally be in the Silo. You can't do much to worry me there." Her mouth curls up the slightest bit.

My dad checks on me briefly before leaving. He tucks my blankets under and around me tightly from my shoulders to my feet the way he used to when I was little and I thought monsters might be able to slither under the covers if there were any gaps.

"Lyla burrito," he says with a smile, and then presses his lips into my hair. "Get some rest."

"You'll be back first thing tomorrow morning, right?"

"Before the sun's even all the way up," he promises.

My mom follows him to the door. "Be just a minute, sweetie," she tells me.

I fiddle with my bed while I wait for her to come back from walking my dad to the truck. The buttons that lift it are entertaining. I raise my feet higher than my head and then my head higher than my feet before all of the movement makes me dizzy and sick. I stare at the ceiling and then out the window. Television's out. Even if I wanted to watch, I couldn't. My mom gave the nurses the remote as soon as she came across it. Pioneer would want us to keep the Community's rules, especially here. Eventually I stare out at the hallway and watch the nurses go back and forth. It's pretty quiet. I don't see any other people. I wonder how many other people are out there in rooms just like mine.

I wish I had my sketchbook so I could sketch some of the nurses, but it's all the way across the room in my backpack. I'm not up to getting out of bed and retrieving it. Instead I settle for the tiny notepad in my bedside table with CULVER CREEK HOSPITAL written across the top and the pen that was with it when I found it. But then I don't know what to draw, and besides, it's really hard to concentrate. I end up making random doodles, a maze of squiggly lines and circles.

"Knock, knock."

Cody's in my doorway, leaning against the frame. My mouth drops open, but no sound comes out. *What is he doing here?* is my first thought, but a close second is, *I must look awful.*

"I wanted to see if you were okay," he says. He fiddles with a plastic Walmart bag that he's got gathered up in one hand.

"How did you know how to find me?"

He laughs and rubs his chin. "Uh, you were in a car accident—it was pretty much a given that you'd end up here."

"I mean how did you know which room?" I say as my face fills with heat. "Do they just let anyone have that information?"

His ears start turning red. He looks back at the door. "My dad kinda has some pull around here . . . but listen, if you'd rather I go, I will. I wasn't trying to stalk you or anything. I just . . . saw you go down in the parking lot. I needed to know that you weren't seriously hurt, you know?"

He flashes me a tiny smile and I smile back.

"So how are you?" he asks as he inches closer to my bed.

"Bored," I say. "Hospitals are really, really boring."

"Well, I think I might be able to help with that," he says. He holds up the Walmart bag before handing it to me. Inside are three magazines and the book I was looking at in the store.

"Thought Mr. Spandex could keep things interesting." He points to the book cover. We both laugh.

"Thanks."

I don't know what to do. I should give it back to him. I can't exactly keep this stuff in plain sight for my mom to see. Plus, enough stuff's gone wrong already, why make it worse? On the other hand, if I can manage to hide them and smuggle them out tomorrow, I'll still be able to keep my promise to Marie and for once look like the daring, adventurous one, especially after they find out that I got hit by a car and survived. Cody obviously went to some trouble to bring them to me, and I don't want to be rude and give them back.

The room has gone silent again.

"Um, I really wish you could stay, but my mom'll be back any minute now and she isn't real big on strangers."

"I noticed. Protective, isn't she?"

"Protective is an understatement," I say. "At least when it comes to me."

"How about if I promise to keep one eye on the hallway at all times? Can I stay then?"

I don't respond, but he makes no attempt to leave. I'm disappointed with myself over how happy this makes me.

"I get it. You keep to yourselves at all costs, right? No fraternizing with strangers."

I don't know what to say to this, so I just ignore it altogether. "Thanks again for these." I smooth my hand across the glossy book cover.

His mouth curls up at one end and my stomach rolls over. "My pleasure."

*I need to tell him to go. Now. Thank him and say goodbye. Mom'll be back any minute.*

Cody sits on the edge of the bed. His hip touches my leg and a thrill runs through me when he doesn't move it away. This is so stupid and yet I obviously don't care. If I did, he'd already be gone. I would've kicked him out right away.

"Honestly, I'm glad I had an excuse to try and see you again," he says.

"Why?" I really want to know. I can't imagine why he would want to see me, even though I can name at least a dozen reasons why I want him to keep trying.

"Truthfully?" He blushes. "I don't know. I mean, you're not exactly like any other girls I know. And you might be fairly cute, which helps." His blush spreads and he smiles. "But I think mostly it's because you sort of intrigue me. You're more smothered by your parents and your situation than I've ever been by mine, and yet you don't seem to notice that much . . . or even really mind. I don't get it."

I'm not sure if this is a compliment or not. I decide to hold on to the part where he said he thought I was cute.

"I guess I want to figure you out." He winks at me and I melt a little.

He looks toward the door. "Listen, my dad's gonna be coming in here in a few minutes to talk to you about the accident and then I'm guessing your parents will be back in here too. I was thinking . . . maybe afterward—after your parents leave—I can come back?"

"Um, I don't see how. My mom's not leaving. She's staying in here all night," I sigh. It seems like all we keep doing is finding more ways to say goodbye.

He frowns and we both get quiet before a slow grin spreads across his face. "What if I can manage to get you out of your room with her blessing?"

I snort. "Impossible." I lie back on my pillow and stare at the ceiling.

"We'll see," he says.

There are some noises out in the hall beyond the door, and both of us jump a little. Cody leans over and pats my shoulder. Our faces are so close that for a moment I'm sure he might kiss me.

"I'll see you soon," he whispers, and then he's up and out the door before I remember how to breathe.

I hide the magazines and book under my mattress. I'm definitely keeping them now.

Cody isn't gone for more than a minute or two before my mom emerges from the hallway. The time between his leaving and her returning is short enough to make me squirm. *Did she see him?* She looks agitated but not completely flipped out. I barely have time to feel relieved, though, because the door opens all over again and Cody's dad walks in.

I didn't pay much attention to him when I saw him last. I was too wrapped up in Cody. He's a great tree trunk of a man, much larger than I remember. Maybe it's because I'm lying down and he's standing up or maybe it's because the room is fairly narrow, but he seems giant-sized. He leans over the bed and holds out his hand.

"Hey there, Lyla. Nice to see you again. Sure wish we were meeting back up over more pleasant circumstances, though."

I shake his hand. His grip is firm and warm. I look for Cody in his face, but they don't seem to resemble one another much. Cody's features are sharper, finer. The sheriff's are all broad strokes: wide nose, wider chin, full cheeks. His hair is close-cropped and equal parts gray and black.

"Mind if I sit?" He points to the chair before sitting in it. It creaks loudly under his weight. "So, how're you feeling?"

"She's sore, but fine. The doctor said that if she doesn't show signs of swelling or a more severe concussion, she can go home tomorrow," Mom answers for me before I can even open my mouth.

The sheriff smiles at her. "That's good . . . real good.

Ma'am, I'd like to have a moment here with Lyla. Alone. If that's all right?"

"Why? I'm sure I can help you more than she can. She's a bit fuzzy about what happened," Mom says with a smile that's just a little too wide for her face.

"Strictly procedural stuff, ma'am. I just need her take on things so I know whether or not the driver involved needs to be charged with anything. You're more than welcome to stay, it's just I know the nurses needed to ask you some questions and I thought maybe since I'm here with Lyla this might be the perfect time. I'm sure it won't take long at all and then you can help me fill in any gaps right after. I'll be out of your hair just as soon as I get what I need for my report."

His smile matches hers. His voice is firm. Reluctantly, my mom folds. She huffs out a breath. "All right. Fine. But I'll be right outside if you need me." She gives me a long look on her way out. I nod just a little to let her know that I'll be careful.

The sheriff wrestles his way out of his seat and walks over to the door. He waits for my mom to go all the way out into the hall and then shuts it. He smiles at me as he returns to his seat. I try to occupy myself with straightening the covers over my legs so I won't look nervous.

He watches me for a moment.

"There's no need to be nervous. I'm just going to ask you a few questions. Nothing too difficult, okay?"

I nod. He seems satisfied and leans back in his chair. "Let's start with what you remember about the accident."

I tell him about our trip to the Walmart. I briefly mention seeing Cody inside and my cheeks burst into flame, but if he notices, he doesn't react. He keeps his expression neutral as I talk, all the way up to the end, when I describe crossing the parking lot. I leave out the part about seeing Cody again and how it made me turn around. I say I forgot something in the truck and went back for it.

After I'm done, he asks me some questions about what I'd noticed about the car before it hit me. Did it seem like it was going fast? Had I noticed it at all when I crossed the parking lot the first time?

My nerves have just started to settle down when he leans forward and looks at my neck. "Medics said you have a pretty ugly gash on the back of your neck there—not from this accident. How'd that happen?"

I can't keep my hands from traveling to the fresh bandage on my neck. Pioneer's punishment. "Oh, that. That's nothing. Really. I don't even really remember getting it." I try to smile. "I think I brushed up against a nail or something in the barn and it scratched me."

The sheriff looks at me carefully. "That must've been some nail. What were you doing—scratching up against it like a cat?"

I look away, out the window at the tree outside. "Uh . . . yep, I mean no, I just, um, brushed up against it . . . like I said."

Turns out I am the world's worst liar.

He nods to himself. I can see his head bobbing out of the corner of my eye. "Okay, Lyla, one more question and then I promise I'll let you get some rest."

I nod. I try to infuse my expression with innocence, banish any panic in it.

"Is there any chance that you walked in front of that car on purpose?" He looks at me closely.

I burst out laughing. "You think I just tried to *kill myself*?" This is the most ridiculous question anyone's ever asked me. If he only knew the kind of extreme lengths my family's been through my whole life just to survive the apocalypse, he'd think it was a hilarious and stupid question too.

"Maybe you only meant to get someone's attention. Is anything going on out there in Mandrodage Meadows that I should know about? Something about your leader, Pioneer? 'Cause if there is and you need help—if you're in danger—I can promise you that I will do everything in my power to keep you safe. You just say the word."

He looks down at his fingers while he waits for my answer. He's managed to pick at the side of one of them and now there's a quarter-inch sliver of skin sticking up. He yanks at it with his thumb and forefinger until it comes off. I watch as a tiny red blood splotch forms in its absence. "All I need is for you to tell me what's going on."

I shake my head. "Nothing. Nothing's going on. It was an accident. I wasn't watching where I was going today. I was distracted. That's all. Nothing intentional about it, I swear."

He stands up and brushes his hands over his pants. "If you're sure. Well then, I guess we're done here." He smiles. "Just try to be careful from now on, okay? I sure wouldn't want to hear about you having any more accidents. And watch out for those nails. I'm thinkin' that it might be time for you to start paying closer attention to the world around you."

I force myself to nod and smile back. He opens the door to leave and my mom practically falls in. "Ma'am." He nods at her to join him as he leaves.

My mom follows him into the hall. I can hear her voice and then her laughter, forced and high-pitched. I cringe. We're doing a horrible job of convincing him that we're not hiding anything. I replay the last half hour in my head. I dissect each of my answers to his questions. I tell myself that there's no need to worry about anything. He has no real reason to be too suspicious of us. He'll probably just write up his report and forget all about us once we leave Culver Creek. In a few weeks he'll have much bigger problems to deal with. So why do I feel like we're a little piece of skin, sticking up just enough to make him want to pick?

*Then you will know the truth and the truth will set you free.*
*—John 8:32*

# TWENTY

After the sheriff leaves, my mom grills me for over an hour. She wants to know what he said and then what I said verbatim. I decide not to tell her about his last two questions. I'll wait and tell her when my dad comes back instead. She can't do anything about it now anyway—except freak out, and that'll only make us look weirder.

She relaxes some after she's satisfied that most of what he wanted to know had nothing to do with Mandrodage Meadows, but she doesn't leave the room again. She's convinced that the nurses know where we're from and are whispering about us.

"I can't wait to be back home. I absolutely hate being stuck out here. With them." She wrinkles her nose like the whole place and everyone in it stinks.

"We will be tomorrow," I say.

"Well, tomorrow can't come quickly enough." She sighs and goes to the window. "I won't be able to relax properly until we're halfway home."

The afternoon lingers forever. There's nothing to do,

so I make myself sleep a little even though it'll mean being awake longer later. I can't stand watching my mom pace and sigh and pace and sigh. I find myself wishing she'd just leave for a while. It'd be easier to pass the time without her hovering. And besides, the sheriff, the sound of traffic outside my window, the chatter of strangers down the hall, remind me too much of New York. Karen and all that happened back then feel too close here somehow. In Mandrodage Meadows we can keep our memories away, leave them outside the gate, but not here. Here we can't avoid them. They snake around us, squeezing the air out of the room, making it impossible to really forget.

When they bring Mom and me a tray of food around dinnertime, I practically jump out of bed to meet them. Eating will give us something to focus on, something to do. We eat slowly, pretending to savor the tasteless meat loaf and mashed potatoes. I scrape my Jell-O cup until I can't tell what flavor it was anymore. The cup's completely clean. Mom plays with hers, pulling the spoon in and out like the sucking sound it makes fascinates or repulses her.

"Disgusting," she mutters before sliding the tray away.

We haven't talked much for hours. Mom's concerned about eavesdroppers. The magazines and book under my mattress are making me feel edgy. I want to shove them farther under. Every time my mom leans forward in her chair, I wonder if she's spotted a bit of paper poking out. It's excruciating.

Eventually Mom gives up trying to stay awake and

fiddles with her chair until it slides out into a very narrow, very hard-looking bed. She starts spreading out the sheets the nurses gave her. I am nowhere near tired after my long afternoon nap, but I fake a yawn anyway. I'd rather sit in the dark and listen to her sleep than sit around and have to stare at her or play hangman one more time.

Just as we're turning out the lights—at the uncharacteristically early hour of seven—a nurse pops her head into the room. She's really young and pretty, completely opposite all of the other nurses I've seen today. Her hair reminds me a little of Cody's. It's the same medley of browns that his is. She smiles at me and winks, which surprises me. Honestly, it's a little weird.

"Sorry to bother you ladies, but I need to take"—she makes a big show of checking the clipboard in her hands— "Lyla down for a few more tests."

My mom starts to stand up.

"No need to get up, ma'am. I'll just take her for a little while. And you can't really go with her to the testing room anyway. We're taking a few more X-rays." She smiles at my mom. "Get some rest; I'll come get you if we need you." She leans back against the door until it opens all the way and rolls a wheelchair inside.

"Can't I just walk?" I complain.

"'Fraid not, hospital policy," she says. She helps peel back my covers and I exhale heavily, but settle into the chair. I had X-rays earlier and the process was pretty tedious, but it's better than staring at the ceiling.

"Okay, let's roll." I smile at my own pun, but no one else seems to get or notice it.

Mom looks like she's about to tag along anyway, but then stops herself. It has to be because she thinks it'll look odd if she goes. She perches on the edge of the chair-bed. Her posture is so rigid that it looks unnatural.

"Relax, Mom, I'll be right back. I'm fine, the X-rays will prove it." I want the nurse to think her odd behavior is a direct result of worry and not paranoia.

Once we're in the hallway, the nurse leans down by my ear. "Ready for a little adventure?"

I turn back to look at her. "What?"

"Cody sent me. I'm his sister, Taylor." She bounces a little on her toes as she talks. It makes her seem even younger.

"You aren't really a nurse, are you?" I ask.

"Um, technically, no. But I am planning on studying to be one and I do work here part-time . . . just not as a nurse."

I look at the nurses' station. For the moment no one's there.

"I waited until the coast was clear," Taylor tells me proudly. "We can't have anyone wondering where we're going, now can we?"

My stomach starts to turn rapid somersaults. "Where *are* we going?"

"Somewhere a little more private," Taylor says.

Cody wants to see me. He sent his sister in to basically

kidnap me so he could. I should stop her, jump out of the chair, and turn around. His dad's the sheriff. He's too close to the one person who could spell big trouble for my family and the rest of the Community. But his face flashes across my brain and I can't make myself get up and turn around.

Taylor's still chattering on and on. "You've done a real number on my brother, you know? He's been hanging out here all day begging me to help him see you. He promised to do my chores for the next month if I managed to get you out of your room and away from your mom." She pauses. "Is it true—are you one of those people that live way out on the prairie in that commune-type place?"

I nod.

"Wow, that's weir . . . I mean different." She hesitates a little and seems to consider her next words carefully. "So, what's the story? Why isolate yourselves all the way out there?"

I give her the usual spiel about how we want to live simply.

"So you're, like, kind of Amish?"

"What?"

"You know, the people with the horses and buggies that dress all old-fashioned and won't use electricity or technology. They think it's evil or something. Do you?"

I shake my head. "Um, no, we don't. We came here in a truck. And I usually wear jeans or shorts. And we like electricity. A lot."

She shrugs. "So then you're not like a cult or something?"

That's the second time one of them has used that word. Pioneer has always said that they would. He says any religious or political group—any group at all where people are passionate about something—is considered one. He says it's because people who lack passion and commitment can't understand those who have it. No matter what we say, they won't change their minds. And if we're not careful, they'll see it as a reason to persecute us.

"Absolutely not," I say as mildly as I can because it's the response I've been taught, but I'm still irritated by the question. What does it matter to her either way? We're not hurting anybody, at least not those who leave us alone. In fact, the only people who seem intent on hurting someone are the people here and places like it—first with their words, like right now, and later with their weapons—or cars. It seems Pioneer is right about that.

We roll down the halls in silence for a moment. I concentrate on my hands, which are in my lap.

"I'm sorry, that was a pretty rude question. Sometimes my mouth goes off before my head can censor it. I was just curious."

"Really, there's nothing to be curious about," I say.

"That's not what my dad says."

My heart just about stops. She's confirmed what I already suspected. The sheriff isn't just going to forget about us.

We stop in front of an elevator and get on once it opens.

"We're almost there," Taylor says as she presses the button for the ninth floor.

It's only now that it dawns on me that I'm wearing a hospital gown . . . and nothing much else. "Um, but my clothes. I can't see your brother looking like this."

Taylor bursts out laughing. "Oh, man, sorry, I almost forgot." She hits the elevator's stop button and starts pulling off the scrubs she's wearing. She doesn't even flinch when the elevator starts buzzing at us.

"Whoa, I didn't mean you needed to give me *your* clothes." I hold up a hand to stop her, but she's already shimmied out of everything. She has on a pair of very tight stretch pants and a long T-shirt.

"No problem, they weren't mine anyway. I borrowed them from the locker room." She holds the clothes out to me. I recoil. The last thing I need is to be caught with stolen clothes.

Taylor sighs. "Oh, don't get your panties in a twist. They belong to a friend. Trust me, she won't care. She lives for this forbidden-romantic-interlude kind of Shakespearean crap. And I live for less chores, so hurry up and change so we can get you to my brother and make everybody happy."

I can feel myself blushing. Is that what I'm about to do? Have a romantic interlude? It sounds medieval . . . and scarily exciting. I pull on the scrubs and stand next to her. I can't sit in the chair anymore, I'm too nervous. I'm swaying a little, and the elevator feels like it's moving side to side now, but I manage to keep my balance. Taylor starts the elevator back up again and we ride the rest of the way in silence.

When the doors open, we walk out into a completely deserted hallway. It smells new, like sawdust and fresh paint.

"This floor just got remodeled. No one's using it yet. It doesn't reopen until next week, which means you guys will have it all to yourselves." She grins at me.

She leads me down to the end of the hallway and into a room with a bunch of hard sofas and chairs on one side and a row of vending machines and a small kitchenette on the other. Cody's on one of the sofas. He stands up and grins. "Told you I'd find a way to see you again."

Taylor rolls her eyes. "Yes, you're the king of smooth, little brother. You have one hour. Don't waste it. Bring her down to five when you're done—and don't be late. I have a date of my own tonight."

*A date.* Her words only add to my nervousness. I can't have a date, not with him or anyone else. I'm intended. I'm Will's. I don't move from the doorway. I put a hand on the frame and try to make myself go, but then Cody's grinning at me again and I'm letting him lead me farther into the room. What is it about this boy that makes me put aside all common sense?

"Sorry I had to have my sister come get you, but I couldn't really come myself. Something tells me your mom would've freaked out." He motions for me to sit down on one of the pea-green sofas. I sit at the very edge and watch as he settles down beside me. It's so quiet for a moment that the silence almost seems to become a solid thing between us, but then my stomach growls out of nowhere. Loudly. I put my hands around it and cringe.

"Hungry?" Cody chuckles, and then jumps back up and walks over to the vending machines. I notice that one of them has a familiar design on it. The same one that's on the Coke cans from Marie's little party the other night. *Coke. Yum.*

"Um, I'd love a Coke," I say shyly.

He slips some coins into the Coke machine and then a few more into another one. Then he stoops over and collects my snack and spreads it out on the thin wooden table in front of me. I examine the little bag there. "Cheetos?"

Cody plucks it from my fingers and pulls it open. "Yeah."

When I don't react, he gapes at me. "You've never had them, have you?"

I shake my head.

"Well then, you're in for a treat. They are by far my favorite junk food."

I peer into the bag at what look like orange-coated caveman clubs. They don't look like they should be edible. They look sort of disgusting. I wrinkle up my nose.

"Hey, don't knock 'em till you try 'em," Cody says. "Allow me to educate you in the fine art of snacking."

"I didn't realize there was any art involved in eating." I can't help smiling at him. He makes me feel happy for no particular reason. It's a little like when I'm with Will, only so much better. It starts to dawn on me that this is what it feels like to really like someone. This is how I should feel about Will, but don't. It's Cody I want, and no amount of rationalizing will change that. Whatever this is isn't rational at all—it's crazy, stupid, reckless . . . and somehow perfectly *right*.

"Snacking I get, but this . . ." I pick up a single Cheeto and dangle it in front of my face. "I don't know *what* this is."

Cody chuckles. "It's food . . . in the loosest sense of the word. It's horrible for you and has absolutely no redeeming qualities except that it tastes good. Once you have one, you'll want another, trust me."

He's basically describing my reaction to him. He's my Cheeto—bad for me, but now that I have a taste for him, I can't leave him alone.

"What?" He smiles at me.

"Nothing," I say, and pop a Cheeto into my mouth. If I'm going to destroy myself, I might as well do it thoroughly.

Cody watches me. "Good?"

I think about it. "Yeah, it kinda is."

He grins and then dips his hand into the bag, pulls out a handful. I shake my head and pick up the Coke. I take a big, long sip and sigh. It's cold, which makes it even better this time. I think I'm in love with this drink. It is the one thing I wish like crazy I could smuggle back with me by the truckload.

"Wow, you're like a soda junkie," Cody says, his eyes wide, and I laugh so hard that some of the soda fizzes into my nose and makes it burn. My eyes water. Jeez, what is my deal with getting soda up my nose? I seriously need to be careful when I'm drinking this stuff.

"You make junk food seem new and sort of fascinating," Cody says softly. "Does it ever bother you that there's so much that you've never experienced?"

I lean back against the stiff sofa. My answer comes out in a rush. "I can't really be bothered by something if I don't know that it exists. I like where I live and how I live. The smaller your world is, the safer it is, you know? I may not know about every kind of junk food or movie or book, but I don't have to worry about someone taking someone that I love, or eating something that might ultimately kill me, or wondering every morning if someone will come to my school with a gun and shoot me or my friends, or if a group of terrorists will come and blow up the building where my parents work. The world can be a pretty scary place to live. It's a lot less scary when there isn't so much of it open to you." It's the closest I'll come to telling him about Karen or how we came to be in Mandrodage Meadows.

He nods slowly. "I guess I see what you're saying . . . but those things don't happen all the time to everybody. And I don't see how being somewhere smaller and more controlled keeps you from trouble. If anything, it gives you less room to run. Eventually everybody has to deal with something unpleasant. I don't think hiding away from those things means that they won't find you."

I don't know what to say to this. My cheeks burn. Maybe I'm not explaining myself right, because what he's saying makes a sort of sense and now I'm looking at what I said in a different light. I shake my head, try to organize my thoughts so I can make him see what I do. But in order to answer him fully, I'd have to tell him exactly why we're out in the middle of nowhere. I'd have to tell him about the end of the world. I want to—a lot—but it's not my secret to tell, at least not wholly.

"Can we talk about something else?" I ask.

"Can I ask you just one more thing? Then I promise we can talk about something else? You can even ask me something uncomfortable . . . like whether I wear boxers or briefs."

I can't help smiling. "You're assuming that I'm interested in the answer to that question."

Cody smiles back. "I'm not assuming anything. I *know*."

I roll my eyes and he laughs.

"Okay," he says, "last question. Who decides what you can and can't have where you live?"

I frown. "What do you mean?"

"I mean, does that Pioneer guy make all the rules or do you all get a say?"

"I . . . I mean we . . . I guess Pioneer decides, but we

put him in charge." I bite my lip. I feel like I'm walking into a trap.

"So what happens if you disagree with him?"

"Hey, I don't have to answer that one. You said only one question more and then it was my turn," I remind him. I don't like where his questions are headed. It's like he's trying to say something's wrong with the way we do things. But how would he know? He doesn't really know me or Pioneer or any of us. "I mean, maybe we could decide more things on our own, but I'm not sure why it's so important. Pioneer's always done right by us . . . or at least tried."

"But what if he's wrong?"

I exhale slowly. This is not what I thought we'd be talking about. I'm not sure what exactly I was hoping for . . . maybe kissing, which goes to show where my head was at when I agreed to this whole thing. "He never is." I try not to let the creeping doubt that his questions are creating overcome me. This conversation is starting to feel dangerous.

"Everyone's wrong sometimes," Cody says, his eyes watching me a little too closely.

"Well, *he* isn't."

His questions are getting under my skin now, simultaneously frustrating and irritating me.

"How do you know? If he only exposes you to what he wants to, how do you know?" he presses.

I shrug my shoulders. I want this conversation to end.

Now. "We just do. He's always been honest with us, even when it's about something unpleasant."

"Oh? So you know he's been in jail before, then?"

I recoil. "You're lying. Why would you say that?"

"You didn't know, did you? My dad's been doing some checking. Turns out he beat a man almost to death once. A man he used to work with."

I fold my arms and try to look like this bit of information doesn't shock me. *Why didn't Pioneer tell us this? We have no secrets this big that we've kept from him.* "Well . . . that was a long time ago. He's never done anything like that since I've known him." I push away thoughts of my punishment for sneaking out. I fight the urge to rub the bandage at the back of my neck. *That was different. Not the same thing at all. I deserved it. He didn't want to have to punish us that harshly . . . did he?*

"Maybe he had a good reason to do it," I say.

Cody shakes his head sadly. "He almost killed him. Is there any reason that's good enough to keep beating a man who isn't fighting back?"

I barely have time to process this before he starts talking again. "He was a gas station attendant back then. He dropped out of high school. Never kept a job for more than a year or two. So how does a guy like that end up in charge of twenty-some families? And why would he want to move you all to the middle of nowhere? You have to admit, it looks strange, Lyla."

I can't process all that he's said. It's too much. He's made

Pioneer a stranger and I don't like it. This isn't the Pioneer that took me in and kept me safe or the man who gave me Indy. This man Cody's talking about sounds like a monster, and I can't reconcile my version of Pioneer with his. I need to get out of this room. I need some room to breathe.

"I don't want to talk about this anymore," I snap, and my head starts pounding. I don't feel very good all of a sudden. "I want to go back now." I stand up so suddenly that I get dizzy again. I lean over to grab the table in front of me and knock over my Coke instead.

Cody grabs some paper towels from the countertop and starts wiping it up. "I'm sorry. This is not how I wanted this to go at all." His eyes move up to mine. He gives me a weak smile.

"Well, that makes two of us," I say.

He shakes his head slowly. "It's just . . . I like you. A lot, actually. And once you leave here, I probably won't see you again for a while . . . if ever."

He has no idea how true this statement is. It makes me a little sad all of a sudden and softens my anger.

"Basically, one guy is making my seeing you impossible and I just don't get it." He stands up so that he's looking down at me. Our bodies are almost touching. "And when my dad told me about his record and that gash on your neck . . . it worried me. I just feel like you need protecting or something."

"The neck thing was my fault," I say defensively. "I did something I shouldn't have."

"But, see, that doesn't make me feel any better, especially if it was some kind of punishment or something."

"But none of this has anything to do with you. I'm not asking you to look out for me. I'm fine, really. The Community and Pioneer are all I need." I stare up at him and try to look like I mean what I say. He doesn't move; he just stays so close that I can feel our body heat mingling between us. Then he inches a little closer. "Why are you here then, Lyla?"

I open my mouth to speak, but no words come. I want to lean in, touch his lips with my own, feel the rough scruff on his chin with my hand. But I make myself move away. "I'm here because I was in an accident," I say.

"That's not what I meant."

I bite my lip and work to keep my expression neutral, distant. I can't let him get any closer to me. I've been fooling myself. I shouldn't spend this time with him, no matter how brief it is. He's got too many questions that I can't answer, and so does his dad. I'm only making things worse by being here. "I know what you meant," I say. "I made a mistake."

"I don't think you believe that, not really," he says softly. He moves forward. When I try to back away, I bump right into the wall behind me. Cody moves one hand up to my face and gently traces my jawline with his fingers. My skin feels like it's fizzing. Dozens of tiny goose bumps erupt on my arms. My mistake was thinking that

I could just turn off my feelings for him and walk away. I can't. I like him. Right or wrong. Dangerous or not. His questions—his dad's—aren't enough to make it stop.

He leans in a little closer and his lips touch mine. It's a quick, barely there kiss, but it's enough. I smile against his mouth. I never imagined it could feel like this. God help me, but I can almost understand why those girls on the romance books swoon. My knees really do feel weak.

"I just want to make sure that you're safe, Lyla," he whispers.

He wants to make sure that *I'm* safe.

In a few weeks he'll be dead or dying—and I know it. I'm keeping his future a secret, not allowing him even the smallest chance to survive. Cody doesn't deserve to die. He's not evil. I'm sure of it. He's nothing like the man who took Karen. He deserves to live. I *want* him to live. How can we be so sure that the Brethren didn't choose Cody too? Maybe that's why I'm so drawn to him.

If what Cody says is true, Pioneer beat a man almost to death and still became the Brethren's prophet. If he gets a shot at redemption, why can't Cody or Taylor or any of the other people I've met today? So, what do I do?

It takes me less than a second to decide. "There's something I need to tell you. . . ."

Cody and I sit back down on the sofa. I tell him about the impending reversal in the earth's rotation, about the Brethren, Pioneer's visions, all of it. I even explain how

Pioneer found my family and how he's helped us. I want him to see that at his core, Pioneer's a good man and that we aren't strange, we're just surviving.

It's odd—saying it out loud. I don't know if I'm making it sound right. Coming from Pioneer, it sounded so much better. I need to make him believe, but he doesn't look as concerned as I thought he'd be. I try to think of another way to word it so I'll get a better reaction than this one, but I can't think of any. If he could only listen to Pioneer, he'd see, he'd understand.

Cody doesn't say anything for a long time. I expected him to argue now or maybe to laugh and tell me that I'm crazy. It's what Pioneer said would happen if we told the Outsiders, but he doesn't do any of these things. Instead he scoots closer to me and wraps his arms around me. I lean into his chest. "I'm sorry about your sister," he finally says.

I look up at his face, examine it cautiously. Does he believe me? And if he does, what do we do now?

His eyes are dark, unreadable. "So, Pioneer's the only one who's had these . . . visions . . . of the, um, future?"

I nod.

"So how can you be so sure that he's right?"

I blow out a breath. And there it is. He doesn't really believe me. "Because there's science to back it up . . . I mean, look at global warming. I think even you have to admit that all of the natural disasters that happened last week are a pretty good indicator."

"What disasters?" Cody looks confused.

"Don't you listen to the news? The earthquakes in Indonesia and Japan? The hurricane in New Orleans?"

Cody scratches his head. "Lyla, nothing like that happened last week. The last time there was an earthquake in Indonesia was years ago, same with New Orleans. The Japan one is more recent, but still, even it happened a while ago. . . . Did he tell you that they *just* happened?"

"You have to be mistaken." I feel my world compressing, the air in the room becoming nonexistent. "These have to be new ones. They just happened last week. I watched it on the news."

Cody shakes his head, looks at me with concern. "No, Lyla. They didn't happen. Not last week. If all of those things happened in one week, we'd all still be talking about it. It'd be all over the news right now. I mean, on the news, did they ever mention what day it was?"

I try to think back. They must have. Pioneer wouldn't deliberately show us something years out of date, would he? What would be the point?

"I can't remember," I admit.

"He showed you old footage, Lyla. It isn't hard to do. He wants to keep you all in line and scared." Cody walks to the other side of the room and rummages through a backpack there before pulling out something thin and black with a screen on one side. "He's lying to all of you . . . and I can prove it."

> To me death is not a fearful thing. It's living that's cursed.
> —Jim Jones, leader of Peoples Temple

# TWENTY-ONE

Fingers curl around mine and I'm vaguely aware of someone standing beside the bed. It must be morning. I barely slept but now I'm reluctant to wake up; my eyes feel crusted over.

"Wake up, Little Owl." The voice isn't my mom's. It's Pioneer's.

I force my eyes open. It's his hand on mine. He's smiling down at me, but his forehead is all creased. I count the lines there—three lines. This probably means that he's mad but not ballistic. I relax my shoulders and lean back on the pillow again. My accident hasn't completely sent him over the edge . . . at least not yet.

I rub at my face and try not to look at Pioneer again, but I can feel him watching me. Cody spent the better part of our hour together last night showing me Internet clips from the disasters I told him about. Some of the footage was familiar, but the dates the disasters occurred weren't. It was exactly how Cody said.

When I got back to my room, Mom wanted to know all

about the X-rays and how they went and what the nurses said and did, but I couldn't answer her. I didn't even know how to begin to tell her all the things Cody told me. I had no idea where to start. Instead I just kept rubbing my temples and complaining about my head—which wasn't exactly a diversion. My head was hurting, but so were my stomach and my heart. Eventually she gave up, helped me get into bed, and fell asleep herself.

I was awake for most of the night, everything I'd seen replaying on a loop in my head. I kept hearing Pioneer's speech before he showed us the news clips. He seemed as shell-shocked as we were. I still can't quite believe that he purposely lied. *Is it possible that he was somehow duped as well?*

Cody didn't think so. He wanted to come back today, to bring his dad and see if there might be any way to keep me here at least one more day while they figure things out. I told him to stay away. I need time to think about everything, process it. I need to decide what I really believe. But it looks like my time is already up.

"Seems you've gotten yourself into quite a pickle here, Little Owl," he says.

*That's* the understatement of the century. I almost laugh—seems to me I've been in a pickle since the shooting range. At this point I'm pretty confident that I'm in a whole barrel full.

"How are you feeling?" he asks when I don't reply.

"Like Indy's galloped across my head a few times," I say.

"What exactly happened?"

I sigh. I'm tired of explaining things to people. First the sheriff, then Cody, and now Pioneer. My thoughts feel disjointed and I can't focus on any one thing—except for figuring out who exactly I should believe.

"I just wasn't watching where I was going, that's all. It was a very, very stupid accident."

Pioneer's eyes narrow. "And Sheriff Crowley? He stopped by, I hear."

"Yes."

Pioneer's face hardens as he leans over me. My parents are behind him, standing close to the bathroom and whispering to one another. They can't see Pioneer's face. The abrupt change in his expression chills me, especially now that I know what he's capable of.

"This was not the time to be careless, Lyla," he says in a low voice.

I swallow and nod.

"What did he ask you?"

"He wanted to know exactly how the accident happened."

"And?"

I hesitate a fraction of a second too long. He picks up my hand and holds it in his. Then he squeezes it a little too hard. I bite my lip.

"He wanted to know if I walked in front of it on purpose," I say through my teeth. Crying out won't do me any good. My parents are on Pioneer's side when it comes to things that put the Community at risk.

"He *what?*" Mom's voice raises an octave at the end. Apparently she's been listening to us after all. I wonder if she saw him squeezing my hand. "That's absurd! You didn't tell me that."

*Didn't I?* I can't remember. I thought I did.

Pioneer ignores my mom's outburst. "And did you?"

"Of course not!" I cry.

"Then why did he ask you that?"

"I don't know."

"He had to have given you some reason," he presses. He squeezes my hand even harder.

"Ouch," I say through gritted teeth. "You're hurting me."

"Tell him, Lyla," Dad warns.

"He . . . he saw my neck, you know, the wound there from last week," I blurt.

Pioneer's face pales a little and his eyes catch fire. His forehead creases go from three to five. "And what did you say about it?"

"I said I had an accident during chores, but he didn't buy it. He thinks maybe you hurt me."

My parents and Pioneer share a look. Then Pioneer rakes a hand through his hair. "Well, we're all in a pretty pickle now. That man has been trying to figure us out for a while. I suspected it before, but once he came out to visit, I knew for certain. Seems like now he's ready to come for us, guns blazing. And he won't quit until he's torn us apart, of that I'm sure."

"So what do we do?" Mom's lip quivers. She looks younger than me for a moment.

"We leave here. Now."

"But we're supposed to get her discharge papers. Shouldn't we stay and sign them so they don't have another reason to come after us?" Dad asks.

"You're not getting what's happening here," Pioneer snaps. "That sheriff is coming for me. He's going to tell people that I'm evil, that I've abused your child and everyone else's. He'll tell all the world that you're fools for following me. And he will make them believe it too. They'll say they are saving you when they come into Mandrodage Meadows, killing whoever fights them in their zeal to do what's *right*. He's determined to split our family up now, no matter how much it costs him or us. Don't you see? We're on the brink of war with a doomed man. He's not going to just let us leave today if he can help it. We have to go prepare the Community for the fight that's coming. We can't waste any time. Because until the last days, he has more resources than we do. He can win right now and he knows it."

My mom sobs into my dad's chest.

Pioneer goes to the shelf where my clothes are neatly folded. He throws them onto the bed. "Put these on quick, girl."

I don't know what to do. Everything's happening so

fast. In the end I do what I'm used to, what I've always done when I'm panicked. I obey Pioneer. The room tilts a little as I scramble out of bed with my clothes and rush to the bathroom. We'll be gone in a few minutes. I won't see Cody again. I'd thought maybe we might have some time to see each other today. I didn't say goodbye. Now I won't get to.

I shut myself in the bathroom and lean against the door. I try to breathe, but I'm gasping instead. I'm leaving with a man I'm not sure I totally believe anymore. I haven't been able to tell my parents about the disasters, to show them the real footage or talk to them about the dates. I'm still not sure it's enough to make them doubt everything he's said all this time.

Once I'm dressed, Pioneer and my parents head out into the hall. I follow until I realize that I've forgotten my backpack. Once I'm in the room, I realize I forgot something else too. The magazines and book. I consider leaving them, but can't. Cody brought them for me. It's all I have of him and I can't leave them behind. I quickly stuff them into the bottom of my pack and pull my sketchbook and various other items over them to make them harder to spot. I slip the pack over one shoulder and head out into the hallway.

Pioneer and my parents are down the hall by the elevators. They motion for me. I glance over at the nurses' station. There's only one nurse there and her head is down, the pencil in her hand moving quickly over her paper. I don't hesitate, I just walk past, head up, pace brisk but not at a run, not yet. Once I'm out of her sight line, I jog to where they are, trying desperately not to bounce off the right side wall and then the left. Why won't this hallway stop rocking? I'm out of breath instantly. I'm still so, so dizzy. My mom wraps her arm around my shoulder and we walk past the elevators and toward the stairs.

"Hurry now," Pioneer urges in a whisper. He opens the door to the stairs and slams into the sheriff. Both men stumble into the stairwell. Cody is there, halfway down the stairs. He hurries up the last few steps and puts a hand on the sheriff's back to steady him. He looks at me, his eyes full of questions and alarm.

If Pioneer is panicked by any of this, he doesn't show it. He pulls back and glares at the sheriff.

"You all seem to be in something of a hurry," Sheriff Crowley says.

Pioneer shakes his head and attempts a smile. "Just anxious to get our Lyla home so she can rest. We've all been real worried about her."

"Sure, sure." The sheriff looks from Pioneer to me. "How you doin' this morning?"

"Good," I say. I try to keep my eyes on him and not Cody. My parents and Pioneer are watching.

"Wait!" The nurse who was at the desk when we passed comes running down the hall. "You haven't been discharged yet."

The sheriff's left eyebrow shoots up. "Well now, you *were* in a hurry, weren't you?"

Pioneer glares at him but says nothing.

"The doctor needs to check on you one last time before he signs your papers, and your parents need to go down to the billing office."

She leads us back down the hallway and we have no choice but to follow. My parents veer off at the elevators and make their way to the billing office, while Pioneer accompanies me back to my room. I'm pretty sure he won't let me out of his sight until we're gone. The sheriff and Cody are close on our heels.

My stomach won't stop trembling. Anger rolls off Pioneer in waves. There's a confrontation brewing between the sheriff and Pioneer. I can feel it gathering like a storm cloud above us. The longer we're all together, the bigger the cloud gets.

"I'd like to speak to Lyla one last time while you're all waiting to go," Sheriff Crowley says as we walk.

"Absolutely not." Pioneer stops walking and stares at him. "She's been through enough."

"I can see that. Seems like she's had several accidents recently, not just the car." He gestures toward my neck.

Pioneer's eyes flash. "Exactly what are you implying?"

Sheriff Crowley looks him squarely in the eyes. "That living in Mandrodage Meadows might be a bit dangerous."

"Listen, I don't know where this is coming from. I took

you on a tour of our development myself. What exactly do you think is so dangerous? Clean living?" Pioneer says.

The sheriff shakes his head. "Well then, if you don't have anything to hide, maybe you'd like to answer a few of my questions yourself, Mr. Cross?"

Mr. Cross. That's his real name. Mr. Alan Cross. I remember it from last night.

Pioneer looks dumbstruck for a second, but the sheriff just keeps staring at him, the challenge plain on his face.

Pioneer looks over at me. If I go with him, I'll get to hear his take on all that Cody and the sheriff have found out. "Lyla, go sit on that chair over there and wait for me." *Strange, I thought for sure that he'd make me stay by his side.* "I'll go, but your boy can't wait with her," Pioneer says to the sheriff. "And we'll talk right over there." He points to the other end of the nurses' station, still in plain view of my chair.

Cody's dad gives him a look and Cody nods and walks toward the bank of elevators. But then as Pioneer and his dad turn around, he ducks down and hurries over to the low wall on this side of the nurses' station and sits on the floor where they can't see him but I can. I lean over and pretend to rub my temples. Out of the corner of my eye, I can see Pioneer look over at me, but then the sheriff says something and Pioneer's eyes snap over to him.

"Are you okay?" Cody whispers, almost too low for me to hear.

I nod into my hands.

"Lyla, you don't have to go back with him. My dad says he can keep you here if you say Pioneer hurt you. I mean, he did do that to your neck, didn't he? I don't think you should go home. Not right now."

I peer out at him through the curtain I've made with my hair so Pioneer can't see my face very well. "Why not?"

Cody looks uncomfortable. "I overheard my Dad talking about you guys in his office yesterday when I was working the phones at the station. He's going out to Mandrodage Meadows again. Soon. And so is the rest of the force plus some people from the ATF."

"The who?"

"The Bureau of Alcohol, Tobacco, and Firearms. They think Pioneer's purchased some illegal weapons and gun parts. Dad had a few tips called in a while back—that's why we came out to visit you all last time, to do an initial scout-out of the place. But until yesterday he didn't have anything more to go on. Then he got a tip from a guy one state over who had been arrested for selling stolen guns this past week. He wanted to try and get out of his charge by narcing on his customer list. You guys were mentioned. I took the call from the guy working that case when it came in and just sort of . . . forgot to hang up. Dad's got more than enough now to search your place thoroughly."

I let his words sink in. Our worst fears are coming true. They're going to invade Mandrodage Meadows. And I know that my family and friends won't let them without a fight. We won't have to wait for the end anymore.

It's already here. If these people have their way, they will force a fight that could quite possibly kill us all.

Anger flares inside me. I'm angry at Pioneer for buying the guns and attracting more attention than any of the rest of us ever could. I'm angry at the sheriff for coming after us, and I'm even angry at Cody for making me doubt Pioneer and the Community, for trying to convince me to leave them. All three of them have taken away everything that's ever made me feel safe. Now I feel like I don't have solid ground to stand on anymore.

"Lyla, do you understand what I'm saying?" Cody whispers.

I look over at Pioneer and the sheriff. They're in the midst of a very intense conversation. I can't hear their words. I can't even really process Cody's. I don't understand. All I know for sure is that I can't stay here. My whole world is back at Mandrodage Meadows. I can't betray it for a boy I barely know just because Pioneer said some things that weren't exactly true. I have to go back and warn everyone about what's coming. I have to tell them about what Pioneer's done, about who he is, so that they can decide for themselves what to do next. I can't choose to be safe while everyone else is in danger.

"I have to go home," I say.

Crouching low, Cody scurries over to where I'm sitting. He grabs my hand. "No, you don't. Lyla, please. This can't end well. It won't end well."

Before I have a chance to answer, Pioneer is suddenly

next to us, grabbing my arm and pulling me away from Cody.

"I thought I told you to stay away from her," he says in a low voice.

"Let go of her," Cody fires back, his eyes just as dangerous and unstable as Pioneer's.

"I'm okay, Cody. Please, just go, okay? I'm fine." I look at Sheriff Crowley. "Really, everything is fine. You've got this all wrong. All we want is to be left alone. We're not hurting any of you, so please, just let us go home."

Pioneer looks pleased by my speech. Cody and Sheriff Crowley don't. I have to make them leave us alone—for all of our sakes. "Thank you both for your concern, but I don't need it. I'm right where I want to be." Maybe this is not entirely true, maybe I'm right where I *need* to be, but I don't clarify.

I look at Cody. I try to put my goodbye in my face. I hope he sees it and recognizes it for what it is. He needs to stop trying to rescue me. I'm not even sure that I can be, not anymore.

*We've lived as no other people, lived and loved. We've had as much of this world as you're going to get. Let's just be done with it.*
—Jim Jones

# TWENTY-TWO

Pioneer drives us home. I lie across the backseat, my head in my mom's lap. I'm dizzy and sick, but I'm not sure if it's because of the concussion or my confrontations with Sheriff Crowley and Pioneer or the realization that I won't ever see Cody again.

We are driving uncharacteristically fast. Normally we obey the speed limit at all costs to avoid getting pulled over and attracting attention. But after the hospital and all that's happened, Pioneer doesn't care anymore. His hands grip the steering wheel. They're white around the knuckles. He hasn't spoken since we left Culver Creek. Dad's tried to draw him out a few times, but now we're all silent and it's so uncomfortable that I can barely stand it.

I need to tell them all about what Cody said. I need to warn them. But I want to tell my parents first, without Pioneer listening in. I'm hoping they'll know what to do next. Still, carrying the information around is weighing on me. I'll be glad when it's not my responsibility anymore.

When we finally pull up to Mandrodage Meadows, I practically leap from the car and then instantly regret it because my head aches in protest.

Every person in the Community seems to be out in the streets, packing their golf carts with boxes full of stuff—blankets and clothes.

"We're moving all of our things into the shelter now," Pioneer says as he shuts his car door and follows us into the street. "Tomorrow will be our final day above ground."

*Did he just say 'tomorrow'?* I knew he would speed things up, but this is so much faster than I expected.

I can tell by my mom's expression that she wasn't aware of this either. I start to walk away from the car. I'm anxious to get home. I want to tell her what I know.

"Don't forget your things, Little Owl," Pioneer says, interrupting my thoughts. He's holding up my backpack. I have to work not to look completely alarmed at how close he is to the contraband I've smuggled here. I'd let it completely slip my mind. I make myself smile at him and take the pack. "Thanks, I almost forgot."

"Don't worry, it's my job to remind you," he says.

I shoulder my pack. Pioneer is staring at me. Does he sense my doubts about the Silo and the end? Does he somehow suspect what happened between Cody and me? I try to walk away from him slowly, casually, but I can feel the stiffness of my gait betraying my inner panic, exposing me to him.

"We need to get underground before Sheriff Crowley

comes here and does any more investigating," Pioneer tells us. He steps in front of me, blocking my way. "And when we are safely in the Silo tomorrow, you will tell me everything that went on at that hospital. Understand?"

Mr. Whitcomb rushes up to us and whispers something in Pioneer's ear. Then Pioneer strides off without another word. There will be an awful lot to do between now and tomorrow. He must be anxious to get a head start. He's walking toward the stables. *Indy*. This is the longest I've gone without seeing him. I strain to get a look at the corral, to see if I can spot him. He's normally out having his exercise about now. But the corral's empty. With all that's happening, I guess our normal routine is going to suffer. I'll have to bring him an extra helping of carrots later to reassure him, just as soon as I'm done talking with my parents. I don't want to think about having to say goodbye to him. Maybe after my talk with my parents, I won't have to. I fidget as they gather their things. I'm ready to get home, to tell them everything Cody told me.

"Lyla!" Suddenly Will runs up and scoops me into a gentle hug. "I was so worried." He kisses me lightly on the mouth. I'm too startled to kiss back . . . and maybe just a little too guilty.

"You're okay?" He searches my face.

"I'm fine," I say for what feels like the hundredth time since the accident. Actually, the more people ask, the less fine I feel. And anyway, I can't look at him directly.

Will gives me a strange look and puts me down.

"I'm just a little sick . . . and so tired," I say.

He smiles softly. "Sure. I get it. I'll let you go get some rest. I guess come tomorrow you'll have lots of time to tell me all about what happened."

He kisses my forehead. I don't pull away, although I want to. I watch him turn and amble off in the general direction of his house. Then I turn and follow my parents home.

Once we're safely inside, I ask my parents if we can talk, and we all sit down at the kitchen table. After I spend a minute debating the best way to explain things to them, I just blurt it out. There is no good way.

"That boy at the hospital, Cody, said that his dad is investigating us. They think we've got some kind of illegal weapons or something. They'll be coming out here again tomorrow to search the place really well."

When I mention the weapons, my dad winces like maybe he knows about them and gets why we might be in trouble. My heart starts jack-rabbiting in my chest. I was hoping that maybe they'd laugh off what I said and then spend the next few minutes convincing me that I'm mistaken, but they don't.

I tell them about the sheriff's questions about the accident. I have trouble meeting their eyes when I tell them that he thinks Pioneer's been hurting me. My mom looks furious, but my dad does something that I don't expect. He gets up from the table and walks over to the kitchen door's frame and rests his head on it and closes his eyes. The look on his face makes me want to put my arms around him. He looks so sad. I leave out my meeting with Cody. I make it sound like the sheriff told me about the earthquakes and the hurricane and their separate occurrence dates. I don't want them to suspect my feelings for Cody. And I don't trust myself to talk about him without getting upset.

"I'm sure Pioneer had good reason for telling us what he did and showing us the news clips all together," Mom says. "He probably meant it as a reassurance. Sealing ourselves in the Silo is scary. For all of us. I think he just wanted us to feel as confident as possible about it." Her smile barely falters. I'm beginning to think maybe she won't ever question anything that Pioneer does. I wonder what it feels like to be that certain of him.

"It was a kindness, really," she adds.

"If the sheriff and the ATF do come here, it'll be a major problem," Dad says. "They will try to force us to leave. This sort of thing's happened before to people like us. It could be Waco all over again. It's why we've tried so hard to stay under their radar." He shakes his head. "I warned Pioneer about buying those guns the way he did. It was a big risk." He gets up from the table and walks over to the back window. He stares out into the backyard.

"But we'll be underground now by the time they come," Mom says. "They don't know about the Silo, right?"

She looks at me for confirmation and I try not to hesitate before I nod. I don't want to admit that I told them much more than I was supposed to. I need some more time to figure things out. "They never mentioned it to me."

"If we hide the Silo's entryway really, really well, they may think that we just ran off." She's unusually calm. I can't figure it out. Maybe she doesn't totally believe that they'll come at all, or maybe she just has that much confidence in the Silo's ability to protect us. Either way, I'm not sure she's facing up to reality.

"So we're really going into the Silo tomorrow?" I don't know what I was hoping for, but I am beginning to realize that it wasn't this.

They both look at me.

"Of course, why wouldn't we?" Mom asks.

And all I can say is, "I don't know, I guess." Maybe my attraction to Cody is clouding my judgment more than I thought. They don't seem rocked by what I've told them at all. I try to push away the lingering doubt that I have, but it's not easy. My chest keeps clenching uncomfortably. I wish I could just lie down and sleep, forget the past two days altogether.

Dad leaves right away to tell Pioneer what I've told him. Then Mom puts me to work filling boxes with our pictures, blankets, and clothes. We load them into a golf cart and drive them over to the Silo. It doesn't take long to put everything away. We don't have much to unpack. I look around our tiny rooms and try to imagine them as home. I can't. All I want is to be outside in the open air, in the stables with Indy. *That* still feels like home, like life. This place . . . feels strangely like death.

We finish preparing our private quarters and then help everyone else move what we need from the clubhouse. I visit the stables when I can. The horses are restless and ill-tempered. None of them have been let out all day.

I go into the tack room to get Indy's saddle. At least I can work him out before I have to help with dinner. But when I open the tack room door, all the saddles, blankets, and reins are gone—as well as all the rifles we keep there. I'll have to ride him bareback.

I put my hand on Indy's side and lead him out. The other horses bang on their stall doors and whinny. They want out too, but I can't take them all by myself. Still, I resolve to remind my dad to put them in the corrals before we enter the Silo for good. They can't be cooped up in their stalls until someone comes out here again. The way the sheriff talked, it might only be a couple of days, but I don't want to rely on that. It'll be hard enough to say goodbye to Indy today without worrying if he's okay. I don't like leaving him out here, but I don't have a choice. The Silo's no place for animals.

I grab Indy's mane and pull myself up onto his back. I nudge him in the flanks and he takes off. We barely miss the corral's fence as we thunder past. I work to guide him with my legs. It's almost as if he can sense the changes we're making and he's balking at them. I try not to think about what will happen to him and the other horses once we're underground. The sheriff will take them with him into town. But they only have weeks left no matter what. I don't want Indy to die.

Pioneer said that the end will come quickly. It makes sense to me. I can't imagine that the Brethren would let them suffer, not the animals. If I thought they might, leaving Indy and the others would be unbearable. It almost is now.

I'm crying. I wipe at my face and I lean over to bury my head in Indy's mane. He's panting hard now and slowing to a stop.

"I don't want to leave you, boy," I whisper. Maybe I won't have to. If the sheriff and Cody are right, this isn't the end. "This isn't goodbye," I tell him. "It can't be."

Once word gets out about the impending raid, there's some discussion about sealing ourselves in right away and not waiting for morning. But ultimately, if we're going to make it look like we abandoned Mandrodage Meadows and made a run for it, there are too many loose ends to tie up tonight. We have to do something with our trucks and trailers or they'll know that we haven't actually left. Some of the men decide to drive them farther out into the prairie, maybe try to sink them in the lake that's not far from where we are. They decide to take a few horses and then ride them back. This should buy us a little time, get us closer to the point when our whereabouts will be the least of the sheriff's concerns.

Dad stays gone for the rest of the day. Mom and I stay

busy transporting books and food from the clubhouse to the Silo's library area and kitchen. Eventually we stop for a late supper. We eat all fresh things—apples, lettuce, cucumbers, tomatoes, and corn. I try to enjoy it. After all, I won't get to eat these kinds of foods much longer, especially if we can't immediately get the hydroponics garden up and working inside of the Silo. Still, the food sticks in my mouth and throat like pieces of rock. We're running headlong toward our future now, and despite my parents' continued confidence in it, I'm getting more and more terrified that we're making a mistake.

*Pain's not bad. It teaches you things. I understand that.*
—Charles Manson, leader of the Family

# TWENTY-THREE

Someone's screaming.

At least, I think that's what I hear before there are a series of hard clapping sounds. The screaming is almost too high-pitched and at first I think it is a small child, but the volume seems impossibly loud. It's eerie, inhuman . . . and besides, there are no children here, not anymore. Whatever it is, it wakes me from a sound sleep. Now my heart's thundering in my chest and I'm trembling with the kind of intuition that seems to accompany this kind of interrupted sleep. Something's very wrong.

*The raid.*

Can they have come for us this quickly?

I look out my open window. The screaming's stopped. There's nothing now but the sound of the trees shushing together in the breeze and the singing chatter of the crickets. The moon's bright and flat enough to look unreal. I wrap my arms around myself. My oversized nightshirt seems too thin; the air's finally turned cold.

The street is empty. It's still the middle of the night.

I'm sure that everyone else is sleeping and yet there's an undercurrent of energy riding the wind outside, making the hairs on the back of my neck stiffen and rise. I squint out at the darkest shadows, sure that I'll see men with guns and uniforms, but everything's still. The shadows are empty.

I tiptoe to my parents' room. Mom's there, but Dad's not. I don't wake her up to ask her where he is. Whatever's woken me up and put me on edge feels urgent. She might try to keep me close and stop me from investigating on my own.

I throw on some clothes and creep downstairs. I check the few rooms there just in case, but Dad isn't in the house at all. I open the front door. The screams start again briefly, dying out just as quickly as the ones that woke me up. There's the clapping sound all over again. Like fireworks going off . . . or gunshots.

I walk across the porch and jump down into the yard. I start heading in the direction that the sounds are coming from. Where are the night guards? The streets aren't just empty, they're deserted. I look toward the front of the development. The gate is still closed. There's no real sign that there's trouble, just those screams and clapping sounds. I hold my stomach and try to calm the queasy feeling there. I'm still dizzy; the street heaves up to meet my feet and I realize that I'm walking funny, high-stepping to make sure that I don't stumble. Still, I have to keep going. I need to know who's screaming and why.

I walk past the clubhouse and on to the stables. The quiet here is overwhelming. Every stall is empty. *Where are the animals?*

I start to jog past the pigpens, chicken coop, and corral, which are equally bare, their doors gaping open. When my dizziness doesn't get the best of me, I run toward the orchard, increasing my speed with every step.

Beyond the back wall of the development, just past the entrance to the Silo, the sky is glowing. I can hear voices . . . and there's something else. Fire. I can smell the smoke from where I'm standing.

I'm shaking, I don't know why. I manage to climb the apple tree closest to the wall and perch on the highest branch that's sturdy enough to support me. There are bright red apples all around me, ready to be picked, but it's too late for us to take them with us into the shelter. I move the branches and look out at the prairie.

I'm expecting to see police cars and trucks, maybe floodlights and men in flak jackets—like in the movies. I'm that sure that the sheriff has already made his way here. But instead there are several large bonfires blazing. Our trucks are parked by them and I can see people standing around the edge, although they're too far away to make out clearly.

At first I can't figure out what's going on. Then I notice the animals. The fire closest to them sends flickering shadows across their sides, but I can still make out the familiar shapes of their chests and legs. They are lying so close together that they're practically on top of one another. And they aren't moving.

None of what I'm seeing makes sense. I grip the branches so hard that the bark bites into my palms. A slippery sickness wraps around my stomach and squeezes.

I watch as two men begin to stack wood around the animals and between them. I can't see them clearly enough to know exactly who they are. I think one of them might be Mr. Whitcomb. He strikes a match. I can see the pinprick of light. Then he leans down and lights a bunch of . . . hay maybe, or prairie grass. It flares, yellow and orange flame engulfing it in seconds. Then he pushes it into the pile of bodies. They've tucked wood around them. I can see it now. Flames leap upward and lick at the sky before wrapping themselves around the animals.

I can see Mr. Whitcomb clearly now. He's folded his arms and is staring grimly into the fire. The man next to him peels away from the lopsided circle once he's through laying down wood. He staggers away from the bonfire and hunches over. I see the familiar shock of blond hair in the firelight and realize that it's Will. He's vomiting. And then everything hits me all at once, with a terrible jolt. They've killed our animals and are now setting them on fire.

The air should smell bad, like sulfur or rot, but it doesn't. It smells like roasting meat, like some kind of morbid feast, and somehow this makes everything that's just happened worse. I gag and hunch over the side of the branch I'm on. I rid myself of my own meager dinner.

Tears sting my eyes and my mouth won't close. Once I've thrown up everything, the screams come—from somewhere deep inside of me, the place that Indy claimed a long time ago.

I'm not sure how long I've been screaming when I'm finally able to stop, but Will's seen me and so have the others. My dad is running toward the wall, but I don't want him anywhere near me. I don't want any of them near me ever again. I scramble awkwardly down the tree, lose my grip and fall the rest of the way, landing hard on my butt. Bright hot pain travels up my back, making me sick to my stomach all over again. I'm crying, deep, body-shaking sobs.

Indy's gone.

They killed him.

They killed them all.

It was the animals that were screaming. The sounds still echo in my ears. I'm running, but I have no idea where to go. Lights are coming on in the houses now. I spin around in a circle and drop to my knees.

*"Indy, Indy!"* I wail. I'm hunched over in the middle of the street and I don't care. I can't care about anything, not now.

I thought that we came here to get away from all of the ugly in this world. This was supposed to be our haven. This was supposed to be better. *We* were supposed to be better. But this, right here, is the worst thing I've ever seen. And there isn't a shelter insulated enough to protect me from it.

> We've been terribly betrayed, but we've tried and . . .
> if this only works one day, it was worthwhile.
>
> —Jim Jones

# TWENTY-FOUR

I'm not sure how long I'm on the ground, but when I finally become aware of more than just my grief, I'm surrounded by people. My mom's got her arms around me, alternately stroking and shushing me. I push up and away from her and stare at the crowd.

"They killed Indy. The animals, they burned them," I say. I search face after face for some sign of the same outrage I feel, but they just look at me.

"Calm down, Lyla. Let me explain," Dad says as he crouches down beside me.

"You murdered them! They knew, they were screaming and scared. You shot them and then you . . . you . . . b-b-burned them!" I scream.

Dad looks up at the crowd. "We had to, Lyla. Please try to understand."

"I don't want to understand! I hope I never do. How could you?"

Dad sits back on his heels and closes his eyes, takes a

deep breath. "We enter the Silo tomorrow. You've always known that we can't take them in there with us. Would you rather we just left them to slowly starve? This was the humane thing to do."

I cover my ears. "No, no, no! Don't you try to make it sound kind. *They were screaming!*"

The men stare at me, each of them trying not to look guilty, but failing. Will's standing just past my dad, his face pale and sickly. He won't look at me. I remember how he vomited into the grass. Does he hate what just happened as much as I do? Why didn't he try to stop them?

"Will, how could you let them? How could you?"

He seems to sink into himself. I can tell he hates what happened. He obviously didn't make the decision to do this, but it doesn't matter. He was a still a part of it and right now I hate him, hate all of them.

"Lyla . . . ," Will says miserably.

"I don't want to hear it! Just leave me alone, Will Richardson!" I shout at him. "I can't even look at you anymore."

"Lyla, that's enough," Dad says quietly. "He did what he had to do; we all did. You can't be a child about this."

"I don't understand any of this anymore. What are we doing here? What kind of life is this?" I say.

My mother's hand flutters in my hair. "You're upset, sweetie. You have every right to be, but once we're underground, once you've had time to think about all of this, it'll all make sense, I promise."

"None of this will ever make sense. I thought we came

here to escape all of the ugliness out there, but we can't, can we? It's here too. We pretend like it's all okay—this place, our routines—but it's built on lies. How many of you knew about the animals? How many of you kept it from the rest of us? From me? How can we trust each other if some of us are hiding things?" I start crying again. "How are we better than the people in town when we treat each other exactly the same way in the end?"

"Sweetie, it's been an upsetting morning, but if you'll just come inside the house, we can talk about it while we pack the last of our things," Mom pleads.

"You're not listening! Pioneer could be lying about everything. No one outside of this place is preparing for the apocalypse. How can he be the only one who knows about it? Would the Brethren really choose someone who's been in jail as their messenger?" I can hear a few people gasp. Others glare at me.

I look over at my parents. My mom looks stricken, like I've just slapped her. "Any lies he may have told I'm sure were for the good of the Community." She shakes her head. "This is not the time for this, Lyla Hamilton."

"This is the *perfect* time for this. How can you not see what's happening? We don't have to go into the Silo today. We can wait and see, talk to the Outsiders and decide for ourselves what's really true. We don't have to obey him and never question what he says, don't you see?"

"Pioneer is a good man!" Mom yells, and because she rarely ever raises her voice, it's enough to silence me. "He kept us safe for ten years. He took us out of that city after Karen"—she swallows hard—"disappeared. He made our lives good again. It is the end of the world. I've known it was coming ever since your sister and those towers. How can so much evil go unpunished? And you know what? I'm glad it's the end, Lyla. I want it. I've wanted it for so long. Once it's all gone, I'll never have to worry about losing someone I love again. We'll be together. We'll be safe in the Silo, where none of them can ever hurt us again."

I stare at my mom openmouthed. Her face is flushed, her eyes wild and too large in her pinched face. For the first time I really see just how desperate she is to cut all ties with the outside world for good. If we could've moved into the Silo right when we moved here ten years ago, she probably would have. This is what she's been wanting all along.

"It's easy to make accusations when the person you're accusing isn't there to defend themselves, isn't it?" Pioneer's voice booms across the open space and I can't help cringing. *How much has he heard?* He's standing in the doorway of my house and he's got my backpack in one hand. "You've had your say. Now I think it might be time for me to have mine."

The crowd's eyes swivel from me to him. They don't believe me. I can feel it.

"Please, everyone," I say, "just consider the possibility that he's got things wrong. Why can't we wait until we're sure before going underground? Why are we rushing?"

Pioneer runs into the street. He slaps me hard across the face and I stumble backward. My head throbs in protest and my brain feels tender inside my head. I back away from Pioneer and hold my hand up to my flaming cheek. No one comes to my rescue or even looks at me, not even my parents.

"Unfortunately, our Lyla has been corrupted. Of course, I blame myself. Had I not asked her to give the sheriff's son a tour of our development the other day, we may have managed to avoid all of this. That boy has turned her head and influenced her against us. The sheriff planned it. He sent his son to spy and to lead her away. I should have recognized it that day. He wants to stop us. He wants to come in and take our shelter . . . it became clear yesterday morning when I went to the hospital for Lyla. And he won't stop, not until he's displaced us and taken all we've worked for for himself and his kind. I'm starting to think he even arranged for Lyla's little accident so that he could get more information out of her."

"He's lying! I'm not saying any of this because of Cody or the sheriff. Please believe me," I say. I look at my parents and they look from me to Pioneer and back again.

Pioneer throws a pitying smile at me and shakes his head. I glare at him. Then he unzips my backpack and drops the contents onto the grass. He stoops over and picks up one of the magazines and the book I got for Marie. "You see what she's brought back with her, what she's stolen? She has been breaking our rules, influencing Will and the other kids to sneak out in the middle of the night, arranging secret meetings with the sheriff's son, probably letting him have his way with her even though she's intended for someone else."

My cheeks burn. "He did *not* have his way with me. And I didn't steal anything. Someone gave the books to me."

"This someone?" Pioneer's holding up my sketchbook, which is flipped open to my portrait of Cody.

Will looks at the paper and then at me. My feelings for Cody are crystal clear in the care I took in drawing him and the expression I captured on his face. Will blinks a few times and his jaw tightens. He looks so hurt, so angry, that I can't help reaching out to him. "Will, I . . ."

He brushes away my hand and pushes past the crowd and runs toward the lake.

"Lyla?" Mom is looking at me like she doesn't know who I am anymore.

"Mom, it's not exactly like he says. I didn't steal anything. Please believe me. I would never steal. I . . ."

"But the boy?" she presses. "I saw you with him in the store . . . and I knew . . . but I brushed it away. And then he was at the hospital today, wasn't he? I'd almost forgotten until now. Oh, Lyla, what have you done?"

She says this like I have any control over who I'm attracted to, as if I can shut my feelings off like a faucet. How can she blame any of this on me? Why can't she believe me and not him?

I look down at my feet. I don't know what to say.

Pioneer is now holding up the money Marie gave me and letting it fall through his fingers. I hear several people gasp and I know that I'm finished. I look like the liar now, not Pioneer. It's all too much for my mom. She turns away from me to bury her head in my dad's chest.

"Dad . . ." I will him to look at me, but he's still staring at the money. Even if he did look at me, what can I really say? Do I tell them it's Marie's money? Who would believe it now?

I look up and search the crowd for Marie. She's standing beside her parents. Her eyes meet mine and I can almost feel her fear. She's waiting for me to call her out, to tell everyone that she's the one who wanted the books and magazines. But she won't volunteer herself. And I realize that I can't turn her in. I'm in trouble no matter what. The money doesn't explain away the portrait of Cody. Bringing her into this will only make things worse. So I shake my head slightly at her and turn to face Pioneer.

"I won't explain the money. I didn't steal it, though." I turn toward the crowd. "I know what this looks like, but it isn't how he says. The sheriff doesn't want to take the Silo from us. He's afraid for us. Explain to me how a man who spent years in jail for almost beating a man to death can be the Brethren's prophet! If the Brethren were really using him, wouldn't they speak to us as well and tell us that he's the one? Why have we given up everything to this man? How can you trust anyone who makes it impossible to question them and then has to lie to get you to do what he wants?"

I'm using the same questions on them that the sheriff and Cody used on me. And saying them out loud makes me more certain that they're questions that we need to ask. I'm not sure why I never thought of them before, why it took an Outsider to get me to see the chinks in Pioneer's armor. Now if only I can get everyone else to see what I do.

Pioneer's eyes burn so bright that for a second I think they might actually manage to bore a hole in my chest, but then he swallows hard and forces a smile onto his face. "I don't have to explain myself to you or anyone else. The Brethren chose *me*. They speak to *me*. How dare you question their will! I am not the one who is hiding things here. I know I am an imperfect man. I never said I wasn't. But I am not the one who is endangering the entire Community over some teenage crush. It is all because of you that that sheriff will show up here again. Where is your concern for what happens then? If he can manage it, he will separate us and force us to leave our home. Do you really think anyone here wants that? Except, of course, for you?"

I don't know what to say. I can feel everyone staring at me, their faces hard and angry. No matter what I say, it won't matter. They believe Pioneer. I'm the liar. I'm the one they're unsure of. Pioneer's already won and he knows it. He lips curl up slightly, just enough for me to notice his satisfaction.

"I'm sorry, Little Owl. Really I am. I've failed you. I

should've nipped this in the bud as soon as I suspected. I've always been too soft where you're concerned, but I promise you now that I will do right by you and teach you the lessons I should have a long time ago."

He nods and Mr. Whitcomb and Mr. Brown grab my arms before I have a chance to run.

"Wait, don't do this. Mom, Dad, please! Help me!" I beg, but Pioneer's got his arms around both of my parents and is turning them away from me as he whispers something in their ears.

"Don't let him do this. I'm sorry! We just need to talk about this. Please don't let them take me!"

*Dad!*

*Mom!*

*Will!*

*Please!*

I wait for someone to step forward and help me. My dad looks back at me and for just a moment I'm sure he'll break away from Pioneer and come get me, but the others block the way, form a wall in between us until I can't see him anymore. They won't let him help me. I've done the unthinkable. I've questioned our whole existence. And for that I have to pay.

Children, it will not hurt.
If you'd be . . . if you'll be quiet. If you'll be quiet.
—Jim Jones

# TWENTY-FIVE

Mr. Whitcomb and Mr. Brown pull me through the crowd and toward the back of the development. Behind us, the crowd is still milling around, watching Pioneer talk to my family and whispering to one another.

I struggle to catch my parents' eyes one last time before I'm out of their sight line, but they're looking in the opposite direction, toward the entrance to the development. Actually, several people are now looking in that direction. The front gate is swinging open and Brian's running through it from the guard station with his gun raised over his head.

"They're coming! They're coming!" he shouts.

All eyes are on him as he rushes up to Pioneer, his face bright with panic. "There're at least ten trucks and some other cars coming. We've got maybe five minutes."

There's a moment of utter silence and then I can almost see the moment where everyone's shock and disbelief turns to terror.

Pioneer claps his hands to get their attention. "Everyone, please, we can't panic. We knew this was coming. There's not enough time to get everyone into the Silo without leading them right to us." He lowers his head and puts his hands on his hips like I've seen runners do after a long race. "We're out of choices. Our only option now is to fight. If we go on the offensive first and open fire, we can buy ourselves some time. They'll have to retreat and regroup and then we can enter the Silo."

People begin running for their homes to get their rifles. Those with guns on them already rush to the developments' walls and the front gate. They fall into shooting positions with their rifles drawn, their faces set. Brian runs back to close the front gate.

"Get her out of here!" Pioneer yells when he sees me still standing in the middle of the road with Mr. Brown and Mr. Whitcomb. Mr. Brown snaps out of his daze and yanks me toward the path that leads to the Silo.

I have just enough time to see my dad run back out of our house and hand my mom her gun. Together, they turn and run toward the wall. Mom looks back at me once, and only for a second, but the disappointment and fear in her face are clear. Tears prick my eyes. I try not to wonder if we'll see each other again. I don't want them to get hurt. I never wanted anyone to get hurt.

We're almost to the Silo when a flood of gunfire echoes out across the development. I jump and the men glance at each other. They quicken their pace, anxious to get back and help the others. Tears flood my cheeks and my palms grow slick. How can I just sit inside the Silo and wait while everyone else is out here fighting and maybe even dying?

There's a small cell in the supply room on the bottom floor of the Silo. Pioneer said we needed it just in case someone breaks the rules while we're underground. That's where they take me now. I'll be the first person to enter the Silo for good.

At first I try to struggle, to get free, but Mr. Whitcomb's grip is too tight and Mr. Brown is carrying a gun. I don't think he would actually use it on me. He's known me forever. I'm friends with his daughter. But I'm not confident enough to test him. His eyes are strange—wild. And the way that they're moving in his head, not focusing on any one thing, unsettles me.

They throw me into the cell and then hurry out without a word. The supply room door slams shut behind them and then everything is quiet—deafeningly quiet.

I'm more alone than I have ever been. It scares me. I try to get my heart to stop pounding in my chest. I can't fight what's happening. I'm not sure how I thought I could. Cody, Culver Creek, and all the rest of the world up there are quickly becoming more dream than reality now, something that won't ever be mine. I'm part of the Community and, like it or not, my fate is tied to it.

I strain my ears to catch some noise, anything that might hint at what's happening above me, but I'm too deeply buried. I have no idea if the fight's still raging or if it's already over. I press my hands to my eyes and try to block out the images that play over and over in my mind of my dad and mom and Will and Marie bleeding out on the ground.

My stomach roils and there's a sour taste in my mouth. The waiting and worrying are making me sick. *How many people will I lose today? Will the last thing they think about me be that I betrayed them?*

I pace back and forth. The cell is closing in on me. There's just enough room for a small cot—and a bucket with a toilet seat on top, which I avoid looking at as much as possible. I don't even want to think about using it. I pace until my legs ache and I'm dizzy from changing directions every few steps. But each time I walk the length of the cell, it seems to shrink a little more. I want to scream, but I can't. I bite my lip hard enough to make it bleed instead. If I start screaming, I might never stop.

*What's going on up there? Why is no one coming? It's been at least an hour already, hasn't it?* I kick out at the wall with my foot. It feels good, so I do it again and again. I kick and kick until I'm out of breath. I need to get out of here. I can't be stuck down here while everyone else is in danger. They could all be dead right now. How would I know? I suck in breath after breath as I start pacing again. My chest constricts a little each time, shrinks like the cell walls. I need air. I can't get enough air. I'm alone and everyone I love could be dead or dying. I'm as good as buried alive. My breathing gets faster and faster until I have to sit down and put my head between my knees. I struggle to pull myself back together.

After a while I lose track of how long I've been in the cell. I can't decide if it's been hours or almost a day when Pioneer finally shows up. He's dirty and, from the looks of him, exhausted. His eyes are the only bright thing about him. He walks toward my cell. A kind of manic energy lurks in his expression. I shrink from the bars on instinct.

"What's going on?" I croak. I can barely get out the words. I'm not sure that I really want to know now that I actually can.

"What's going on?" He chuckles. His laughter is a little too high-pitched and it makes me tremble. "The wolves came to our door, that's what's going on. But we beat 'em back." He nods more to himself than to me. "We kept 'em out. Of course, they're still out there . . . creeping, creeping, ready to blow our house down as soon as we tire."

He seems to be lost in his own thoughts, talking in metaphors that I don't understand. A chill runs through me and I hug myself.

"Is anyone . . . is everyone okay?" I make myself ask.

Pioneer looks at me. "Do you still care, Little Owl? Are you really worried about your family or is it the wolves you fear for?"

He's scaring me now. I don't like the way he's looking at me or the weird tension in his voice.

"My parents? Will? Marie?" I press.

"All alive and well—no thanks to you. But you know

that I can't keep them that way, Little Owl, not anymore."
He shakes his head sadly and my whole body feels frozen.

"What are you saying?"

Pioneer presses his forehead to the bars and peers in
at me. "I'm saying that the sheriff won't retreat. Sealing
ourselves in the Silo won't keep them away. They'll find
the entrance eventually, and when we refuse to let them
in, they will blow, blow, *blow* our house down. We can't
hide from them or fight them, not like I'd hoped. There's
far too many of them."

I lean back against the wall and try not to cry. "What
do we do?"

"*I* will do whatever it takes to keep those wolves from
coming in here and separating us, from brainwashing all of
you until you don't know what's true anymore. I will not
let all of the good in my Community become tainted." Pioneer looks up at the ceiling. Tears course down his cheeks.

"All I have ever done is to teach you what's right. I
wanted to help you avoid the Brethren's ultimate judgment. They gave all of us this one chance. . . . Why did you
help those wolves take it all away?"

I slump down onto the cot. How did everything get so
messed up? I didn't mean for things to happen this way.
I didn't know. My throat gets thick and tears flood my
eyes. I don't know what to say. I stare at the floor and try
to swallow, try to breathe, try to think. "I don't know . . .
I wasn't trying to hurt anyone. Please, I . . ." I can't finish.
There's nothing I can say that'll make any of this better.

Pioneer leans forward and looks at me. His face is still wet with tears, but his eyes are darting around the room, focused on nothing and everything at the same time. "I will do whatever it takes to keep them from taking what's ours. No matter what. Even if that means that our plan has to be . . . adapted now."

I'm not sure what he means by this, but I know I don't like it.

"The Brethren are speaking to me now, Little Owl. Right here. They mean for us to return to the earth from which we have sprung and become a part of it again." He barks out a laugh all at once. It sounds shrill, empty. "The new beginning we seek won't happen on this earth. No . . . it is being prepared for us beyond this place." He nods to himself. It's like he's forgotten for the moment that I'm even in the room with him. "Building the Silo was a test of our obedience. We have done what they asked and now they mean to reward us, but we have to be ready to come to them first. It's the ultimate test."

He's up and pacing the room. The room feels electrified. Dangerous.

"What are you saying?" I ask. I stay away from the cell's bars. I don't want to get too close to him. "We're supposed to survive."

"Not anymore," he says simply. "Not anymore."

I rush up to the bars and grip them tightly, try to shake them even though they can't move. "No one wants that! No one will do this. This isn't what we're here for!" I'm shouting. If I could reach over and slap him, I would. This is all so very wrong.

Pioneer shakes his head sadly. "You can't see what I do, Little Owl. But you will. All of you will. They've told me what to do now. And I am ready. I will do what must be done—for all of our sakes."

"This is crazy! Please! Dying can't be what they want for us. You're wrong. This is wrong!" I'm jumping up and down. I need to get out of here. I pull at the cell door and it rattles, but doesn't give.

Pioneer doesn't seem to hear me. His sudden calm is terrifying.

"You'll see, it will be wonderful—so much more than we could have ever imagined. I can make the transition peaceful. Yes . . . no one needs to be scared. It will be like . . . like falling asleep and waking in the sweetest of dreams. They're waiting for us. It's time we go to meet them."

I don't know what more to do or say. I'm stuck. I can't get out no matter how hard I shake the bars. Pioneer has gone over the edge. He's going to kill everyone and all I can do is watch—just like with Indy. No one will even know to fight him off. I scream, loud and long. I pull at the bars until my fingers feel sore, and then I kick them with my feet. I can feel my mind wanting to let go, and it takes all my willpower not to let it. I shake my head from side to side and then lean it against the bars.

*Think, Lyla, think. There has to be some way to get out of here.*

Pioneer waits for me to stop thrashing around, then he leans in close to the bars, close enough so that I can feel his breath on my face and smell his sweat. "Your doubt has brought me clarity, Little Owl. Thank you for that. This new direction we're taking is because of you. And in honor of that, I think I will save your departure from this world for last."

He pats my fingers with his palm and turns to leave.

"Wait!" I shout. I need to keep him here with me.

I can't let him walk away. But I have no other choice. In desperation I take the toilet seat off the bucket, thread it through the bars, and throw it at him. He doesn't do more than hesitate by the door as it lands at his feet. I missed. He looks back and wiggles his fingers at me—a very unsettling goodbye. Then he turns out the lights and steps out into the dimly lit hall. His silhouette lingers in the doorway for a moment.

"I think you should enjoy a little darkness now so that you may truly appreciate the coming light," he says. Then he disappears into the hall. The door swings shut behind him with a soft thud.

The room is pitch-black. I can't see anything, not even my own body. I scream again, but the sound seems to get swallowed up by the dark.

I'm trapped and alone.

Buried.

The Silo was never meant to be a shelter. I understand that now. It was always meant to be a tomb.

> How very much I've tried my best to give you a good life.
> But in spite of all my trying, a handful of people with
> their lies have made our lives impossible.
>
> —Jim Jones

# TWENTY-SIX

The darkness and silence are complete after Pioneer leaves. If anyone is in the rooms above me, I can't hear them. There's only the impenetrable black and the staccato rhythm of my heart.

More time passes. I can't be sure how much because there's no way to know. I've started talking out loud to the empty room to try to distract myself and keep my claustrophobia at bay. At first I was screaming over and over to be let out, but if I can't hear anyone, they probably can't hear me either. And the screaming, even though it's coming from my own chest, is frightening to hear. It makes my panic grow until I feel like I might explode into a million bits.

I go back to pacing the small cell.

"Someone will come. Someone will be here soon. He won't do what he said. He can't." I say these things out loud over and over, but it isn't really helping. The dark is

266

a living thing around me, fluid and full of shadowy shapes that I know probably aren't real, but even so, I'm starting to wonder. I press my hands to my eyes because I can't tell anymore if they're open or closed.

I pace my cell, counting out the steps it takes to go from wall to wall. Seven forward, seven to the left, seven to the right. I run my hands along the bars and then the wall and then the bars again as I walk, stopping only after I count five hundred steps. Then I lie on the cot, pull my feet to my chest, and try to make myself calm down. I close my eyes. I can't stand staring into the darkness any-more. And my head. It feels worse than when I hit it in the parking lot. Without trying, I fall asleep.

Some time later, a sliver of light wakes me up. My eyes scrunch in protest and I place a hand across my face, shrinking back into the cot. I want to cry with relief. I'm not completely alone. Someone's come. But then I remem-ber what Pioneer said about saving me for last. He's come for me. I scramble off the cot and pull it on its side in front of me like a barrier. I don't know how else to protect myself. There's nowhere to hide.

"Pioneer?" I say when I can't stand the anticipation any longer. My voice is raspy at first; my throat's dry from lack of water and use.

"Lyla?"

It's Will. I break down, my sobs coming in fits and starts.

He opens the supply room door wider and props it

open with a large can of peaches. He doesn't turn the overhead lights on yet and I'm glad, because my eyes are still adjusting to the indirect light from the stairwell. It hurts and I have to shield my eyes.

"Pioneer said that I should bring you some water." Will holds out a cup and waits.

I stand up and shuffle closer to the bars once my eyes adjust. I take the cup from him and sip. It's warm, but I could cry it tastes so good. "Thanks. Where is Pioneer now? What's happening? Is everyone okay? You're not hurt, are you?"

Will shrugs. He looks weary and miserable. "I'm not hurt. I don't know how everyone else is just yet. It was pretty crazy out there. We're scaled in. The sheriff pulled back a while ago and we just left everything and came here. But Pioneer says that they'll try to get in soon."

I lean my head against the bars. I was hoping everyone was still outside. I was hoping that somehow I could convince Will to tell them about Pioneer's new plans and that they could run from Mandrodage Meadows, take their chances with the sheriff. Live.

"Will, you have to get me out of here. Pioneer's losing it. He's planning something awful and we need to warn everyone."

"Shut up!" Will yells. I stagger backward as if I've been slapped. "Pioneer warned me you'd do this. You'll say anything, won't you? When did you get like this, Lyla?

How could you let yourself turn on him—on all of us—so easily?"

"Will, I'm not, I promise I'm not. Please believe me. He's planning on killing all of us now so that we won't leave here. Ever. We have to stop him." My head hurts. A lot. Talking is making it worse. I press my hands to my temples and try to make it stop. I need to make him hear me. "Please, Will, there's no time."

Will doesn't seem to be listening. "You were mine, Lyla. We were supposed to get married someday. How could you even look at anyone else?"

It hits me then—how much I've hurt him. He really does love me. Not in the friendship-type way that I love him, but in the deeper, more romantic way that I don't. I've always known that he liked me more, but it's so much stronger than I suspected. The center of my chest aches. Will is one of my best friends and I've hurt him, wounded him enough that he may never forgive me. But now is not the time to talk about any of this. I need to get him to focus on Pioneer. I need to get him to help me find a way out of here and then go and warn the others.

"Will, none of this matters right now. Listen to me! Pioneer's going to kill us. Not the sheriff, not the men outside. Pioneer."

"Why should I believe you? You call him a liar, but you're the liar, Lyla."

"What happened with Cody . . . ," I begin.

"Just shut up! Don't you say his name. I don't want to hear it!" Will shouts. He looks up at me. His eyes are shiny with tears. Then he turns and walks further into the supply room, keeping his back to me. "You're never going to love me like I love you, are you?"

His question shocks me. He turns back again, his eyes angry, but sad too. "Are you?"

I wish the cell bars weren't between us. I want to go over and put my hand in his, to make him see that I will always care for him. I work to soften my answer. "I don't know, Will. I've always hoped that I could someday."

He swallows a few times before he speaks. "Well, I'm not sure I want to be your consolation prize anymore. I deserve better than that, Lyla."

"I know, you're right, you do," I say. I'd convinced myself that he was somehow oblivious to my true feelings, but now I know he's always known. I can't imagine how much it's hurt him these past few years. I am cruel and selfish and utterly unworthy of his devotion. I've failed him. I've failed everyone.

"I am so, so sorry," I say because it's all I can say. "What's wrong with me, Will? Why couldn't I just be what everyone needed me to be?"

"Don't do that," Will snaps. "You can't ask me to pity you now. I won't. You got yourself and all of the rest of us into this mess. For what? So you could play at being a regular teenager? Well, you're not. None of us are. We're chosen. And yes, that means sacrificing some things. But we have all had to do that. Don't pretend that you're the only one who's struggled with what Pioneer asked of you. It's not our place to question him or the Brethren's plan. You have and now see where it's gotten us—underground months early with Outsiders breathing down our necks. We're gonna have to keep fighting them off to keep ourselves safe now. You get that, right? We'll be fighting until the end of days. They'll find a way in eventually, it's just a matter of time. And it's all your fault."

He's still convinced that Pioneer is sticking to the original plan. He won't believe a word I've said. He's not going to get me out. He's not going to warn the others. I have only my word as proof of what Pioneer's planning, and my word is meaningless in the face of his anger and hurt.

I sink down onto the cot. No one will believe me if Will doesn't. Maybe he's right. Maybe I'm to blame for what's happening. If I hadn't questioned Pioneer or let Cody in and told him everything, we might've been okay. Pioneer wouldn't be planning to kill everyone. Will wouldn't hate me. My parents wouldn't doubt me. I've started something I can't stop now. No matter what, it won't end well—for any of us.

Will hits one of the supply shelves with his palm. "You've ruined everything." He rushes toward the supply room door, but stops long enough to turn the lights out again. He's gone and I'm alone in the dark—which is exactly where I belong.

# TWENTY-SEVEN

It's only when I wake with a start that I realize I was asleep
again. I keep doing that. Falling asleep. It scares me, but I
can't stop it from happening.

There's noise in the stairwell. I bolt upright on the cot
and listen. Someone's coming. I shrink into the corner of
the cell and watch as the supply room door swings open.
A thin slice of weak light shoots into the open space and
then a shadowy figure slides in after it before pulling the
door shut.

"Whoa," I hear someone whisper before there's a click
and a flashlight turns on. The cone of light it casts bounces
off the storage shelves for a few minutes. I can't see who's
holding it, but I know it's not Pioneer. Whoever it is is
much shorter than he is.

"Over here," I whisper, and the light finally lands on
my cell. I put my face to the bars. I feel relief wash over
me. Pioneer hasn't hurt anyone yet. I still have time,
another chance.

"Hello?" I ask.

"Ssshhh!" someone whispers. The light swings backward and illuminates Marie's face. "I am toast if anyone finds out I'm down here. I'm gonna have to leave the lights out just in case, sorry."

She puts a hand on mine. "How are you?"

"Not good," I say, and open my mouth to say more, but she cuts me off.

"I'm so sorry about before. I should've stuck up for you. I should've told them the books and magazines were mine."

"No, you did the exact right thing. We'd just both be in here right now."

"And I'm sorry about Indy. I didn't know . . . most of us didn't. My dad said that Pioneer only told the men and even then he only told them just before they had to . . . kill them."

"I'm sorry too. Marie, where's Pioneer?"

She shrugs. "I haven't seen him in hours. Things are out of hand right now, Lyla. Your townie boy's dad showed up here a few hours ago and he wasn't alone."

"I know, I saw Brian come in just before they took me here."

"There was gunfire. Everyone was shooting. It wasn't like target practice. I was so freaked out. I could barely aim the gun, I was shaking so hard. Will and Brian did better, but I don't think that they actually hit anyone." Her eyes are wide and scared, but excited too. It reminds me a little of Pioneer's face earlier when he talked about our new mission. But she has no idea what Pioneer's planning next.

"Marie, listen to me," I say before she can start talking again. "We have to get everyone out of the Silo."

I'm hoping that she'll listen better than Will did. I need someone to believe me. I don't want to fight this fight alone. And I need her to open my cell.

"Why would we want to do that? They're still out there, Lyla."

"Pioneer's had a new vision. He told me when he came down here last. The Brethren told him that in order for us to be with them, we had to die now."

Marie stares at me. "I know you're desperate to get out of here, but seriously, Lyla, accusing Pioneer of something like that is just crazy."

I exhale loudly. She doesn't get it. "Marie, I'm being serious! We're not safe in here."

Marie makes a face and cuts me off. "You can't start all that again. Pioneer's doing what he has to. You like that boy, I get it, and it sucks that you can't see him again. But this is not the way to handle it. You're just getting yourself into more trouble."

I drop my face into my hands. Why did I think that I could get her to listen? I make a frustrated sound into my palms.

Marie comes closer to the cell. Her flashlight dances

across my cot. "Everything will be better now that we're underground, Lyla, you'll see. We can both start over. I can't exactly sneak magazines and stuff anymore and you can't see that boy. It'll be easier now. No more temptations, right?" She looks at me hopefully. "It'll be good." She's convincing herself as much as me.

"No, it won't! We've been friends for a long time, Marie. Look at me. Do I look like I'm lying to you?" I move until I'm just on the other side of the bars from her. We stare at each other.

Marie stills and her smile fades away. "You're really serious, aren't you?"

"That's what I've been trying to tell you. You have to get me out of here. We have to go warn the others." I'm feeling hopeful again. With Marie to back me up, I should be able to get at least some of our friends and family to believe me.

Marie's just staring at the bars, her face slack with shock.

"Marie?" I say, and pat her hand to try to snap her out of it. "Marie! I don't think that we have a lot of time."

She looks up at me, her eyes bright with fear. "What're we going to do? We're sealed in here. It's already too late." She grips the bars and her flashlight slides upward, caught between her hand and the iron. It sends a perfect circle of light bouncing across the ceiling. I can't see her as clearly now. She's more shadow than person.

"I don't want to die, Lyla. I thought being in here meant that I wouldn't have to." She starts to cry.

I place both of my hands over hers. "We don't have to die. That's just it. Not if we all tell him together that we don't want this. He can't make all of us do what he wants, not at the same time, not on his own."

"But won't we just die in a couple of months anyway when the world ends? We won't be able to come back in here then."

"I'm not really sure that the end is coming anymore. Don't you think it's possible after everything that's happened that he's wrong? I think that's why he's fighting so hard to keep us here."

"But what if he isn't wrong?" she presses.

"It comes down to whether or not you're ready to die today. I'm not. If the world ends, we can't fight it, but we can fight one man. We can choose to live this day and every day after it that we have left. And besides, is being sealed inside this place really going to be living at all? We can't even be sure how long we'll have to be down here. If we're stuck here the rest of our lives, will we feel like we've had any kind of life at all? I don't think just surviving like that is enough, Marie, not for any of us."

"But I'm scared," Marie says. Her voice trembles.

"I am too. I'm terrified of standing up to him. I'm terrified of dying. But it's like he said that day out at target practice. Even lambs have to be lions sometimes. We have to fight that fear. If we hadn't been so scared of the rest of the world in the first place, we might not have given Pioneer so much control over us. It's time to take it back." I tighten my grip on her hands. "If we do it together, it won't be so bad. Please, will you help me stop him?"

She sniffles loudly, but she doesn't take her hands away from mine. I smile at her and hope that I look braver than I feel.

"Okay, lions it is, I guess . . . roar?" Her voice is shaky and that last word comes out more like a question than a statement. Her eyes meet mine and we both laugh, the high, hysterical kind reserved for times like this one when you have to either laugh or else scream.

"I came down here to get you out anyway." She smiles through her tears. "I mean, I figured that with all the commotion, no one would notice right away, and by the time they did, you could've laid so low that they would see you weren't gonna cause any more trouble. But I suppose that was some ridiculously faulty thinking, since I haven't even sprung you yet and you've already convinced me to come over to the dark side."

I grin at her. "I love you, Marie."

"And I love you. Now stand back." She puts a hand in her pocket and pulls out a key. "Did you know that there are backup keys to everything in Mandrodage Meadows? Pioneer had my dad get them made one time when we were on a supply run. I knew he had to have them stashed somewhere. Took me most of the afternoon to figure out where. Turns out they were in the armory. I saw them when I turned in my gun earlier."

"You had to turn in your gun?" He doesn't want anyone armed now. I shiver when it hits me how thoroughly he's planned this next step . . . almost like it was something he's been considering for longer than just today.

"We all had to. Pioneer's idea. He said we wouldn't need them anymore today. But I guess that's because of what you said he's planning." She still can't bring herself to say it out loud.

Marie moves toward the lock. She shines the flashlight on it and leans over. "I'll have you out in—"

Her voice cuts off as the darkness behind her begins to move. Her chest bounces off the bars in front of me and her back arches backward like it's on a string. The flashlight drops and spins across the floor.

"Marie, what happened? What is it?" I yell. My eyes follow the arcing path of the flashlight as it travels across the floor. A hand and Pioneer's familiar plaid shirt materialize for a second. In the hand is a knife. Rimmed in blood. He was here all this time, even before Marie came in. Why didn't I hear him come in? I must've been asleep. Was he waiting down here to see if someone would help me?

And now he's stabbed Marie.

"No, no, no, no, NO!" I scream. "Leave her alone!"

The flashlight is still rolling across the floor, illuminating bits and pieces of Pioneer and Marie. Marie makes a small sound in the dark. I strain against the bars and try to reach out, grab Pioneer if I can. I want to keep him from her, but he dances out of the way.

Eventually the light stops on Marie. Her mouth is open. Nothing comes out but a rush of air. Then Pioneer's foot hits the flashlight and it spins away again and she's swallowed up by shadows. When the flashlight illuminates her body the next time, she crumples forward onto the ground. I crouch down on my side of the bars and reach for her.

"Marie!" The flashlight slows to a stop beside her slumping form. She looks at me. Her mouth is still open and trying to form a word or a scream or both. A thin line of red blood leaks from the corner of her lips and drips off of her cheek, which is now resting on the floor just outside my cell.

Pioneer picks up the flashlight. Marie manages to turn her head and her eyes go wide when she sees Pioneer standing there. I don't think she knew it was him until just now. He bends down beside her and gently moves the hair from her face. He sets the flashlight down beside them so that it shines on them both and then he looks at me. His eyes meet mine and they're resolute. Empty.

"DON'T YOU TOUCH HER!" I scream. I pull at the bars, try to shake them loose.

"She was going to let you out. It would have ruined my new plan," he says. He looks from me to her again. "I can't say that I'm surprised, though. Close as you two always were, it was only a matter of time before she followed your bad example."

He looks down at Marie, his expression full of tenderness. "You are the first of us to travel on, dear one. May you take comfort in knowing that we will join you soon. No need to be scared now. You won't have to be alone while you wait. I sent Drew on ahead of you last year. He'll be waiting for you."

I gasp and Marie's body spasms. We thought he'd just left—all those magazines and Marie's hope that she'd see him in one of them—and he was already gone. Pioneer was preparing for this day even then. I blink as tears fill my eyes.

Pioneer leans over and kisses Marie's cheek gently. The pain in her face is almost more than I can take. She tries to turn away but he holds her face in his hands.

"LEAVE HER ALONE!" I yell, but he doesn't even look up.

Pioneer's lips move, but the words coming out are too soft for me to make out. Marie is struggling to move, to get away from him, but he sits on her and holds her shoulders down. She moves her hands to his, to pull his hands away, I think, but her fingers are shaking and she's having difficulty working them. Her breath is wet sounding and whistling strangely.

Pioneer's lips keep right on moving silently, prayerfully. He puts one hand over Marie's eyes before he lifts the knife up to her neck. He clears his throat. "Travel safely to the Brethren in peace." He says these last words like a benediction, and I throw myself against the bars. My head swims and my legs go weak.

"*Marie!*" I scream with everything I have.

Pioneer takes a deep breath and then moves the knife from left to right in one fluid motion, opening up Marie's throat. Her body jerks. I want to scream, but I can't. I can't move. I can't think. It's as if I'm made of glass and everything inside of me is shattering. I press so hard against the bars that it hurts, but I keep pressing against them anyway. *Marie.*

When it's over, the floor is wet with blood and Marie's pale green shirt is bright red. Pioneer's face is blood spattered and wild. His hands still grip the knife, but it's down at his side now. He's looming over her, watching her chest for signs of movement, but there are none.

Anger bubbles inside of me, lava hot and violent. I pick up the cot and throw it against the bars. The room seems to be spinning. I can feel my grip on reality loosening. She trusted him and he betrayed her. He's the evil we should've been running from all along. How could we not see it? How could we not know? He has to pay. Somehow he has to pay for all of it.

Pioneer stares at the blood on his knife. His hands are shaking. Tears roll down his face. It's like he's actually mourning her. Slowly he picks up the flashlight, stands, and walks to the back of the supply room. He returns a moment later with garbage bags and a roll of paper towels.

He wipes off his hands and face, then begins peeling off one garbage bag from the box at a time and laying them over Marie like a shroud.

I watch him numbly. I can't make sense of what just happened. This cannot be real.

"This is your fault. She could have just gone to sleep with the rest of us. If she hadn't come down here to set you free, none of this would've happened." His voice cracks. "But I knew that she would. I just knew it, that's why I waited down here for her to come." He stares at me so hard that I back up a little. "What have you become, girl? Some kind of demon? My own Judas sent to betray me in my darkest hour?" Spittle flies from his mouth and suddenly he lunges forward toward my cell. I shrink backward even further. He shines the flashlight in my face so that I can't see him anymore, and I pull myself as far into the corner of the cell and as far away from the bars as possible.

"Well, I won't let you, do you hear me, demon? I won't let you tear the Community apart!" he yells.

He can't reach me from where he is, but still I can't stop shaking and crying. He slit Marie's throat to save her soul, and now he's bent on saving mine as well.

Suddenly there's a knock on the door to the supply room.

"Pioneer? We need to talk."

It's Mr. Whitcomb. The door begins to open. Pioneer shuts the flashlight off, plunging the room into total blackness again. I had meant to scream and get Mr. Whitcomb's attention, but now I don't know what Pioneer will do. He may have gotten the knife again. If I try to warn Mr. Whitcomb, will he kill him now too?

I squint into the darkness and try to see where Pioneer is, but it's impossible.

"I'm here, Sonny," Pioneer says, and he rushes toward Mr. Whitcomb's silhouette in the doorway. He pushes him back into the stairwell. The door slams shut behind them. I can hear them running up the steps.

They've left me in the dark again—only this time I'm not alone.

# TWENTY-EIGHT

I don't want to believe that Marie's gone. For a long time I
sit against the bars and call to her, hoping somehow she'll
answer. I try to tell myself that she's just unconscious. But
she doesn't wake up. Now there's only silence, a vast ocean
of it. I'm drowning in it.

I cry until I have no more tears. I'm rocking back and
forth against the bars. It's all over now. This is the end.

*Maybe that's good.*

*Maybe it should be the end.*

I'm not sure that I can get past what just happened. I
don't want to carry around the image of Marie's bloodied
body or Indy screaming. But both are seared into my brain
and on constant replay. I just want it all to go away.

The dark is scarier now. I keep thinking Pioneer is in
here too even though I just saw him leave. How long did
he sit in this room and listen to me cry and talk to myself?
He'd had a knife for all of that time. Was he going to use
it on me after he killed Marie? And what about now? Has

he already found a way to get rid of Mr. Whitcomb? Could he be coming back down the stairs at this very moment? I listen and wait, but I can't hear anything other than my own labored breaths.

I promise myself that if he is somehow in here with me again, I will fight. I will do whatever it takes to make him hurt. He has to pay for what he did to Marie, to Indy, to all of us. He made us think there was a better way to live, a better life, when all he was really doing was sentencing us all to death.

When he doesn't materialize in front of my cell and jab his knife through the bars, I start to think about what I should do next. I need to get out of this cell. I need to expose Pioneer for what he really is. I need to save whoever I can so that Marie's death counts for something.

*The key.*

Marie had a key. An image of it flashes across my brain. Pioneer didn't take it. He'd forgotten to retrieve it before Mr. Whitcomb came along. She must still have it in her pocket or her hand. If I can reach her, I can get it and get out of here.

"I'm sorry, Marie. About all of this," I say. My voice sounds overly loud in the silence, hollow.

I lean against the bars and put one arm out as far as it will reach so I can feel around the floor in front of me. My hand lands in sticky wet—blood—and I recoil. I have to make myself put my hand out again. I strain against the bars, crying out when my hands don't land on anything substantial, but I don't quit. I keep grasping at the floor, pulling my arm out as far as it will go. My shoulder screams a protest, but I can't give up. Not now. Just a little bit farther. I gasp, my lips parting just enough for me to taste the metal bar beside my face. I put my foot on the cot beside me and press myself harder into the narrow opening between bars. Just when I'm beginning to be afraid that my cheekbone will break, my fingers finally, finally graze fabric. It's stiff with blood, but it still bends as I grab hold and pull. I can hear the trash bags that Pioneer used to cover her rustle. The sound makes me jump. At first nothing moves and I pull harder with both hands, my fingers cramping with the effort. I feel Marie inch forward just a little. It's enough to help my fingers find better purchase. Slowly I slide her forward until I can reach her pocket. It's empty. She'd been holding the key in her fingers. I let my hand travel the length of her arm. I put my hand over hers. Her fingers are cold at the tips, but her palm is still warm. I bite back a fresh round of sobs. Tucked in her hand is the key. I slide it out and pull it back to me.

It takes a few minutes to wrangle the key into the lock. My hands are shaking so badly that I have to lean against the bars to steady them, but then the door opens and I'm free. I feel my way from the cell to the door and switch the overhead light on. It takes several minutes before I can open my eyes and several more before I can actually focus on anything. I'm not sure how long I was in the dark. Hours? Days? It feels like forever.

Marie's body is almost too much to take now with the lights on. There's so much blood on the floor. I stare at her sneakers, which are sticking out past the garbage bags. I can't decide if I should leave her covered up or not. I keep thinking that she can't breathe under the bags even though I know she's dead. I kneel down beside her and finally tuck the garbage bags around her like a blanket, leaving her face uncovered. Her skin is ashen and milk pale against her dark hair; the caramel tone it usually has is gone. I stroke her cheek. It still feels unbelievable, wrong that she's gone, that Pioneer did this to her.

"I'm going to stop him," I whisper into her face. "I promise." I lean down and kiss her cheek.

I stare at Pioneer's knife, lying between Marie and the door. I should take it with me, but the blade is red. Marie's blood. Suddenly I can't make myself pick it up. I don't want to take it with me. I don't want to ever see it again.

I stand up and open the door to the stairwell. The light is on, but dim. The air is stuffy and close and shadows blanket the twists and turns ahead of me. I start moving slowly upward, careful to stay on the balls of my feet and make as little noise as possible. I feel like Pioneer is lurking behind every turn in the stairs, waiting to come at me with his knife—even though the knife is still on the ground next to Marie. My heart stutters to a stop as I peek around the corners. Pioneer's not there. Now that I know I'm still alone, I'm not sure where to go.

My parents. I can go to them first. They may be my

only hope for reinforcements right now. They'll listen to me; they have to. I'll explain everything and they'll know I'm not lying. I can bring them down to the supply room and show them Marie if I have to.

Our living compartments are two floors up. I head there first, hoping to catch them alone. I can't talk to them in front of the others, and if anyone else knows I'm out, they'll tell Pioneer. I climb the stairs as fast as I can. I ease open the stairwell door that leads to our rooms. It's quiet, dark. There's no sign of anyone; still, I study the hallway and the doors leading to our neighbors' compartments. I leave the overhead light off and tiptoe across the burgundy-carpeted floor, being careful to listen as I pass each door. Several of the doors already sport wreaths of dried flowers, signs that the others have taken up residence and are trying to make their spaces as welcoming as possible. Our door is still plain, unadorned. The dark navy paneling on it gleams. I twist the knob and peek in.

My parents are sitting at the tiny table on the right where our small kitchenette is situated. My mom has her hand up to my dad's forehead. The cotton ball in her fingers is wet and tinged pink with blood. She freezes when she sees me. Her blue-green eyes are large in her head and her mouth drops open. She looks horrified. It's only now that I realize that my shirt and hands are still stained with Marie's blood.

"Lyla! Are you okay?"

She clambers out of her seat and rushes toward me,

stops short of hugging me and lets her hands flutter about my arms and waist. "Where are you hurt?"

"I'm not," I say. "The blood's not mine."

I can't say that it's Marie's. The words won't come out. Instead I start crying hysterically. I'm a little shocked that I have any tears left. I thought I'd managed to use them all up in the supply room. My parents descend on me, wrapping me in a tight hug between them.

"What's happened?" my dad asks.

I look up at his face. There's a long, angry red mark on his temple, but otherwise he doesn't seem to be hurt. The relief I feel only makes my crying jag worse. His forehead wrinkles and he stares into my face. "Lyla, what's happened?"

"H-h-he k-k-killed h-h-her," I manage to say between sobs.

"Who killed who?" Dad says more gruffly.

"Who are we talking about?" my mom says in a voice that's unnaturally high-pitched.

I try to regain control of myself. I have too much to tell them. I can't let myself get any more unglued. "Pioneer killed Marie."

My parents glance at each other. I can see the look of doubt that passes between them, so I hurry to tell them everything that's happened before I can worry too much about them not believing me. I tell them about the cell and Pioneer's and Will's visits and Marie's. The words are coming so fast now that they're practically overlapping one another. I don't stop until I talk myself to where I am now—with them—then I grow silent.

"But why would Pioneer do something like this?" Mom looks completely confused.

"You think I'm making it up?"

"No, it's just . . . why? He wants to save us. It doesn't make sense."

"He thinks we have no chance of staying in the Silo now. He thinks that the sheriff and the others will force us out. He's convinced that no matter what, we're going to die."

My dad shakes his head. "But why would he kill Marie the way you say he did?"

The way he asks the question hurts. He's struggling with my story and that means they both think I might be lying. "He killed her because she came to let me out. He was waiting down there in the dark with me like he knew she'd be coming. For hours. She's still down there. I can show you."

They both look at my shirt at the same time like they're finally starting to believe that I'm really covered in blood; I can see the horror flood across their faces.

Dad lets out a shaky breath. "Well then, we have to confront him. I know that I'm not ready to hand over my life because we've hit a snag. If we have to leave the Silo, then we'll cross that bridge when we come to it."

Dad pushes his hair up out of his eyes and winces as his hand grazes his wound. He's sweating like crazy.

We all are. It dawns on me that the air isn't circulating. That's why the stairwell was so stuffy. Pioneer's turned off the air.

"The air's not working anymore, Dad," I say.

He looks up and puts a hand to the vents. He frowns. "No air means no oxygen. We'll suffocate in here. What did he say to you about his plans exactly?"

"He said it was time we all went to sleep, traveled to the next place, where the Brethren would be waiting."

Dad's face is sickly under the fluorescent overhead lights. "Carbon monoxide," he says more to himself than to us. "The oxygen levels will start dropping now, and if he keeps the generators running . . . the carbon monoxide won't dissipate. We'll die in a matter of hours." He leans back against the kitchenette's counter. "That's why we closed off the emergency tunnels already . . . not because the sheriff would find them. It was to reduce the air circulation even faster. We don't have a lot of time."

"Emergency tunnels?" I ask.

Mom leans in to listen. Seems my dad has kept some secrets too.

"When we built this place, we needed to have two escape hatches apart from the main entrance. In case of fire or, like now, if the air isn't circulating properly. There's one in the supply room and another that leads out of the medical center. I drew them into the plans myself. Pioneer wanted it kept a secret so that he could be sure no one would breach them during our stay here unless absolutely necessary—you know, in case someone panicked over being cooped up so long and tried to escape. That's originally why we had the cell built too."

"But we can use them now to leave," I say. I feel the first faint glimmers of hope. We might not even have to confront Pioneer if we can get to the rest of the Community first. We can sneak out as many people as possible and then just let the sheriff deal with Pioneer.

"There's a coded lock on each door, but yes, if we can figure out his code, we can use them to leave the Silo. Although I'm not sure we will be able to convince everyone to come along even if what you're saying is the truth." Dad glances at my mom. I look from him to her and back again.

"Why not? He's about to kill all of us. Why would anyone just give up and stay once they know that? He murdered Marie. That has to be enough to make them listen."

"Because giving up is easier than having to go back out there," Mom says quietly. Her eyes are shimmering with tears and she looks frightened. "Because the world's evil and capable of much worse than what Pioneer's done. If the sheriff forces us out, we'll have to live in it again . . . at least for a few weeks before the end, and then we'll die anyway. Maybe he's right to let this be it." She walks over to the front door and grabs Karen's shoes, cradles them. "Do you think Karen will be waiting for us?"

I stare at her. "Mom, Pioneer could be wrong, don't you

see? About all of it. The apocalypse might not be coming. Shouldn't we make sure before we just accept it?"

"But he can't be wrong!" Mom yells. "No world where children are taken from their own doorsteps, from the families that love them, can remain in existence. Terrorists crash planes into buildings, men hit their wives and children, teenagers shoot their classmates, and countries war with one another. The Brethren won't just keep letting it all happen. They can't, do you understand me?"

Mom's face crumples and she presses the shoes against her cheeks. She's crying harder than I've seen her cry in a long time, like somehow she's been storing up this hurt all these years and she can't hold it back any longer. Her cries are harsh and angry, painful to hear.

"But why would the Brethren wipe out the world and let Pioneer go? He killed Marie. He stabbed her and left her on the floor. How is that good? How is he not just as evil as the people who took Karen? We haven't escaped anything here. We can't run away from all the bad things, because there will always be more. We have to deal with them and survive."

"But what if I can't? What if I don't want to anymore?" Mom says into her hands. She buries her head in my dad's chest. His eyes meet mine. The pain in them is every bit as raw as my mom's, but his eyes are dry. He believes me, I can see it in his face, and he wants out just as much as I do.

"Mom, please! I don't want to die in here. Can you

just try for me?" I want so much for her to wrap me in her arms and rock me the way she used to when I was little. I want her to promise me that everything will be okay. I need the mom she was before, the one I barely remember anymore, who laughed and danced and told stories. When we moved here, I thought she could be okay again, but she's never quite pulled herself back together and now she never will.

"Mom!" I ask again, my voice cracking.

"I can't, Lyla. I'm sorry." She won't look at me. "I do love you, but I just can't."

I lunge forward and yank Karen's shoes out of her hands. "These stupid shoes! Why do you keep carrying them around? Karen's dead! She is never coming back. These shoes aren't a reminder of her; they're an excuse for you to give up. And don't you dare say you love me! You can't and still choose this."

I hurl the shoes across the room. They hit the wall and land underneath the kitchenette's small table. Mom turns her back on me and rushes to pick them up. She carefully brushes the worn suede back into place and then tucks them against her chest again.

"So that's it? You're going to choose your dead daughter over the one who's living and breathing and right in front of you? I spent my *whole life* trying to make sure you never had to go through anything like her death ever again. I stayed inside the house after she went missing; I came here and followed Pioneer. I did whatever you asked me to do. I would've even gone into the Silo for good to make you happy, but you never cared, did you? You brought us here so you could stop living."

The truth of what I've just said rips me apart. I stare at her, hoping that she'll at least try to argue with me, that she'll find a way to make things right, but she just hangs her head and rubs her thumb across those stupid shoes.

She begins to talk without looking at me. "You can't understand. You're just a kid. I lost a child. You don't just get over that."

"No, *you* don't understand! You lost Karen, but you still had me."

She tries to move a little closer to me, but I don't want to be anywhere near her right now and I back away.

"I *do* love you," she whispers. "Find a way out, Lyla. I want you to. You deserve more than I could ever give you."

I fold my arms around myself to keep from reaching out to her. I still want her to come around—so badly, but I can see that she won't. Her arms drop to her sides and she walks past me to the bedroom area and closes the door behind her. She's taken Karen's shoes with her. I'm finally beginning to understand. She died when Karen did and all these years we've just been living with her ghost.

Dad stares at the door. "I'll talk to her."

"It won't do any good. I think she's wanted this all along," I say, my voice shakier than I want it to be. "Are you coming?"

I move toward the door.

"I have to stay with her, Lyla. She's my wife," Dad says softly.

"And I'm your daughter. You're telling me neither of you are going? This is crazy! You'd both rather stay here and die?"

"No, of course not. You'll bring help . . . but if somehow you can't, I can't just let her die down here all alone."

Dad looks tortured and guilty, but I don't care. I want to shake him or hit him. I want to make him come with me.

"You're asking me to survive your death and hers? On top of Karen's, Marie's, and Indy's?" My voice breaks. I can't believe he's doing this. I can't lose my entire family in one day. It's too much.

"You'll do it because you survive. It's what you do. You were the only one who actually managed it after Karen and now again with Pioneer. You'll survive us too if you have to."

"I was never completely alone before," I say. "Dad . . . please."

My dad looks close to wavering, but then he shakes his head. "You'll find help. And I swear that I will do what I can from down here to keep us alive until then. I can talk to the others and show them Marie. You need me down here. You can't get everyone out all at the same time anyway. There's not enough time. You have to get help. The faster you go, the sooner all of this will be over."

"Daddy . . ." My voice breaks and I fold in on myself.

He pulls me close. His voice is thick and he has a hard

time speaking at first. "I want you to go, Lyla. Find the exit and leave. Get help. You have to go now, because there's not a lot of time left."

He's right. I can feel the closeness in the air. I might be imagining it, but every breath I take feels less . . . right. The oxygen levels could already be dropping.

Dad walks over to the wall and pulls out one of the storage drawers built into it. There are rolled-up papers inside along with flashlights and pens, candles and matches. He pulls out one of the large paper rolls and opens it.

"These are the building plans for the Silo. We're here." He points to our compartment's location. "The closest emergency hatch is in the supply room on this wall. Pioneer's hidden it pretty well behind supply shelving, so you'll have to move things to get to it. There's a combination lock on it. If Pioneer hasn't changed it since we originally set it, it could be this."

Dad pulls out a pen and writes a series of numbers onto the side of the plans. I recognize them. It's the date the world's supposed to end.

"When you get up to the surface, give the plans to the sheriff. He'll know what to do from there." Dad plants a kiss on the top of my head. "Be careful. And no matter what, don't stop until you're out."

I nod and take the papers, folding them so they'll fit inside my jeans pocket.

"I love you," Dad says. "Your mother does too—I mean that. She's just been broken for a long time."

"Sure, whatever you say," I say bitterly.

"People don't always react the way you want them to when they're hurting. Don't give up on her."

"Why not? She's already given up on me." I look past him at the closed door to the bedroom. "I need to go."

I can't stay in this tiny space with them any longer or I might not be able to keep my courage. As it is, I can't think about the possibility that I might never see them again. My feet are having a hard enough time taking the few steps forward to the front door.

"Be careful," Dad says from behind me. The way the silence hangs in the air makes me think he's about to say something more, but then he doesn't and I'm opening the door and looking to see if anyone's in the hallway.

"Wait." Dad pulls me close, hugs me so hard that I can't breathe. "I love you."

"Me too," I say, but I feel like I'm choking on the words.

I step out into the hallway, thick with heat and darker than I'd like it to be. I fly toward the stairs. I don't look back. I can't. The only thing I can do now is run.

# TWENTY-NINE

Once I'm in the stairwell, it dawns on me that the Silo is too quiet. Why are my parents the only people I've run into so far? I linger on the landing for a moment. If Pioneer's already put things in motion, do I really have time to get the sheriff down here? I need someone else to go with me. I can't do this alone, despite what my dad thinks.

If I can just talk to Will and show him Marie, he'll help me. Even angry, he's not deluded enough to keep following Pioneer after this . . . at least I don't think that he is. And Brian. Once he knows, he'll help me for sure. I need to at least get them and then they can go with me above ground to get help. Instead of going down the stairs, I go up. I'll check some of the other floors first and then go to the emergency tunnel. Will will be in the medical rooms, especially if there are already some wounded there after the gunfight. He's been training with Mr. Kincaid for the last few years.

I open the door to the second level of personal

compartments on my way up. All of the doors here are shut tight as well. It's just as eerily quiet as the other floor. Then I run up to the next level, where the medical rooms are. When I crack open the door, I finally see people. They're gathered outside of the medical rooms' double doors. I'd forgotten that some family members would gather here too and wait for word. I'm not sure I want to know who's hurt. I can't keep losing people.

It won't be easy to get to Will now. But I do see Brian milling around with the others. I'll talk to him first— except now that he's in front of me, I don't know what I should say, how to break the news about Marie. His mom is huddled with Mrs. Whitcomb and some other ladies. She's crying.

Pioneer is nowhere in sight, so I walk into the midst of them. The ladies notice me at about the same time and their faces settle into identical glares.

"You! This is all your fault. How dare you be anywhere near here right now! He's dead because of you. You killed my husband!" Brian's mom screams at me. Brian goes to stand beside her; his hand settles on her shoulder. He looks awful. I swallow hard. He doesn't even know about Marie yet. He's lost two of the people he loves most in one day.

"Your dad?" I ask Brian.

"Was shot out there . . . during the fight." Brian looks shrunken, defeated.

"You shouldn't be in here with us. You should be

outside with Them." Brian's mom points a shaky finger at me. I start to back away.

"She doesn't deserve salvation. She should be dead, not my Steven." She's wailing and the others rally around her, comforting her.

I was wrong to try to talk to anyone else. I should've realized. They won't listen to me. The only way I can help any of them now is to leave. I have no choice but to do this on my own.

Before they can move toward me, I turn and throw myself back into the stairwell and down the stairs. I manage to make it to the supply room door before I hear their voices on the stairs. They're coming for me. I rush into the supply room and flick on the light. I begin moving the closest set of shelves in front of the door. I have to knock off half of the canned goods on it before I make any real progress. Then I take a set of two-by-fours from a stack of lumber in the corner and wedge them between the door and the thick steel bar at the bottom of my cell. It should buy me some time. I move farther into the room and trip over Marie. I didn't have time to explain what happened to her to Brian or the rest of them. What if, when they manage to get in, they think it was me, that I killed her? I have to leave quickly.

I begin searching the enormous back wall, my dad's plans in my hand. I pull bags of flour away off of the shelves there and upend baskets full of onions and potatoes. Behind me I hear the supply room door jiggle.

"She's locked herself in somehow," someone yells.

"Door's jammed," someone else yells back.

I think Mr. Brown is the one talking, but I can't be sure. His voice is garbled like it's underwater, either because the door is so thick or because panic roars in my ears. I work faster, pulling boxes of rice and pasta away from the shelves. One bursts open and rice spills out on the cement. I clamber over the slippery grains, trying to get to the next set of shelves.

The door begins jumping in its frame. They're trying to kick it in. I don't have much time. My teeth start chattering. I'm more afraid than I've ever been. It's strange, what I fear most right now isn't the outside world, but my own friends and neighbors, people I've trusted.

When I sweep a long line of canned goods onto the floor, the escape hatch materializes from behind them. It's round and large like a manhole cover, with a latch and padlock on one side. I jiggle the shelving unit in front of it as much as I can without stopping to take any more supplies off it. It's heavy, but still I manage to inch it forward enough to get behind it. I pick up the padlock and begin working it back and forth, entering in Pioneer's end date. I pull down and nothing happens. The combination's wrong. The supply door shudders behind me again. Loudly. I'm about out of time and I have no idea what numbers to try next. I wipe my forehead. My shirt is damp and sticking to me. The heat is becoming unbearable. My breaths are starting to feel shallow.

*Think. Come on, think, think, THINK!*

I roll through another set of numbers, Pioneer's birthday. It's wrong.

I hit the hatch with the flat of my hand in frustration. What good is an emergency hatch if you can't use it in an actual emergency?

One of the two-by-fours holding the door closed bounces, then shifts out of place. The other one looks dangerously close to doing the same. I turn back to the lock and begin trying every combination I can think of. None of them work.

"Open this door, Lyla!" It's Pioneer. If I don't figure the lock out soon, I'm as good as dead.

I don't answer. I rack my brains for some set of numbers with meaning. If he used significant numbers before, chances are he's done it this time too. He probably changed the lock in the last few days, after he knew we would be inside the Silo for good.

It hits me then.

The first combination was the day we were originally supposed to be sealed in here. So maybe . . . I try today's date. It doesn't work. But then maybe we've already been in here for a day. It's hard to tell. I try the dates for every day this week. *Come on, come on, come on.* I start to shake as I try the last one. I'm out of ideas. It's all over. My fingers struggle to line each number up with the arrow, but when I reach the last one, the lock hangs open. It worked!

I throw the lock on the ground just as the other

two-by-four shifts away from the door. The only thing keeping the people in the stairwell out now is a shelving unit, and since I was able to move it across the door alone, it won't be long before the men on the other side of the door get it moved back out of the way.

I swing open the emergency hatch, throw my flashlight and Dad's map out in front of me, and dive into the black space beyond the door. It's dank and smells of dirt and worms.

I switch on my flashlight. I'm at the bottom of a long cement cylinder. There are iron rungs on one side of it. They form a narrow ladder to the top. I can't see where the cylinder ends, but I'm guessing it's as tall as the Silo itself, which means I'll be climbing for a while.

I put the flashlight in my waistband and the map back in my pocket and start making my way up.

I try not to think of how high up I'll be at the top or that there's obviously something blocking the exit up there since it's so dark—something Dad neglected to mention before. I just climb.

Hand over hand.

One foot and then the other.

My hands are sweaty. They keep slipping as I move upward by degrees. The air here is worse than the air inside the rest of the Silo. I'm practically smothering. And my head is pounding again. It feels tender and achy. Between the concussion and the lack of breathable air, I have to battle to keep the flurry of black dots that swarm just outside of my sight line from blinding me completely. I'm not sure if I have enough air to make the climb, but I don't have any choice. I have to keep going up.

I've made decent progress by the time I hear people yelling down below me. I look down in time for a large, bright round beam of light to block out my vision. I startle and have to hook an arm around one ladder rung to keep from falling. I can't see anything but the light.

"Come back down, Lyla." Pioneer's voice echoes off the walls.

I don't answer. I turn my face toward the cement wall again and focus on the rungs above me.

Hand over hand.

One foot and then another. I am close to the top. I have to be.

Below me a shadow falls over the light. Someone is beginning to climb. I can't see who it is, but it doesn't matter. Whoever it is is coming fast. His silhouette scrambles up the cement tube like a giant spider. My stomach clenches. I try to speed up, but my limbs are stiff with panic. I feel as if I'm actually slowing down.

"You won't be able to get out now," Pioneer yells up. "I can't have you endangering us anymore."

My flashlight's sending jumpy streams of light up ahead of me as I climb. I can see something up ahead—the top of the tube, but there's no door. There's only a thickish-looking fabric that reminds me of spider webbing. It makes me feel like I'm in a trap. Now the spider person's coming to finish me off. I reach up and touch the mesh fabric. There's something heavy behind it. I knock my hand against it. It makes a solid thudding sound, but the board manages to move upward a teensy bit. I test the fabric, try to pull it down, but it's taut and holds fast. I need something to cut it with.

"Your parents are waiting for you, Little Owl," Pioneer calls up.

There's a threat in his voice that makes me falter, but I don't stop. I can't. I pick at the fabric, try to poke a hole through it with my fingers, but it holds.

Below me the spider person becomes visible. It's Mr. Whitcomb. His jaw's clenched shut and his face is beet red. The climb up is starting to catch up with him. I can see it in his eyes, but he's still coming.

I have to get through the fabric now. I grab for the only tool I have, my flashlight. It's a heavy-duty kind—large and encased in steel. I unscrew the top and the tunnel gets darker. I can still see because of the light below, but not enough to work quickly.

I feel the edge of the tubular part and hope that it's rough enough to cut the fabric. Then I loop one arm around the rung beside me and brace my feet—one against the ladder and one on the opposite side of the wall. I move the flashlight casing's edge across the material above me.

I run the flashlight casing back and forth, over and over, in as close to the same spot as possible. I feel some of the nylon threads give way under my assault. I go faster.

Once the tear is big enough to grab onto, I slip my hand inside and tug. The tear grows larger until it runs the length of the space above me. I push at the board beyond it. It moves again, but only a little, not enough to dislodge it.

I move upward as far as I can go, curling my back against it and pushing up with my legs. The board groans against the cement, and bits of sand and dirt trickle down the sides of it.

"Too late," Mr. Whitcomb says below me. He huffs out a breath and lunges upward. His outstretched hand grazes my shoe.

I readjust and kick his hand away. Then I move the board with my back one more time. This time it slants upward. It's really just a sheet of plywood, which seems like an absurd barrier against the outside world, but I guess anything thicker would make upending it from the inside impossible.

More sandy dirt rains down on us. It gets in my eyes and I can't see.

Mr. Whitcomb makes one more grab for my feet and I surge upward. The board slides up and over my back. All at once, dirt covers my head, my mouth, my body. It slips under my shirt and down into my pants and shoes.

Mr. Whitcomb makes a startled sound and I open my eyes. He's fallen down a few rungs. His feet dangle downward, bicycling to get a foothold on one of the rungs or the wall. Daylight streams into the space, lighting the entire tunnel all the way to the bottom. The flashlight and

Pioneer are no longer below us. The dirt has settled at the bottom of the tunnel and the air is starting to clear.

Suddenly Pioneer pokes his head back out of the hatch down there and looks up at me. "I won't let you leave. You belong down here."

A few more feet and he won't have a say. I'm almost there.

I look down one last time. Mr. Whitcomb has regained his footing. He reaches into the back of his waistband and pulls out a gun. He aims it at me.

I cry out and start climbing again, but the rungs are coated in dirt now and treacherous. My feet slip out from under me. I struggle to keep my hands on the rungs.

I've almost made it.

I close my eyes and wait for the gun to go off, for the bullet to hit me, but then there's a flurry of movement above me—the sound of dozens of heavy feet pounding the ground outside. I open my eyes and blink. The brightness above me hurts my eyes, makes my head hurt. Suddenly the circle of powder-blue sky above me is blotted out by a man wearing a black helmet. Then there's a loud thunderclap sound behind me and the man's face disappears again.

Mr. Whitcomb shot at me.

I wait to feel pain, but there's nothing. He must've missed. I look down at him as he struggles to regain his balance and shoot again.

"Help!" I yell up at the sky, to the people I can't see.

I scramble up as best I can, my feet slipping more than climbing. My ears are buzzing an alarm inside my head. The gunfire has temporarily deafened me.

My fingers finally find the grassy lip of the tube and then hands grab hold of mine and haul me upward. My legs hang out over the mouth of the tube for a moment. The right one catches fire. I scream, but I can't really hear myself as I slide across the grass. The man holding my hands is shouting something at me, but I can't hear him either. The buzzing in my ears has increased to an all-out roar.

I roll over onto my back, smacking my head hard against the ground in the process. I watch as two other men point their guns down into the Silo and shoot. Someone crouches down by my leg and carefully rolls up my jeans.

There's a sizable chunk of skin missing from my calf. Mr. Whitcomb managed to hit me after all.

I gag, but nothing comes out, just a thin line of spittle. Bright, hot pain blossoms in my leg and spreads, and I roll back and forth on reflex, like the movement will somehow lessen the pain. I wish to faint, for the tiny dots of darkness that have been bordering my vision all day to finally grow and blot out the world. But for the first time in a long time, I am completely and utterly wide-awake.

The man who rolled up my jeans scoops me up in his arms before I have time to protest. He takes off toward the stable at a run. I cry out as my leg hits the side of his body, bouncing against it in time with his strides.

"Almost . . . there," he says, exhaling after each word.

His face is turning red with exertion. "Sorry . . . I know it hurts." His eyes are focused on the stable. He's running like I still might be in danger.

I look over his shoulder at the place where the tunnel to the Silo is. There are still men gathered around the lip of it, but they've stopped shooting for now. And there are police and cars and trucks scattered everywhere—across the corral and down by the clubhouse. I feel like I've just emerged into a combat zone. It's like something out of one of Pioneer's movies. Above me a helicopter passes low enough to send my hair flying, and I have to tuck my head into the man's chest to keep strands of it from whipping into my eyes.

I made it.

I got out.

But the rest of my family is still underground, and they're running out of time.

# THIRTY

The stable is crowded. Noisy. There are a dozen tense conversations happening around me all at once, each one distorted by a steady rhythm of static from walkie-talkies, and there are men with grim expressions on their faces crowded into every corner. They all seem to be on important errands, rushing in and out, setting down boxes filled with equipment and tacking up maps and images of the corral and orchards on the walls.

Two tables have been set up at the far end by the tack room. I can see the sheriff behind one of them. He's surrounded by a group of men with black jackets on. I stare at the white lettering: ATF. I don't know what the letters stand for, but I remember my dad—or was it Cody?—mentioning them and my stomach quivers. Up until now I've thought of all these men as the enemies. Now I'm supposed to trust them in order to save my family and friends.

"You're safe now." I look up at the man who has carried me into the stable and try to relax my grip on his neck, but I can't make my hands loosen. He's smiling down at me in spite of this, trying to make me feel better. He's still breathing heavy from our jog here, and his breath smells like cigarette smoke. It doesn't put me at ease.

"I need to talk to those men," I say, and point to where the sheriff and the others are standing. "Right now!" I know that I sound too demanding, but I don't have time to be polite.

The urgency in my voice startles the man and he leans back a bit to look at me before picking up his pace again. He sets me down on the bench behind the tables, the one where I used to sit and sketch Indy and the other horses.

*Don't think about that now. You have to keep it together.*

Time's running out, I can feel it. I can't quite catch my breath and I know that underneath us, in the Silo, breathing is even harder.

"Sheriff!" I say as loudly as I can, and he turns. When he sees that it's me, he rushes to where I am. I talk the whole time he's coming. I have to make them hurry. "Pioneer turned off the air down there. He closed off the circulation vents. They can't breathe." Every man at the table behind the sheriff stops talking and looks at me. I want to stand up, but the minute I put weight on my leg it catches fire and I wince, so I roll onto my hip and pull the map Dad gave me out of my back pocket. I wave it at the men. "I brought you a map of the Silo. Here. Please, you have to hurry!" I keep talking as he unfolds the map and looks it over. I tell him about the horses and about Pioneer locking me in the cell and about Marie. By the time I stop talking,

312

he's not the only one listening. All the men in the stable are staring at me.

The sheriff looks over at one of the other men and then takes the map from my hand. "How long ago did he do this, Lyla?"

I try to think back, but I don't have an answer. I was in the supply room cell long enough to lose track of time completely. I'm still not entirely sure what day it is or how long it's been since everyone went underground. "I . . . I don't know. But it was already getting hard to breathe when I left."

The sheriff pats my leg. "You did good. It was a brave thing you did getting this to us. And I promise you that we will do whatever we can to get your family out of there safely. Do you understand? We'll get them out."

I want to believe him, trust him in spite of all the things Pioneer and my parents have said about people like him, but I don't see how he can be so sure of himself. I bite my lip to try to keep my tears in check. "Just hurry, please," I beg him.

He pats my leg one more time and stands up. "Hey, where are the medics? This girl needs some attention. Now."

Two men enter the stable carrying medical bags. They crouch down by my leg and examine it. The one with my leg in his hands looks up at me after a moment's poking and prodding and smiles. "Lucky shot, actually. It missed the bone completely. Cut right through the flesh. You'll be right as rain again in no time."

I stare down at my leg. How can getting shot ever be lucky, no matter what the injury? My calf is wet and sticky and still throbbing. I can see the open mouth of the wound, almost perfectly round and raw. It's still bleeding. My white sock has turned bright red with blood, and my shoe is stained a gory tie-dye. Nausea creeps into my stomach all over again and I look away.

"We'll get you cleaned up and bandaged—for now—and then when it's safe to move you, we'll get you over to the hospital and get that closed up properly. You're gonna be just fine."

"I'm not going anywhere," I tell them. I try to sound sure, brave. "Not until they get my family out of there."

The men exchange a look that leads me to believe that the sheriff was being overly confident before when he said he'd get everyone out. They avoid meeting my eyes and get to work on my leg. I grip the side of the bench and try not to completely lose it. If I get too worked up, I won't be able to help the sheriff if he needs me. They try to give me pain medication, but I don't want it. I don't like how it made me feel when I was in the hospital, all thick-headed and tired. I have to stay alert and strong. I turn my attention toward the sheriff and the men at the table and try to catch snippets of what they're saying, but it's hard to concentrate. Even the lightest pressure put on my leg hurts and I end up crying out.

"You can hold my hand if you want."

Suddenly Cody is right beside me, standing next to the

bench. The very sight of him loosens my control over my tears, and my face crumples in an instant. I start sobbing. Loudly. He sits next to me and gathers me in his arms. He doesn't say anything and I'm glad. The last thing that I want him to do is tell me that it'll be okay. We both know that it's more likely that it won't. A lie won't make me feel better.

"What're you doing here?" I ask between sobs.

"I had to come. I couldn't watch all this play out on the news and wonder if you were okay. So I, um . . . borrowed my dad's cruiser and here I am. He hasn't noticed I'm here yet, right?"

I look over his shoulder. I don't see the sheriff any-where. "I don't think so."

Cody reaches up and strokes my hair slowly. "Everyone else is still down there, huh?"

I nod into his chest. "My parents wouldn't come with me. My mom wouldn't go at all and my dad wouldn't go without her. And when I tried to get the others, they . . . They blame me for all of this." I'm crying even harder now.

"They won't once they know the truth," Cody says quietly.

"WHAT ARE YOU DOING HERE?"

The sheriff is looming over us all of a sudden. I can feel Cody stiffen.

"It is way too dangerous for you to be here, Cody. You will turn around and head for home. Immediately!"

"If she's here, then I'm staying," Cody says quietly.

"That is not your decision to make!" the sheriff yells. His face is bright red. It's the first time I've seen him angry, and it's scary.

"I'm not leaving!" Cody raises his voice. "You have bigger things to worry about right now than me. Let me stay with her. She shouldn't have to sit here and wait all alone. We'll stay in the stable, I swear. How much danger can we really be in in here? Your guys are everywhere."

The sheriff opens his mouth to argue but doesn't get so much as one word out before there's a loud boom outside. The earth under our feet vibrates and dust rushes into the stable, turning everyone into a grimy silhouette. I have to close my eyes to protect them. Cody pulls me closer. When I open my eyes again, it looks like the stable has been through a brown blizzard. Dirt is everywhere.

"They've collapsed the tunnel, sir!" a man yells from outside, and suddenly everyone scrambles toward the corral.

"Stay here!" the sheriff yells at me and Cody before turning to follow the others out.

I cough and cover up my nose and mouth with my sleeve to keep from swallowing more dust. "My mom and dad!" I holler through the fabric. The sheriff can't hear me; the sleeve muffles my words. I try to get up and follow him in spite of his order not to, but Cody won't let me go—and neither will my leg.

"My dad's right, we need to stay put." He's yelling even

though I'm right beside him, and his voice echoes in the sudden quiet inside the stable. I can hear shouting outside and the hum of a helicopter somewhere overhead, but I can't see anything but the empty stalls and the litter of papers, walkie-talkies, and coffee cups strewn across the tables in front of us. I'm not sure I can just sit here and wait. There has to be something we can do to help. Anything. I suck in a breath and double over into a fresh round of coughs. I feel like my lungs are coated with dirt.

"There's gotta be some water around here." Cody stands up and begins to look around, picking up scattered papers as he goes and putting them back onto the tables. He manages to find a half-empty bottle of water somewhere. He wipes the dust off it with his sleeve and brings it to me. I drink it slowly. My lungs keep spasming and it's all I can do not to choke.

No one's come back yet. It has me on edge. If everything were okay, you'd think at least a few of the men would have returned. What if the explosion did more damage than Pioneer meant it to? What if most of the Silo collapsed and is buried under a foot of dirt and rock right now? My parents. Will. Brian. They could all be gone. I wrap my arms around myself.

"Cold?" Cody asks.

"Maybe a little," I lie. The truth is that I'm chilled through. My fingers, my nose, my feet are all numb. *Am I going into some kind of shock?* I start to shiver violently and

Cody looks around the table and the stalls; I guess he's looking for a jacket or something.

"There're horse blankets in the tack room. Over there." I point to the wall at the far end of the stable. "Just don't get the one with the blue stripes on it." That blanket was the one I used for Indy, and I can't look at it right now. I won't. It's too much. This is all too much.

Cody moves past the first few stalls and toward the tack room. I look away as he passes Indy's stall. I make myself focus on the table in front of me instead. I hadn't noticed before, but there's a gun sitting there. One of the men must've rushed out without it. I study the dust-coated black handle and the leather holster surrounding it. I can't help thinking about all the guns the men didn't forget, the ones they will take with them when they figure out how to break into the Silo. Those guns will soon be aimed at my family and friends if they don't give themselves up peacefully. And I didn't get a chance to tell anyone other than my parents about Pioneer. I'm sure they think that I killed Marie. They won't see the sheriff and the others as rescuers at all. They'll still see them as intruders. They won't surrender.

I glare at it. I hate guns. I think I always have. I want to throw this gun across the room, get it away from me, but I can't reach it from here. I make a frustrated sound in my throat and try not to let it turn into a scream. I feel like I might be crushed under the weight of it all. I should've stayed underground. I should've tried to make everyone see Pioneer for what he is. I should've made them listen somehow. Instead I ran out and saved my own skin. I'm not brave or heroic. I'm a coward, just like Pioneer always suspected.

A loud thump breaks me out of my thoughts. I look up, expecting to see Cody carrying one of the horse blankets, but the walkway is empty. The tack room door flung wide open. I don't see Cody anywhere.

"Cody?" I call out. There's no answer. "Cody? Are you there?"

Still there's no answer.

I look around the stable. Why isn't he answering? I inch along the bench until I can see the tack room a little better. He's definitely not inside. But something's lying on the floor at the far end of the walkway, a little heap of blue-striped cloth. Indy's blanket. *Where's Cody?*

"Cody?" I try again.

*Something's wrong.*

"He can't hear you," someone says.

And the voice isn't Cody's.

It's Pioneer's.

I straighten up on the bench, my heart in my throat. I scan the stable for him. He's not anywhere, but the last stall door is now slowly swinging open. *How can he be in here? How did he get out?* It doesn't make any sense. And then it hits me—the second emergency tunnel. On the map, it empties out into the stable. My breath catches in my throat. He's here for me.

Pioneer doesn't show himself, but he does start talking again. "Cody's resting," he says. I can hear the grin in his voice. "We needed a little time alone. See, I've come to collect you, Little Owl. We should all be together when we leave this place. It's what the Brethren would want. Even after all you've done, you still belong with me."

"Help!" I yell. "Sheriff, somebody, help!" But even as I yell, I'm drowned out by a second explosion in the corral. The stable fills with dust all over again, but I only cover my eyes for a few seconds. I feel Pioneer lurking in the dimness around me. Stalking me. My eyes burn, but I have to look for him. Outside, the shouts pick back up and the helicopter noise gets louder for a moment before it quickly fades.

"That should buy us a few more minutes," Pioneer says brightly. "You know, it pays to be prepared. I was almost certain that those explosives were overkill, so to speak, but now, well, I'm pretty pleased with that little bit of foresight."

I'm afraid to move or breathe. Pioneer could be in any of the stalls, biding his time until he can rush out and take me by surprise.

The gun.

I glance over at the table and the gun that's just out of reach. I hesitate only briefly before I lunge for it. My leg screams in protest, buckling as soon as I put weight on it, but I still manage to grab the edges of the table and keep myself from going down all the way. My knees slam into the floor and I suck in a breath. I reach across the table and pull the gun toward me. Then I slip it out of its holster and cock it.

"I have a gun." I yell at the stalls. "Don't get any closer or . . . or I'll shoot."

"Oh, now, don't be that way, Little Owl. We both know you're no good at that sort of thing anyway." Pioneer's mocking me. He sounds more amused than scared. It terrifies me.

I lift the gun and point it at the stalls. My hands are shaking and it's bouncing up and down. *Steady, Lyla, steady.* I blow out two quick breaths and concentrate on making my arms stiff and still.

"I'll get to you before you muster up the courage to even try it," Pioneer says, and he sounds a little closer—or am I just imagining it? "See, I won't hesitate before I shoot you. I'm delivering you to the Brethren. There's no shortage of joy in that for me. But you? You seem unsure of where we're all headed, and that makes you unsure about what taking my life really means. You seem to think the only way to save someone is *not* to shoot. You're still that little owl you've always been. Always watching, always afraid to act. You don't have the conviction to do what must be done. Never have, never will . . . but you know I do."

He's right, I'm no good at this. Maybe I can just crawl outside. I look at the wide entrance to the barn. I'd have to pass every stall to get to it. I'll never be able to get there fast enough, not with one bad leg. And Cody's in here somewhere. I can't leave without him. I'm stuck. I have no choice but to defend myself.

A loud boom echoes out of the open stall. Pioneer kicked the side of one of the stalls to try to scare me. It works. I scream and the gun goes off. He laughs. He's trying to keep me scared and distracted. Any minute now he'll come for me. I aim at the stall I think the noise came from. I almost let off another shot, but then think better of it. I don't know how many bullets are left. Better to wait for him to show himself. I go back to concentrating on keeping my hands steady.

"You still gonna try to shoot me?" Pioneer's voice is light, teasing. "Better make that next shot a good one 'cause it's all you're gonna get."

All of a sudden he throws himself over the wall of one stall and into the next. I raise the gun a little, try to aim, but he's too fast. The moment's over. He's closing the distance between us.

I slide my knees a little farther apart and try to keep my balance. He might not be able to get me if I'm quick. He'll have to clear the table first no matter what, and I'll have that extra few seconds to try to shoot again if I miss this time.

"Stop right there!" I shout, but my voice is trembling.

Pioneer laughs. It's overly loud. Confident.

I try to get angry. I want the anger to dilute my fear. I force myself to think about Indy and Marie. I remember

322

the way Marie looked at him right before he slit her throat. And about Cody. He's lying in this barn somewhere hurt . . . maybe even dying. I have to find him, help him.

*I can do this.*

*I have to do this.*

"Lyyy-laaa." Pioneer sings my name softly.

I shiver hard enough that I almost drop the gun. I grip it tighter, then tuck my face close to my arms, keeping my eyes on the sight at the end of the gun. I watch the top of the stall for any signs of movement. My finger twitches on the trigger.

It gets quiet.

I stay very, very still . . . and wait.

A minute goes by, maybe more. I can hear people outside, getting closer. I think about calling to them, but I can't speak. Pioneer won't wait much longer. I can't get distracted. *He's coming for me.*

Suddenly Pioneer leaps up from the second stall with his gun aimed at my head. I don't look at his eyes. I focus on his chest, just the way he taught me to at the range. I pull the trigger at the same time he does. Wood splinters off the walls. I can hear it hitting the ground like rain. Am I hit? I don't think so. . . . He's still coming. I must've missed him too. I take aim again just as Pioneer reaches the tables. He lifts his gun. Our eyes meet. His mouth curves up a little.

*Bang! Bang! Bang!*

For the second time today, I'm deafened by gunfire.

I fired . . . more than once I think . . . but did he? I look down at my chest. I'm surprised when I don't see blood blooming there.

He's missed again.

I'm okay.

I look over to where he was. There's a spray of blood on the inside of the stall door right across from me. Pioneer's slowly pulling himself across the floor and into the opposite stall. He's hurt but alive. His gun is on the floor. He dropped it when I shot him. Still, I keep my gun aimed in his direction just in case.

Men pour into the barn almost immediately. They heard the shots. I can't seem to make my mouth work, so I point toward the stalls. They find Pioneer right away.

He's not moving anymore.

One of the guys who worked on my leg steps forward and begins to open Pioneer's shirt. He feels along his neck for a pulse. He nods. Pioneer is still alive. But I can tell by the way everyone's started rushing around that he might not be soon.

A stretcher seems to materialize out of nowhere. They put Pioneer on it and start rolling him out the door. They go right past me, and when they do, Pioneer's head turns in my direction. He's awake, but his eyes are glassy, his face gray. He looks at me, and that look burns into my brain. I raise the gun again because for a brief, hysterical moment I'm convinced he's going to try to lunge at me.

"You're mine," he says. I don't hear him, but I see his

mouth make the words. My finger twitches on the trigger, but I don't shoot. And then he's gone.

Someone takes the gun from my hands. Someone else leads me back to the bench. I'm shaking all over, my teeth chattering so violently inside my head that I'm afraid I'll bite off my tongue. The man in front of me tries talking to me, but I can't answer him. I just stare out into the barn.

"Cody" is all I manage to say when I can finally get ahold of myself enough to speak.

The sheriff's eyes widen and he goes completely white. He runs down the walkway yelling Cody's name. They find him just beyond the tack room. He's got some bruising around his neck where Pioneer grabbed him, cutting off his airway until he went unconscious, but otherwise he's okay. They set him next to me on the bench, and he rubs his neck and winces.

"You're okay." He says it like he was sure that I wouldn't be. He smiles just a little and reaches up to touch my cheek before leaning back against the wall behind him and closing his eyes. I stare at the quickly darkening bruises on his neck and try to stop shaking.

My parents are still underground. So are Will and everyone else. It isn't over. Pioneer could've trapped them down there or they could still be preparing to fight. They don't know that Pioneer's been shot.

The police find the emergency tunnel down to the Silo without my help. I watch them motion to each other and then talk into their headsets, but I can't hear them. I'm not sure if it's because of the gunshot or my chattering teeth, or if my brain has just decided not to let me hear. They crowd into the last stall and look at the floor where the tunnel is.

After a few minutes of tense silence, they call down into the tunnel and we wait to see if anyone will answer. We're all holding our breath. Then my dad's voice carries up from underground and breaks the spell.

"We're okay and we're unarmed."

Tears roll down my face. I wasn't completely sure that they would stop fighting. A flood of relief overwhelms me and I tip my head back against the wood and smile in the midst of my tears. No one else is going to die. It's over. It's all over.

My friends and family emerge from the Silo one by one. They climb up into the stall wide-eyed and blinking like babies seeing the world for the first time. They huddle together once they're out. I can see the uncertainty in their faces. I know what they're thinking. *What now?* I'm wondering the same thing. I want to rush into their midst and find my parents, but I hang back. I'm not sure what they'll think of me once they know I shot Pioneer.

My parents end up being among the last to leave the Silo. My dad is practically dragging my mom out. She's completely unresponsive. Karen's shoes are still in her hands. When he sees me, he grabs me up in his arms and hugs me for a long time. We're both crying when he finally lets go. My mom stands beside us, but she doesn't move or hug me or even look at me. She doesn't do anything at all. She's just standing there, perfectly still. I try not to let it destroy me. I know this isn't how she wanted this to end, but for now I guess it's enough that she's here, that we all are.

In the Community, life seemed perfect.
I thought the evil lived outside our walls. I was wrong.
—Lyla Hamilton, member of the Community
(Taken from the audiotapes of her interview with Sheriff Crowley,
ten days after the raid on Mandrodage Meadows)

# THIRTY-ONE

On the day Pioneer said that the world would end, we come back to Mandrodage Meadows. It's the tail end of fall, and the last of the warm weather is long gone. Most of the leaves have finished dropping. They make shushing noises under our feet as we walk. Cody says that the forecasters are predicting an early and unusually long winter this year. If today is any indication, they'll be right. There's a chill in the air that hints at the snow we're supposed to get later on in the week. I'm kind of glad that it's cold. Somehow the weather fits the moment—like the whole world is saying goodbye with us.

I didn't want to come back. I wasn't sure that I could be here again. But the counselors thought it would be a good idea and so here we are. They said it would bring us closure. When we watch the sun set in an hour and the world doesn't end, maybe we can finally face the truth. The apocalypse isn't coming. And then we can move on, start over. But they have no idea what they're talking about. There's no starting over. There's just going on. I'm not sure why they can't see that. I guess maybe only people like us can, people conditioned to survive, not overcome.

I follow everyone else down the path that leads to the orchard and the Silo. Mandrodage Meadows looks like it did before we left. It's only been a couple of months since then. It hasn't been long enough for it to look neglected, but already it feels eerie, haunted. There are ghosts here, lingering in the twilight, waiting for us.

My parents are up ahead, but I don't try to catch up to them. Instead I keep a careful distance between me and everyone else. It's better this way for all of us—or at least for all of them.

The day of the raid, five people in the Community died. Three of them—Brian's dad; Julie's Intended, Mark; and Mr. Brown's son, Luke—were killed on the wall when the sheriff and his men first showed up. Marie lost her life trying to free me. Mr. Whitcomb was shot and killed in the tunnel when the sheriff's men opened fire after they pulled me out. I shot Pioneer . . . but he's still alive. I hit him twice in the chest—centimeters from his heart, so close that if he'd breathed a little deeper at the moment that I shot him, he would've died right then. The sheriff told me that he flatlined twice on the way to the hospital anyway, and had to endure several surgeries and a pretty serious infection, but still, he pulled through. The sheriff also says that if anyone else had the complications he's had and survived, the doctors would call it a miracle. They refuse to say that about Pioneer's recovery . . . and neither will I. His survival can't be a miracle. Because that could mean that maybe he really is who he says he is—a prophet or messiah.

But no.

I can't believe that. I won't.

Pioneer won't be here today. He's in the hospital, and even if he wasn't, he'd be in jail. Still, I can feel his presence here too. I pull my jacket closer around me.

*You're mine.*

I've tried to put his last words to me out of my head, but they're stuck in my brain, playing over and over on a loop. I know what it means. He won't let me go. Not while he's still alive. Maybe not ever. I close my eyes and take a breath. He's going to jail. He can't come for me—not anymore. The sheriff said he'd make sure that he never could . . . but still I can't make myself stop jumping at every sound, from looking for him around every dark corner, from thinking that the wind moaning through the trees at night is him calling my name. I wasn't trying to kill him when I shot him. I just wanted to stop him from coming for me, but now I can't help wishing sometimes that I had—then maybe this knot of fear that seems to have settled into my chest would've unraveled and gone away a long time ago.

The others are holding on to each other as we get closer

to the Silo. No one waits or comes back to walk with me. I wonder if they're disappointed that Pioneer's not here. Do they want him and not me? I used to know them well enough to know what they were probably thinking, but I've been kept away from the Community by the sheriff long enough not to feel like a real part of them anymore. He's pretty sure that most of them still blame me for what happened during the raid and that the only way to keep me safe from their anger over it is to keep me separated—at least until their counselors have had time to make them see the truth. He's here now—somewhere out of the sight line of the others—watching the group, keeping his promise to me.

Cody stayed in town today. His dad and my counselor, Mrs. Rosen, wouldn't allow him to come with us even though he lobbied pretty hard to be included. Honestly, I'm glad he stayed behind, but I didn't tell him so. I need to be here alone. I need to say my goodbyes without him hovering anxiously over me. I don't want him to worry if I end up breaking down. He's part of my future, and I need to keep that piece of my life far away from this place.

The group stops and fans out around the Silo's iron door. I drop back a bit more and watch them settle in. I lean against a tree and tuck my head into the collar of my jacket. The cold metal zipper bumps my lips. Mrs. Rosen comes to stand beside me. She had been walking with Heather and Julie because she's their counselor too. I guess now it's my turn to get my hand held.

"How you holding up, Lyla?" She gives me a warm smile and touches her shoulder against mine.

"Fine," I say. I don't elaborate even though she's staring at me, waiting to see if I'll say anything more. I just want her to go back to the group and leave me alone. Eventually she does. She wanted me to talk about my feelings, about how this little trip is making me feel. The truth is that I don't know. I feel too many things to be able to put them into a tidy sentence or two for her. What I want is to be more numb than anything else. If I let all the pain in, it might be too much to bear. One day I'll try, but not now, not yet.

Dr. Freeman, the head of the counseling group, clears his throat to get our attention. He leans against the Silo's door and begins to talk about what he thinks this day means. I can't focus on his words; my mind keeps drifting back to the past—the day I came to Mandrodage Meadows, the day I rode Indy for the first time, the night I danced with Will by the river. And almost as if the memory itself conjures him up, Will is there, standing beside me.

"Weird to be back, isn't it?" Will's talking to me but staring straight ahead. I can only see his profile from where I'm standing. I can't read his expression at all. My heart beats a little faster. I haven't talked to him since we were here, when he left me in the cell. But I've wanted to every single day.

I shrug. I don't know what to say. I'm afraid I'll say the

wrong thing. I don't want him to walk away. There's so much that I've wanted to tell him. I lost Marie and now I'm terrified that I've lost him too, that it's already too late. He was my best friend once upon a time, and part of me keeps hoping somehow he will be again.

Will doesn't seem to notice that I haven't answered him. His eyes are on the Silo door. "I keep thinking that the last couple of months are part of some bad dream. That I'll wake up and we'll be out in the pool playing chicken with Brian and Marie. You have no idea how much I wish that were true." His voice cracks a little.

I swallow hard and try not to cry. This is where he'll blame me for ruining things. This is where he'll say that he hopes he'll never see me again.

He takes a deep breath. "I just want it all back. So much. I'm not like you, Lyla. I'm not strong. I wish I could be. I would've died down there that day if it weren't for you. We all would have."

This is not what I expected him to say at all.

"Can you forgive me for not believing you when you tried to warn me?" Will is hunched over like he's expecting me to say no or to yell at him and tell him to go away. All at once I have the overwhelming urge to hug him.

"I was never mad at you, Will," I say, and then I do hug him. "I thought that you still blamed me for everything. I've missed you. I've missed you so, so much."

He rests his head against my hair and I smile into his jacket. "I missed you too," he says quietly.

"It's almost time," someone calls out, and we pull apart just as the sun touches the tree line.

"I know it's not gonna happen, but I'm still nervous," Will says.

I look up at the sky. There are clouds moving in from the west, but they're still far away from where we are. The sky is a deep blue and the horizon is glowing orange, making the trees look like they're on fire. It's beautiful and vibrant and alive.

I think about what he's said about me being strong. I don't see myself that way. I didn't think anyone else did either. I was always just Little Owl, the observer, the weak link, the one everyone worried about. How did that change? How did I? The whole time we were growing up, I thought Will, Brian, and Marie were the brave ones, and now it turns out that I am? I feel like I'm only just now figuring out who I really am—or maybe who I can be.

"See, it's almost dark. It's not going to happen," Will says, more to himself than to me.

I stare at the Silo's door and then back at the sky.

The weird thing is that it still could. I mean, it won't, of course, but on any given day anything's possible. It's what makes being here—on this planet—scary. We can't predict what will happen. We can't control any of it. Good things. Horrible things. We can only deal with it as it comes. I look at the half circle of people in front of us and try to find the right words for what I'm thinking so I can tell Will, but the moment for talking passes and I lean into him instead.

Now the sun is only a thin sliver of light lingering along the prairie's edge. I watch as it finally gives up the day and disappears. The world grows very still—as if it's waiting too, as if it's still deciding what it wants to do. No one moves. We just stand close to one another and watch the sky.

Gradually the stars come out, one by one until there are too many of them to count. The day has officially ended and we are still here. I smile a little and so does Will, but there is no cheer from the crowd, no sigh of relief, only quiet acceptance.

I take Will's hand in mine. Together, we continue to study the stars overhead. The sky's encrusted with them. I'd almost forgotten how clear they could be out here, away from the lights of the town.

I used to think they were portals that the Brethren used to watch us. Now I think there probably aren't any Brethren at all. I'm not sure if knowing this comforts me or not. What I do know is that looking into a sky like this one gives me hope. If a sky this dark can still be peppered with so much light, maybe this world can be too.

# ACKNOWLEDGMENTS

First let me say that I wouldn't have had the courage to embark on this journey had it not been for my husband, Jay. You never once doubted my writing ability (or at least you had the decency not to tell me) and worked two jobs *for years* so I could focus on this dream. I'll love you forever and always. It's your turn now, honey.

Many thanks to:

My daughters, Samantha and Riley, who remind me daily what life's all about and who can make me laugh even on the worst of days. You are the two halves that make up my heart.

My parents, Tom and Peggy Williams, for being there whenever I've needed you and for naming me after a book character because somehow you always knew I'd love stories. I'm glad I finally listened to you and gave this writing thing a try.

My brother, Tom Williams, and his wife, Erika, for gamely reading this book and the one that came before it. Your support means the world to me.

My in-laws, Alan and Trish Poe, who happily volunteered for playdates with my girls while I toiled, and endured many a conversation on writing with me.

My agent, Lucienne Diver, who will always be my version of a fairy godmother. You are brilliant at making dreams come true.

Suzy Capozzi, who loved this book more than I dared hope anyone would.

My editor, Chelsea Eberly, for taking me on and making me feel comfortable from that very first phone call. I'm lucky to have you.

Mallory Loehr for your support and guidance.

Nicole de las Heras for a cover that made me gasp in a good way when I saw it.

The rest of the Random House team for working tirelessly on this book.

My critique partners: Stefanie Jones, who demanded that there be kissing—Cody and Lyla's hospital "date" is for you; Krystalyn Drown, who has the decency to call me on every weak plot point and challenges me to do better; and Jennifer Baker, who not only improved this book exponentially but also shared recipes and encouragement in equal measure. Ladies, you rock.

The Gunning for Awesome girls who are experts at cheer-leading and consoling: Gemma Cooper, Corinne Duyvis, Lacey Edwards, Deborah Hewitt, Michelle Krys, Lori Lee, Ruth Stevens, Amy Tintera, Kim Welchons, Stephanie Winkelhake, and last but definitely not least Natalie Parker, who helped me figure out where this book truly began and emphatically urged me to KEEP GOING.

Tessa Gratton, who took me under her wing.

The Abbreviated Writers' Group of Wesley Chapel. Every writer needs a safe place to grow. This was mine.

Early readers: Andrea McBride, Jane Juran, Cheryl Van Beek, Diana Geller, Vincent Sultenfuss, and Nancy Haines. Your advice and companionship carried me through.

Kurt Wilt and Patrick Crerand for teaching me how to write purposefully and for showing up to help fledgling writers every other Thursday for years. FOR FREE. You give professors a good name, gentlemen.

Last, all my thanks and praise go to God for blessing me with this wonderful, beautiful life that I lead. It's so much more than I could've ever imagined.

# ABOUT THE AUTHOR

AMY CHRISTINE PARKER earned her degree in elementary education at Southeastern University in Lakeland, Florida, and then proceeded to try out many different jobs, including collectible doll maker, fondue waitress, and inner-city schoolteacher. It wasn't until she became a mom and began making up bedtime stories for her children that she finally realized what she was meant to do. Now Amy writes full-time from her home near Tampa, Florida, where she lives with her husband, their two daughters, and one ridiculously fat cat.

Visit her at amychristineparker.com.